Two Weeks Till Valentine's Again

2nd

Bodie Raue

Published by Bodie Raue, 2026.

This is a work of fiction. Similarities to real people, places, or events are entirely coincidental.

TWO WEEKS TILL VALENTINE'S AGAIN

First edition. January 5, 2026.

ISBN: 979-8989428342

Written by Bodie Raue.

Table of Contents

FEBRUARY 1ST: OLD ACQUAINTANCES

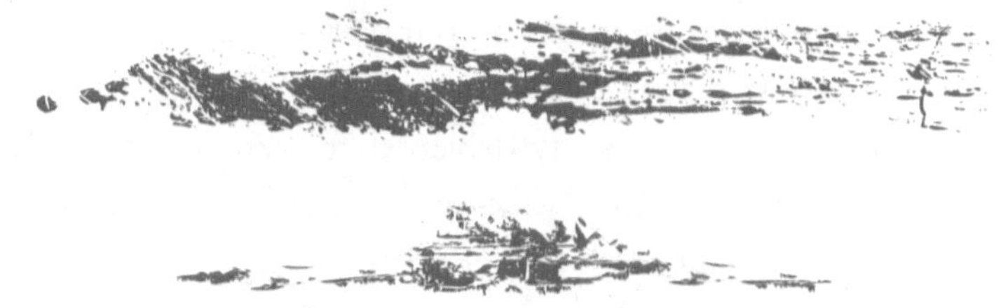

He rides a ragtop with his hair dancing to a bridge-top wind; a big-time smile appears on his face as he races along the roundabout into the outskirts of the city. Mr. Happiness is feeling quite cheerful from the welcoming commitment his customers have been showing him, and why shouldn't he? It is Two Weeks Till Valentine's Again, and he is as much a part of the celebrations as they are. All those devoted couples with their pocketbooks and shopping bags and color-coated cash cards, eager to be spent on passion packages and bawdy house bedrooms.

Preparations are well underway for these enamored travelers, and a tour shop offering a show-and-tell at the most libidinous sites in the city is exactly what Mr. Happiness has to offer them. Start with the 'Spanky in the Fort' and witness a womanizing philanderer take a paddle for his indecent exposure before his superior's wife. Later, attend the 'Pirates Intemperate Desires,' where visiting satyriases leap from ships when promised the virgin spoils of the city. Maybe a springtime frolic through the Fountain of Youth or a forbidden desire experience at the Believe It or Not Museum. But whether the choice be a chocolate basting at Mary Wet's display table or the unwanted solicitation from a few spirits that haven't left the city yet, Mr. Happiness has a tantalizing 'yank and yarn' for them all.

He hits his turn signal and passes below the Valentine's Day banner, parking his car in an alleyway two blocks from his office. He then merrily performs a silly toe tap before the early morning shoppers, placing a batch of freshly printed brochures in his window by nine a.m. Finally, he stands before the doorway, all five feet two inches of him, like a waxwork from a Madame Tussaud's Museum, smartly dressed in his pleated khaki pants, royal blue blazer, and shiny black shoes. He is a simulacrum of success, a man who finds that the allotted hours in the day are never quite long enough to accomplish the complexity of his daily aspirations. A man who is to be honored as the welcoming mat to the city, not so much for his flirtatious advances and late-night dinner dates, but for his engaging personality, generosity, and noteworthy advice toward those in need. A man so consciously infallible and spiritually driven that even the local church has dedicated a song about his nightly walks with the ladies in distress.

Obviously, an important man if his good deeds have warranted a street to be christened in his name – and yet, sculptors are certain to make a mockery of him. Though short in stature and conscious of faith, he is quite tall for a man who finds himself shortened by a twenty-four-hour day length, with many of those hours spent in disobedience to his wife of thirty years and his nine children. The gossip around town is that he is a disreputable cad, a charismatic charlatan, a two-timing scoundrel with half his body beneath one sheet and the other half already in the bed of another. Of course, trying to establish a pure mind and a good heart is not so easy for a man purposeful in preserving more of his offspring. And most undoubtedly, his inappropriate engagements are sure to remain undisclosed while the rumors from his adversaries far surpass what the local newspapers are willing to publish about him.

But apart from the acts of a moosh-mush, happy-pappy, floppy-sloppy, polygamous playboy, there are other amusements in the city that one must not overlook. In fact, just outside his doorway is a nine-year-old opportunist, standing just as he does, with her legs apart, her fingers circled around her eyes, and a very large frown displayed on her face. This mockery annoys Mr. Happiness to no end, but the girl does attract a crowd that he, himself, would not otherwise attract. Besides, it is not so much about the little girl's performance as it is about his sales assistant being late again.

She slips into a light blue emblem jacket and quickly reviews her looks before the mirror. It is Wednesday, so the knee-high go-go boots, along with the short, green cotton skirt, are all requirements for the office today.

She rolls her chestnut hair beneath a white baker boy hat and wraps a yellow scarf around her neck; the chain-ball earrings are of her own choice, of course.

Beatrice Gertrude Backlebond hurries out the front door to her faithless, breathless, Beatle-bug hooptie named Ms. Weary. She and her vehicle have to make the cumbersome, fifty-minute drive to her office each day, and already she senses a delay in the air. The wind has blown the news of an early spring, and as usual, her car is the first to relay the disturbing message. Ms. Weary does not operate well under the weight of a thousand leaves, and unless Beatie can delicately pick off each foliole from her dilapidated frame, Ms. Weary will not exhale a single drop of carbon monoxide to get her there.

After some proper encouragement, however, Ms. Weary does fire up with a wheezing snort. She then coughs her way out to the main road, and from there, it's more about temperamental stalls and accidental rodent flattenings that have her routinely late for work. As a result, Beatie will have to listen to yet another nonsensical speech from her unreasonable boss. Yesterday's speech was in response to Ms. Weary running over the back legs of an indecisive squirrel. A tromping that caused her car to break down and cry for nearly an hour. *We stand up for those that are defenseless, and we scold those that make us late, but when we scold those that are defenseless because they also make us late, then the excuse on one's behalf will always fail to resonate.*

It isn't particularly the career she had been hoping for, but it does pay the bills. Once over the bridge, Beatie guides Ms. Weary through the city streets, pumping her brakes in conjunction with the accelerator to keep her operating. The crosswalks are always a major concern for Beatie, however, because Ms. Weary always refuses to yell at the tourists, despite any encouragement for her to do so.

But it isn't really about Ms. Weary, and Beatie knows this. It's Two Weeks Till Valentine's Again, and as usual, the city becomes one large museum no one ever wants to leave. For two weeks the historical sites are offering unlimited tours, the hotels are offering unlimited stays, the restaurants are offering unlimited-course meals, and even the stores are offering forever fifty-percent-off deals that never run out! And why? Because of Valentine's: an illogical, nonsensical, barf-inducing manifestation that offers what no one has ever been able to promise – an infinite amount of orgasmic cleansing!

Push-Pah!! Every year, it's the same boring, dumb-boring, even more stupid, dumb-boring holiday she has to contend with no matter what holiday it is. It's the same clogged streets, the same crowded crosswalks, the same exponentially growing number of carbon copy people that return every year as if they have arranged to be buried here!

Beatie hits the breaks and forces Ms. Weary to honk at a gaggle of geese. Now she has to find a place to park, then find an angle between an ever-evolving, rotational pull of people, only to be further delayed because some infuriating salesgirl has to sell her a free brochure for fifty cents!! Sure, she has the money; it's just that Mr. Happiness has no problem giving her a lecture for being late, but regarding the little salesgirl outside, he asks only that she not encourage her!

"Sorry, I'm late, Mr. Happiness, people, crosswalks, and more people – it kind of makes for the usual ride here."

"Beatrice, this is no time for excuses when a love once remembered has arrived upon our very office door steps again!"

"I'm not trying to be late, Mr. Happiness; it's just that Ms. Weary hasn't been feeling very well."

"We help those that are sick and mourn those that meet their fate, but when those that are sick meet their fate because we are doomed to be late, well then, we have certainly ruined all of those lives that wish to copulate."

"I'm not sure I understand that one, Mr. Happiness, but if I may..." Beatie looks at Mr. Happiness, whose eyebrows are still raised. "Oh, right, and that is why we are offering the 'Find Me the Lost Beaver Tour' for $150. Taxes not included."

"And we offer this because...?"

"Because finding one's lost beaver is many times the best beaver we can find for them?" Beatie places her coat on the rack and takes a seat behind her desk. Again, it isn't particularly the career she had been hoping for, but it does pay the bills.

"And what about you, Beatrice? Have you not found that one person who is ready to be found?"

"Who?"

"I don't know who; you have to select someone, someone that you can relate to and look forward to spending your time with."

"An acquaintance?"

"Why not?"

"Well, because I have tried that before, and they usually end up never calling again. I don't even know what that's called."

"That's called not finding the right friend. It's not an easy fix, you know. It takes time, but when you do find the right friend, just imagine all the memories you'll have together."

Beatie twists her mouth from side to side. The thought of finding a friend would certainly bring some wanted change to her boring, dismal, mouth-open-sneezing life. But who is she kidding, the talk of meeting anyone before Valentine's just isn't in her future anymore, which may have something to do with her preoccupation for this time-consuming occupation. It has completely stopped her from enjoying the simple things she likes to do – shopping, for one, and by the lack of space in her closet, she is pretty sure she is good at that. And her social life? The living arrangement in Atlantic Beach seems ideal, but the commute to work is almost an hour away. Her closest friends have left for college, and her hairdresser, her only consistent flirt, has the same interest in men she has.

It is noontime and Beatie unravels a napkin containing a small sandwich. She eats it slowly and chews it thoroughly, marveling at the dress in the window across the street. Ebullient is its name, and her delicate fingers are already drawing an image of her wearing such a dress. Using her right hand, she wears the dress down the aisle of her own wedding, and with her left hand, four well-dressed men are escorting her to the alter with a lumpy kid sliding along his back.

Beatie looks up to see a group of tourists laughing at her. Typical 'Ger-schmeebies,' they know nothing about marriage fantasies. She lowers her head to resume her duties of folding the brochures. Of course, a closer inspection of the dress will be required later.

Wednesdays have been rather slow, despite Mr. Happiness' insistence to work through lunch. Naturally, he leaves for an extended break; he does what he wants – it's his office – but while he's away, Beatie has an hour to do whatever she wants.

In her mood, Handel's Passacaglia (i) plays in her mind while she races between the racks of Meeshman's, a second-hand apparel store. They have a wonderful selection of outfits; the only problem is the socialites tend not to contribute around the holidays. Down the road is a Persnicketies; these clothes are said to be 'Popular Wow,' but they are also popularly undiscounted, so the budget-conscious go across the street to Bin Spinky's. It's a favorite among vegetarians, but sadly, their clothes are designed for the slightly malnourished. This is why there is a Bittle Feedle's, next to Barnaby's. They have a great selection of affordable clothing, which is well worth the purchase if one has a sewing machine. Finally, the viewing through the window of Cockle Poodles is always a favorite last stop. Never ever would she be seen in one of their expensive dresses, but it does allow her to pretend to wear a dress to a party she will never be invited to.

The day retreats to the other side of the city and the evening turns sharply in favor of cold. Mr. Happiness has not returned, and annoyingly, there are never any instructions about when to leave. It is half past five already, and Ms. Weary is getting cold. Beatie grabs the office keys and quickly pokes her head out the door. Nothing really unexpected; Mr. Happiness has found pleasure in someone else's backside. A surreptitious affair, perhaps? What will the young lady think of him when his wife finds out? Good news though, while using his hand to measure the lady's back side, Beatie knows a slap is coming – one, two, three, and – run for it!

Beatie is in haste. She has an important evening planned, and it involves finding a good book. Romance novels do bring her the most hope and optimism to her unacquainted life, and Wednesdays are generally the best day to realize this. The library closes at six, but they have an after-hour return slot where she can reach in and retrieve the tastiest of stories. Of course, this method is predicated on a good novel being returned – but there is a splash of good news! One evening, while Ms. Weary was having one of her 'fits,' Beatie found a library that closes at eight. They even have a Reese Witherspoon selection so she can choose six books and return what she doesn't read in two weeks. This should be a chortle-gagging, knee-slapping euphoria, right? No! The book display was empty! Apparently, Reese didn't feel like reading any books this month! Now the choices are Shakespeare's Sonnets, updates in X-ray spectroscopy, or the 240 pages of the Voynich Manuscript written in full Voynichese! Add to this travesty, the library just announced they are closing due to some computer maintenance, expulsion paraphernalia testing! This is absolutely a sneeze-juice-exploding conundrum, and to avoid being incarcerated by some electronically charged execution gate, she has to stumble over a trash can only to have a sticky, moss-laden, puke-smelling, toss-away book spew out and stick to her skirt like fortified vomit cheese! Uggg!! So, now she has to take it with her!!

Ms. Weary starts up without question, and at the stoplight, Beatie looks with curiosity at the book still stuck to her skirt. There are no features to the cover, which she would prefer, but the book does have an amusing title: Change by Way of Means by Lucifer Goggy. The inside cover boasts a collection of words like 'Loneliness' and 'You won't be saved unless you read this book,' and while a good book never has a featureless cover, this book comes with the promise that it does.

At home, Beatie sits on the couch, circling a spoon through a container of Mary Shiver's Coconut Sorbet. The first chapter is fine with a few facts she believes to be indisputable, one being that ghosts do roam the city due to a life of loneliness. It is the following chapter, however, that has her most perplexed. The author assures her that all the memories of her childhood must include loneliness. Beatie recalls her childhood as being very imaginative and supported with lots of toys, and yet for some reason, the author confirms this is not true. In fact, it is loneliness that should be felt wherever she goes. Why? Beatie has never thought about feeling 'lonely' before. True, it is a bit of a damper that she can't share her life with anyone except her stuffed animals, but how does the book know this?

Through the silent hours of the evening, Beatie remains awake, reading with great attentiveness. She collects the last globs in the grooves of the container and then places it in the garbage bin. After finishing a disturbing chapter on the other uses of the hand, she decides not to read any further. Something about the graphically chosen words the author likes to use has her deeply concerned.

Beatie strolls to the window when she hears the sounds of outdoor merriment. There is a scene of young people making their way home from the nightclubs. These are the same people she sees holding hands, lip-sucking, and skin-stroking in her front yard every night. In her romance novels, these people fall in love and live long, titillating lives. Beatie frowns at this and puffs out her lower lip. She cannot help but consider what life would be like if she, too, went out on a night of face sucking.

She sits before her mirror, looking at all the different angles of her face. She is getting on in age, and it shows. Not too long ago she had been a hand model; now she just tries to keep her skin glowing while maintaining a summer tan she hopes will linger into spring.

Beatie leaps into bed with her stuffed animals. It is a good thing her ballet class is tomorrow. She will need a new dress once she passes the Valentine's Ballet auditions. This is all she thinks about, and a visit to Meeshman's, of course. "See, I'm not lonely, Mr. Goggy."

> He stumbles under the burden of his rain-soaked clothes, arriving to an abandoned construction site where many of the buildings have been left unfinished. There is one room with a light emanating from the bottom of the door. He quickly gains entry but discovers that the room is hardly a place for comfort. The floor is a pot of bubbling water, and the walls are cast in a fiery, red glow. This is a room reserved for one's miserable life, not for eternal bliss. The door slams behind him, and a deep voice can be heard from a smoldering pit below. "Breath slowly, it gets pretty hot down here.'

Beauregard Heathan Fox sits up when he hears the sound of a whistle from the train. The light in the cabin brightens his surroundings, and he sees the seats filled with dozing passengers. There is a pair of feet resting between his legs that belong to his traveling companion. She is seated across from him with her head bobbing up and down, exhaling and inhaling with the occasional reverse snort.

A conductor strolls down the aisle checking for tickets, and as soon as he exits, the lights go out again. Bo puts on his mad bomber cap to block out any noise and turns on a light from above. He opens up his logbook of his daily experiences and writes in a few notes:

January 31st, Wednesday. Charleston to Jacksonville by way of the East Coast Express. We are making our way toward the city of St. Augustine, the last stop on our travels before departing back to the UK. Today more than any other day, I feel the strong desire to wake up alone in my own bed.

Bo feels the flap of his hat lift from his ears. His traveling companion, Mia Pearl, has awakened. “I'm bored!” She falls back into her seat with a huff. “I hate myself for being bored. My shrink tells me it's my inability to create an entertaining atmosphere for myself, so I have to manifest my boredom in a way that is destructive to others.”

Bo watches with little amazement as Mia reaches over the seat behind her and snatches a newspaper from a businessman. Naturally, the man gives Bo a dissatisfied look, to which he replies with an indifferent shrug. Mia flips through the pages of the paper until she finds something that interests her. She then tosses the rest of the paper back over the seat.

“Here's some 'printed puke' from the Spectral City Times: Half the residents of St. Augustine have witnessed an apparition, while the other half have reported some sort of a living arrangement with one.” Mia scoffs. “And the llama says? Ghosts! It's what everyone is talking about. Who is everyone anyways? Shouldn't the paper be required to release a list? Seriously, if they came up with just one-one thousands of the billions of people on this planet to support that claim, I might accept their findings.”

Mia unwraps a candy bar from her pocket and takes a bite. She looks up at Bo's inattentiveness, seeing he is more engaged with his logbook than with her concerns. She lifts up an ear flap again and lets out her voice, “I'm not sure you could have said anything different to make your last two months any easier!”

Bo’s eyes go wide with shock as he looks blankly into Mia’s face. “Keira of Perth, Jacobis of Boston, Bon Bon of New Jersey. Aren't those the women you are writing about?”

Bo ignores her comment and continues to write.

“I can only imagine what it was like for those women trying to consummate a relationship with you. Women need constant reassurance, Bo, and you just don't offer that. Of course, if you had the wits to ever consider such a task, you might find yourself in a lasting commitment. Who was the girl from New York? The one who followed you to Charleston only so you could say goodbye to her again?"

"She was not following me, Mar; that was just a coincidence."

"Just a coincidence?! A coincidence is simply a miracle less objectivity, multiplied by subjectivity, equal to all sums of one's mistaken identity. Let's look at the facts; the shaman tells us that..."

Bo pulls both ear flaps down over his ears and lowers his head into his logbook:

> *These events, having taken place on the thirty-first of January, are a stark reminder of how my behavior can be deemed inappropriate by so-called: 'companions'.*

Mia lifts Bo's ear flap again. "It's not an affliction to be alone; it's a choice." Bo, naturally has a smile for everything, which really pisses Mia off. She tosses his hat down the aisle and storms off.

There are never any round edges to Mia's words. They are as pointed as a sharp tongue can be made to deliver them. Amazing that their togetherness was discovered accidentally with the both of them looking for someone else. Yet, despite their disputes, which are many, they find a way to fuse them by the day's end. Their other traveling companion, Samantha, says they are better off together than with anyone else, simply because they are like no one else.

Bo looks up from his logbook and briefly smiles at Samantha several rows away. Her eyes are fixed on him a little longer than deemed comfortable. Her recent engagements have become all too confusing, since she has always preferred the 'look at me and I'll look the other way' approach. Fortunately, the lights go out before it becomes too awkward. Bo closes his book and rests his eyes, thinking about what he will do once he returns home.

FEBRUARY 2nd: WHO ARE YOU?

The cabin comes alive with the announcement they have arrived at the station. Bo clops his way down the aisle in his untied work boots and retrieves his hat before exiting the train.

"Teuchy!" Bo looks up to see Mia already at the far end of the platform. "Let's go!!"

He lugs the two packs through the terminal and sets them on the street outside. It is still dark in the early morning hours, and there is a strong chill in the air that stings his nose.

"We discussed this, you know. Sam is to be our chaperone for the next two weeks."

"I remember mention of it."

Mia lifts up onto the tips of her toes to readjust his hat. "I'm not saying your brain is completely devoid of activity, but sometimes I think the only movement that goes on up there would resemble flies on a turd pile."

"Cute, Mar."

Bo tosses both their backpacks into Samantha's back seat and joins them. The two ladies are having a brief discussion about staying with Sam for two weeks, but because her brother can be a bit intimidating, Mia thinks it best to rent a room elsewhere.

Sam pulls onto a two-way avenue and begins the search for their hotel. When the car slows to a stop, Bo instinctively pushes the back door open with his foot. He grabs the straps of both backpacks and lays them before the hotel steps.

"'Hotel Hospitalario." Mia taps Bo on the shoulder and points to a sign above the door. "Bit of a mouthful, isn't it? 'Ho-spita-lario.'"

Samantha surprises them both by tapping their shoulders. She gives Bo a long kiss on the cheek and adds a second kiss to let him know the first kiss was no accident. Bo and Mia then watch with curiosity as she drives off without pausing at the stop sign.

"Shocking that she would blind side you like that, Bo."

Mia takes several long steps up to the hotel door and gives it a weighty pull. After it refuses to budge, she then taps her knuckles on the glass, followed by a shoulder thrust. After a few kicks with the heel of her foot and a headbutt, she finally walks over to Bo and extracts a heavy tool from his backpack.

"Serious, Mar. My work wrench?"

"Great way to get a response." She cocks her arm back, ready to wield the gadget, when suddenly a gold-painted face appears at the small opening in the door.

"Who you?!" The attendee says.

Bo lifts up both backpacks and bows to the lady, "And a fine diddy-daddle that shines a light on to you too, my good madam."

"I'm Mia Pearl, and this is Bo Fox. Our friend, Samantha Case, called with a reservation?"

The lady grumbles.

Bo and Mia follow behind the little lady as she makes her way toward the check-in desk. Bo dodges a wing from a ceiling fan and looks at the manager with shock, "Has anyone ever lost their head in here?"

Mia snickers at Bo and approaches the counter, "We want a room with separate beds, a bathroom, and a view of a pool."

Bo releases the backpacks to the floor and squints at Mia's hair floating slowly toward the oscillating fan.

"We also want a Telly with access to British Television; plates and utensils with a kitchenette; and our beds turned over daily with two chocolate morsels left on the pillows."

Bo begins stroking his chin, wondering at all if her hair could possibly reach the blades.

"We are also inquiring about a map of the surrounding area, discount coupons to our favorite eateries, and keys to allow us into the hotel after hours."

Bo squeezes his knees together in anguish as the blades catch three hairs, four hairs, then five; but once it reaches up to eight in rapid succession, he lifts a hand to help, "Mar?"

"Shush, Bo!! I want fresh towels and toilets cleaned while we are out..." Mia's face suddenly contorts.

"Mar, are you okay?"

With her teeth clenched and her head tilted sideways, Mia begins a slow walk in a circle trying not to lift off from the floor. Bo recognizes her discomfort, but Mia still waves him off and continues walking with her demands.

"Would a stay of two weeks be too much trouble?"

Comically, once Mia begins skipping along the ground in several full torso spins, the manager finally reaches for the fan switch.

Bo sets Mia down on her two feet and undoes her hair. For the longest minute, Mia just stares at the manager, who returns the same discerning stare back at her. The manager then goes to the closet behind the desk. She retrieves a stick with a hook on the end and hands it to Mia. "You want all those things? You need this. Third floor!"

Mia stamps her foot, "I don't want a stick; I want a key."

Bo slings the backpacks over his shoulders and grabs the stick from the manager. He takes Mia's arm, who still refuses to take her eye off the manager, then he has to pull her aside to avoid bumping into a short, stocky man dressed in dark and purple. She too gives him the evil eye.

"Who were they, Goggy? Is there some reason for giving them the grabber to the attic?"

The little lady shrugs her shoulders and looks anxiously around the counter. "My dinner is missing!"

Bo and Mia rush up and down the hallway looking for an elevator until Bo finally yells out, "Found it!" He places the stick into a ceiling groove and pulls down a retracting door. He then reaches up and pulls down a collection of folded steps and creaking springs.

It is a dimly lit room, made possible only by the morning lights shining through the wallboards. Mia reaches up and pulls on a string, causing a light to reveal the room's contents. It is not at all what she had envisioned for their final two weeks of traveling. There is no drywall, no windows, and the triangular support beams taking up most of the living space don't appear strong enough to hold up the roof. There are two single bed frames with mattresses wrapped in plastic, a bathroom separated by a plastic sheet and a very old television with a video game console attached to it.

"Well, we have stayed in worse." Mia waves the dust about the air and walks toward the kitchenette. She sniffs the plates and turns over a mysterious-looking piece of crockery. She then disappears into a crawl space above the kitchen cabinets and calls back moments later. "There's a window with a view of the parking lot, and I think there's a pool out there too."

Mia leaps down to the floor and retrieves a few bedsheets. She tosses each one like Frisbees onto the beds and looks at Bo sitting on the floor, eating from a plastic container, "Where did you get the food?"

"They were handing it out at the counter." Bo hears a loud thump and looks under Mia's bed to see she is in a catatonic state on the floor. He reaches for his backpack and pulls out his logbook.

Mia has an unpleasant affliction labeled: Myotonic Narcolepsy Rigorous Morti. It is believed to be related to the phenomenon of fainting goats. For five minutes every morning, she falls into a deep slumber with her arms and legs straight out.

Mia walks with her face to the sun, enjoying the earthy smell of an early spring. There are many nice mornings in February, and it just so happens the temperature is twenty degrees Celsius. The attraction of the city before them is an architectural design imparted by the history that existed here two hundred years ago. Simple wood structures that formed bookstores, bakeries, and butcher shops; intricate cobblestone streets that paved the way for pushcarts and pull-carriages; add to that, play parks for people participating in punching matches and popular puzzle games.

Mia reaches into her coat pocket and unfolds a map, quickly identifying a convenience store on the edge of the city. She is hungry, and they are late for where she wants to be. Skirting around tourists, dodging between road signs, and scurrying with one foot in the gutter and the other on the walkway, the two eventually meet in the middle of an empty street. The western section of the city is much quieter than the touristy area, and the old Victorian homes with moss-laden trees add a skeptical feeling that they are no longer in a present-day city. After missing the convenience store for the fifth time, it is by the fortunes of a wild hog breaking through the underbrush that they find a place that may or may not serve food. The building rests upside down on a mansard-style roof, and there is an open window on the second floor that appears to serve as the door.

The store does offer a variety of global newspapers, microwaved foods, water bottles, and many unhealthy knick-knacks that Mia has a taste for. Bo, however, remains with the oddities on the counter that may appear strange to some but intrinsic to those who believe in their magic. He looks at a plaque on the checkout counter and calls for the name: "Cornelius Bumpkin?"

Bo is greeted by a short man with a red bow tie and hair curled about his ears, "Yes! Yes! Those are my magic trinkets from around the world. Some illuminate and some do shake, some put you at ease, and others will keep you awake."

"What is this liquid for?"

"It's used for internal infections." The man lifts the small bottle from a holder and takes a couple of swigs. After a few harsh coughs, he hands it to Bo. "Said to help with sleeping."

Bo takes a sniff of the bottle and scrunches up his face.

"I know what you are looking for. A method for cleansing the body. I have two kits for only $24.95. Half price if you buy it along with a bowel retractor kit."

"What would I need a bowel retractor kit for?"

"I'm not sure. I hear it's great for college parties, though."

"I'll just take this amulet if that would be okay."

"Good choice. The hogstone comes with a year's supply of Boneset. It is said to cure fevers."

"Can you ship it to my mailing address in Scotland?"

Mia stacks what she has gathered on the counter and reaches into Bo's pocket for money.

Mr. Bumpkin tallies up the items. "Are you here on holiday?"

"We're staying at the Hotel 'Ho'spee'tal'." Mia pronunciates.

"I haven't heard of that one. Is that on the beach?"

"Wish it were on a lake." Mia takes a sip of the syrup, and her eyes immediately cross. She grabs a handful of match booklets and stuffs them in her sweat shirt.

They exit the store with Mia walking dizzily down the road. She has the occasional giggle that annoys those she bumps into, but it seems more infuriating when she apologizes with a sweeping bow.

"What was in that bottle, Bo? Makes my brain feel numb." Mia sets the bags down for a moment. "And what is it with you and that rock?!"

"As foretold by the Seers of Scotland: 'With the eye through the hole of the hogstone, all dreams can create a new happiness.'"

"Let me try!" Mia rubs her goofy face, then holds the stone before her eye. She sees two men waving to her from a bowlegged bench. They are dressed in weathered, beaten clothing that she finds disappointing, so she quickly redirects the hole elsewhere. That's when she pleasantly sees a man stretched out in the grass, exercising his thick arms on top of his hands. His wear is a bit concerning, covered in a blue dye from head to foot, but his dark eyes, wavy black hair, and Romanesque nose do intrigue her desires. She nudges Bo and gives him back the hogstone, "They don't make faces like that anymore."

The man sits up with a stick in his hand as Mia approaches with her bags of food. Poking and prying at the plastic containers, Mia quickly responds by pulling out a box of goodies.

"Mar, what are you doing?"

She hands the man various treats and watches him perform a silly dance with a lot of odd kicks.

"Okay, Mar, give him what he wants and let's go."

"My name is Mia Pearl, and this is Bo Fox. We're from the UK."

"I am neither; I am Catalan. Parla Catala." The man stuffs his mouth with several different treats, filling his cheeks until they can hold no more. "Yes, hmm, good. Very good, Mammy."

"Not Mammy; Mia. It was given to me by the nuns at the orphanage. I ran away a lot." Mia opens up a soup container and hands it to him. "So, Catalan, what do you do with your time here?" The man eagerly laps up the soup. "I had servant work in New Smyrna."

Mia takes a seat next to the man. "That sounds rewarding."

"Horrible treatment. It was on an indigo plantation, so I came here with Father Camps."

"I know what that's like. I was forced to work in a garden as a child. So, do you have a place to stay?"

"I live over on Cordova and Tolomato."

"Bo, hand me the map of the city?" Mia spreads the map on the grass. "Wait, this can't be right. This location doesn't meet the zoning requirements for a residence."

Bo takes one of Mia's bags. "Mar, he says he lives on Cordova and Tolomato; let's leave it at that."

"But there's no way. The zoning here doesn't permit the usage of a single-family or a multi-family residence, it's labeled as 'deceased-residential.' Maybe Father Camps had obtained rights to bury someone there, but he can't alter the permit when he doesn't own the ground." Mia looks at the map again and slams her hand down with a loud smack. "I know what's going on here!"

"Mar, let's go!"

"This pisses me off to no end! There was no proper deal done here! Catalan, how long have you lived there?" Mia watches Catalan raise two fingers. "Two years?"

He then motions with his thumb to count higher.

"Twelve? Twenty? Two hundred? Higher? It doesn't matter. I deal with people requiring long-term living arrangements."

"Mar, you lease cemetery space!"

"Bo! Someone is taking advantage of this poor man, and it happens to be someone who wears the cloth! Have you complained to the diocese about this, Catalan?!"

Catalan raises his head from a jar with juice all over his face. "No, cannot. Do you have more of these?"

Mia circles about the lawn, punching at the air. "Do you see this, Bo?! Catalan is being threatened!!"

Bo watches as the man runs his fingers along the inside of the bowl and shakes it up and down. "Mia, leave him be and let's go."

"Where are we going to go while people are suffering?! This is so much the normal case with you! You are never accepting of anyone other than myself, Sam, or your floozy, short-term girlfriends, admit it! Remember how you treated Peetrie in Australia?"

"You really want to talk about Peetrie, Mar?"

"Wow, Catalan, you ate all of our food. Bo, do you have more money?"

She smells of lemon and lime, having doused her work outfit in her favorite fabric softener. She can now start the day with a smile. Beatie had accomplished a lot this morning: the patterns on the kitchen tiles now glisten from a wet mop, the quartz counter top sparkles from a Gunter Gloss shine, and the cherry-stained furniture shimmers from the shellac of an Old English bottle. Now she has the time to practice a few routines for the up-coming Valentine's Day Galla tryouts. The event is only once a year, and who knows if Valentine's Day will be celebrated again? She leaps up and down and does a few odd kicks, racing into her room and then rolling off the bed. After performing a few slides in and out of her closet, she finally finishes her routine by kicking the garbage can across the floor. What to wear? The faded, full-body leotard in the closet and the laceless shoes on the teetering rack have all waited too long to come out. They are now so 'replace-ably' out of fashion that she will have to return to Meeshman's. "Super Yeh!!"

By the time the sun has declared the end of the morning, Beatie is already late for work. She touches up her look with a little shine from the jar and then finds her keys in yesterday's pants. When she finally does get the shift into a gear that works, Beatie and Ms. Weary eventually find a parking spot twelve blocks away from the office. After a drama-filled speech from her boss, it is not long before she is chewing on her sandwich and staring across the street. Oh, how desperately she wants to wear the dress in the window – like right now even! Mr. Happiness is again consumed with his 'barbie-muffin' girlfriend in the back office, so now what? She is not going to wait for this; it's her lunch break, and she has important things to do.

Beatie rocks the door back and forth to create a soft squeak. The assistant manager has dozed off with an unfinished sandwich and a glass of magnesia.

Beatie does not wish to disturb Mrs. Bookafleely, because hurrying into a Meeshman dress is all about secrecy. Yes, secrecy, because Ms. Meeshman has forever banned Beatie from ever approaching one of her pricey dresses. She even said, 'If you can't afford to take it along, then there is no reason for you to try it on.' For this very reason, Beatie won't directly go to the window dress; not yet anyways, she does whisper to it, but that's all.

The store is empty of midday shoppers, which she prefers – always enjoying her own time with only an hour to spare. She has to operate with efficiency, so she begins with the two-tier dresses by the window. Using her nimble fingers, Beatie knows with certainty if a new item has been added, so by the time she reaches the pre-folded smocks and flame-retardant coveralls, she is already pressing her face into the fabric trying to remember its smell. It is at this time, however, that Beatie bumps into a solid object that rocks back and forth but does not fall. Though initially sorry for her clumsiness, she is ultimately disgusted with the interaction. "Oh, no way! Not you, Mannequin!"

Beatie does not like Mannequins, they always appear to be dressed for her but fail to convince. Many of their fashions are outdated and their label descriptions are always inaccurate. She has to get away from mannequins; never once have they ever had her best interest in mind.

Beatie squirts her hands with Meeshman's Moagli Badada Cream and continues on with her search. A reflection of Ebullient on the window suddenly causes her to buckle to her knees. It's just too emotional not being able to go to the dress directly, therefore, she thinks it best to be direct with it in case it's offended. Beatie creeps up behind the display and whispers softly, "Hey, Ebullient? I can't see you right now; Meeshman rules, you know, not mine." Beatie reaches out to shake the sleeve. "Are you listening?" Accidentally, a tag falls to the floor and she quickly retrieves it. Just as she thought, it is only three years old, and it has a foreign name. "Maybe that's why you can't understand me. What else?" Beatie leans forward and extends her nose toward the collar. "You smell perfectly nice." She then puts her arm through the sleeve, and immediately, her eyes roll to the insides of her head. The calm emollients of the fabric are now morphing with her skin. It's so soft that she could even consider sleeping in it.

Beatie accidentally bumps into another solid object, but this one does fall to the floor. "I said not now, Mannequin! Seriously! How silly would I look in that dress at a posh dinner?"

"Beatie?! What's going on over there?!"

"Shhh!" Beatie kicks the mannequin. "Mrs. Snail-bag heard us!"

"Beatie?!"

Beatie pokes her head out of the racks. "Yes, Mrs. Bookafleely. I was just wondering how much the High-water Sissy Pants cost."

Mrs. Bookafleely eases her way down into her chair and watches Beatie duck back into the racks. She knows perfectly well Beatie has no intention of buying anything, and only once did she ever walk out of the store with an item. It was the Muckle-Ma-Geggy, double-chained, Fluvian handbag priced at the stocking charge.

Beatie drops an armful of camises onto the table before the assistant and begins turning each one over.

"Beatrice, you're a grown woman. How about finding someone who can pay for all of this?"

"I'm trying, Mrs. Bookafleely; I just don't know where to go about looking for someone."

"Start with some friends first, and then leave that womanizing confickler who runs the tourist shop you work at."

Beatie turns a shirt inside out and sniffs it. She isn't really listening to Mrs. Bookafleely. The woman's thoughts are never kind, at least not kind enough to let her try on the window dress – but maybe she can! Stealing has never entered her mind before, but there are certainly things worth taking.

"Beatrice, where are you going?!"

Screw Meeshman rules! Beatie grabs the dress from the display window and makes a dash toward the nearest exit. She would have made it too, if not for a solid object hip-checking her onto a chair with rollers. It sends her down a set of stairs and into a dark room she never knew existed. Lifting herself off the cold carpet, she looks in dismay to see moths flipping about on the floor in a slow and flightless death. She also sees a trolley of dresses wrapped in a low-density polyethylene film. Shivering to think that one of those outfits could be hers to wear, Beatie rushes to the ensemble with her nimble fingers a-go. Turns out, these are the same dresses worn by the 'not-so-famous' celebrities in town. The dress in her left hand was worn by the Shrimp Festival Queen, and it still has the shrimp perfume on it! And the dress in her right hand was worn by 'Flee Farmer Bob' at his Bachelorette Party. It even comes with a piglet bonnet!

The crash of the display bars has Mrs. Bookafleely standing in a panic. She hobbles down the ramp and up several steps, soon finding the display bars scattered about the floor. This is where she finds Beatie rolling around in the fallen dresses, rubbing the fabric all over her body and making oinking noises.

"Beatrice Backlebond, what has gotten into you?!" Mrs. Bookafleely limps her way over to Beatie and links a clothing hook onto her belt.

Meeshman's door slams behind Beatie and she quickly sinks to the pavement in disappointment. Several well-dressed people are stepping over her and forcing her to frown. Rich people really do piss her off at times, but she knows that without their existence, she might not have anything to dream about.

Beatie sits calmly in her office seat, bored that nobody is interested in any of their holiday-themed tours. She walks to the window and watches two people holding hands. They are making 'lovey' faces at one another as if they are in love. They do this to her every year at this time and always in the same place. Not this time! Tonight is her ballet class, and she likes doing things other people are too bothered to do.

She looks toward the back office to see Mr. Happiness grooming a different young lady's backside. He apparently finds pleasure in someone else's company besides the one he is obligated to provide for. There is no way Beatie is here for this. She leaves a note with plans she will be back tomorrow.

It is a one-hour ballet session, which seems long enough to get to know the other participants; it's just they don't like to communicate in the usual way. Not that she minds the need to invent new words, but these attendees seem to take it entirely too far. Words like 'Kak Cam' and 'Habari Yako' – is that even tolerable? And then there is this one lady that just makes clicking noises. How do you respond to that? But the biggest communication challenge she finds is with her ballet instructor, Sean Schma Malvenu. Truthfully said, she's a bit of a spinster, and sure, she means well, but what she tries to convey with the whack of a stick has left permanent scars on the slowest of her students. Many of them blame Beatie, because the 'whacking' only began after she started the class.

Ms. Weary stalls several times going over the bridge but is still committed to getting her there. She would have arrived on time too, if it were not for the man in green fatigues slamming his hands down on her hood. He should have never been in the crosswalk anyways, and Ms. Weary agreed.

Ms. Weary putters her way into a parking spot, and after a slow roll between the lines, she coughs herself to sleep. The class is overfilled, so the latecomers will have to wait against the wall. That's just fine; that's their decision. Beatie has to get ready, and that's hers. She desperately wants to be in the main show next week, and there are only a few spots available.

She encircles her arms several times, looking often toward the youngest student leaping about like a baby impala. Beatie doesn't like children being so small and fearless. They should all just become hand models, like the other preschoolers. She stretches her leg over a chair and watches the two-year-old McCocky girl get ready. She is the first one to perform and is always one of Beatie's biggest competitors. There is no doubt about her walking challenges, but one must not underestimate her cuteness. McCocky's social media page has more thumbs up than a basket full of pocket beagles.

"Places, please!" Beatie hears the assistant yell. She settles down in the front row, where she can keep track of all of her mishaps. Already, she counts ten in the first minute, and no way will crying get her any points. "Better wait until next year, McCocky."

Beatie's turn is next. She does a few odd kicks before letting out several loud 'Kak Cams.' Once the lights go down, a stage light appears briefly on Beatie, but then redirects itself to somebody across the room. "She's not even supposed to be here!" Beatie says to herself while slapping a hand across her knee. "That little icky, sticky, dirty-nailed cockapoo was totally responsible for the pinworms in the locker room bench last week!"

Beatie feels a tap on her shoulder and turns with a surprise. "Bonjour! Comment vas-tu! As-tu danse?"

"Mimi! Where have you been?!" Beatie gives her a quick hug. It's Mimi. They have known each other for almost six months now, and Mimi is still yet to use a single word Beatie can understand.

Beatie turns her head back to the floor and squints her eyes in anger. "It's her, Mimi. Cokie Poocock. Just look at her prancing about in those faded leotards and pink plastic shoes. Oh, and of course she chooses the music of Valse des fluers – so demure. Yeh, and go ahead and coil into a backflip five times and see how Bernie Rearburn feels about it. She still has to take the pills for the worms."

"Kookie Peacock?"

"Yeh, that's what I say. Just look at her smiling at everyone with her crooked smile and misdirected teeth."

"Elle n'a que six ans."

Beatie chuckles, "Six arms. Good one, Mimi."

Mimi lifts six fingers and waves them before Beatie's face, "No, six ans. Pas ca. Pas ca."

"Pas Ca? Is that what you just said to me, Mimi?"

"Oui. Pas ca."

Beatie looks at Mimi with intrigued eyes. "I do so like the sound of that word'." Beatie sways her head and flutters her hands back and forth, "So, how are you doing today, Miss Backlbond? Pas Ca! Would you like some Transgruple Delight with your Cheese Spun Gerder? Pas Ca! Pas Ca! That is quite a clever word you've invented there, Mimi; may I use it?" The crowd erupts into a boisterous applause, and Beatie joins in, "Pas Ca!! Pas Ca!!"

It is on the fourth number, by which there are seven, that Beatie's name is finally called. The instructions are few, but there will be three dances, each requiring a different set of leaps. A bit daunting, but those are the rules; get used to it. Beatie holds her shoulders back and her head positioned to the left. She then waits for Miss Malvenu to smack her smacking stick against the wall.

"Hold your stomach in tightly, please!" Calls out the instructor. "Ready and begin!" <SMACK>

On tiptoes, Beatie weaves her fingers through the air, incorporating a well-timed spin before settling back onto her toes. She does this with such grace and zupah that even Beatie herself can't help but let out a soft squeal. Now it's time for the leaps. She races about the room, jumping up and down with a few loud guffaws, inspiring a wanted laugh from the crowd. Now onto the second part.

"Stop!!!" Ms. Malvenu yells before advancing with her smacking stick.

Beatie stands in a frozen position, watching from the corner of her eye as the instructor takes measurements around her feet. She then steps back and orders Beatie to continue, "Deux, trois, quatre, faster!"

Time and time again, Beatie leaps at the insistence of the instructor, and time and time again, the instructor insists that the tips of her toes should barely touch the floor.

It is the third dance now, and Beatie has decided to alter her routine to please the crowd. After a few of the required kicks and spins, now it is time for her to shine. Placing her arms by her side, she races about the room like a fighter jet. No one has ever seen anything like it before, particularly when she leaps into the crowd after being shot down. But now for the finale, which she has prepared just for her instructor. Falling to the floor with her fingers angled as painfully as they will bend, Beatie rolls onto her back in a mouth-frothing convulsion, and then twitches uncontrollably into a death-spiraling silence.

"And twirl and ... fine, whatever, Beatrice." Ms. Malvenu throws up her hands. "Just stand up and curtsy, please."

Beatie leaps to her feet and bounces three times. Never, without a doubt, did she perform to the liking of the audience. The proof? There were a few spins with several loopty-loops, several pointed-toe-heel-bangs, and then who can forget the 'Poisoned Sloth' for the finale? Something she made up in her mother's bathroom after accidentally gargling lamp oil.

Beatie steps forward and curtsies before all the distorted expressions. She then scurries to her chair looking about the room for a reaction. True, their silence does trouble her, but her name being mentioned by Miss Malvenu is certainly gratifying enough.

When the final performer is lifted from the mat, and the surface thoroughly cleaned, Beatie finally relaxes. The great pleasure of being praised for her unprecedented dance is most on her mind, and of course, to be honored to dance in the upcoming Valentine's Hokie Gala. It's really all she thinks about.

A long rack is rolled out across the floor and Beatie gasps with joy. There on display are the Mary Jane's to be issued to those who will perform in the gala next week. Oh, how they sparkle with that extra polish and shine.

Now comes the call to those who performed to the instructor's liking. No way should Squealy Berger get in; she slipped in her own excrement. And Perky-Bust-Little? Be serious! She was spitting up Gerber food on every fall! Good news: neither were accepted. But then comes forth the most infuriating news that Beatie was not expecting. The name Cokie Poocock was called, not just once, but twice; to which Beatie 'booed' both times. Miss Malevenu scolded Beatie and reminded her of her silly and unpracticed routine, but that's just Ms. Malvenu, being Ms. Malvenu. She doesn't really mean it.

Beatie listens to each name called and watches as each pair of shoes are handed out. To those without the footwear, a quick dismissal from general assistant, Larvae Gene Wormscream. Beatie is among those dismissed.

Beatie shakes her head in disbelief at what seemed to be the longest, most horrifying adaptation of a headache. Not being invited to the big show is just too impossible for her to accept. The only logical explanation is that it's a mistake. If she recalls from less than an hour ago, she is pretty sure she nailed it. So why is she shoeless?

Enter general assistant, Wormscream, with a different kind of shoe. A shoe that has an open-toe peep hole with buckles and straps. A shoe that shines, but not in the way one would expect it to. It shines because it wants something. Well, simple solution is to get the right shoe! Beatie pushes her way through all the parents and raises her voice above the screaming children.

"Ms. Malvenu! Ms. Malvenu!"

"Beatrice, this is not a good time."

"But these are not the right shoes! Did I not sway with the lightness of a feather and the grace of a swan?"

"Beatie, you knew when you signed up for this class that I view ballet quite differently than the names you claim are experts. Not a good thing for you, but worth understanding."

"But you can't ignore the great contributions of Jinjie Kicky, Martha Bumbolly, Diddi Gum Babba, and Bubba Farley!"

"Beatrice, I have tried to be nice, but this is just the problem I have with you. I looked up those performers you speak of, and none of them exist."

"Are you sure you're getting the spellings right?"

"Enough of this childishness, Beatie! This is about the past and the future; do you understand me?!"

"No, I don't. Those are opposing words."

"The 'past' is ballet. The 'future' is the new club my uncle is opening downtown. Now, this should be a great way for you to give those extra large ..." Ms. Malvenu places her hands before her breasts, "...some exposure."

"I don't follow you. I have big hands?"

"Larvae Gene will give you the necessary instructions for you to follow. I want you to look at this as a blessing. You will finally become the woman you were always meant to be."

"No, Ms. Malvenu! I pay good money for these ballet lessons!"

"Beatie, I make the decisions about who will best perform in my shows, and that's final!"

"Well, bully for you! I guess I'll be taking my frown now, thank you kindly!"

Ms. Mavenu's angry eyes suddenly stare directly into Beatie's. "Did you just raise your voice to me?"

Beatie covers her mouth and tightly closes her eyes. She knows what's coming. Ms. Malvenu is going to scold her and tell her that she is being lackadaisical, that she doesn't follow instructions properly, and that birds sometimes leave a burning nest to start over again. After that, Ms. Malvenu becomes vague, and her thinking untranslatable. It is then, she says that she has seen better spins from dead animals in a family swimming pool, adding that dung beetles roll excrement with more grace than she does – that Beatie understood.

"Beatrice, there is an address on the back of this card, and I'm doing you a favor. Now I'm sure you will meet a wide array of interesting people there. You will be there, won't you?"

Beatie is not happy, but she will go along with the demands, knowing that she has nothing else to do with her evenings. Ms. Wormscream hands Beatie and Mimi a performance outfit with instructions on how to wear it. She then hands them a musical CD with voice commands. With reluctance, they both take the club's directions.

Beatie sits in her car staring at the T-straps in the seat next to her. The shoes remind her of a reading at the Blue State Library by Buxom Man Beef:

'When you're wearing bad shoes, bad things happen.' That seems to be what these heels are all about. Beatie turns on the ignition, sliding the CD into the music slot and listens to the sound of an orchestra playing. 'Step in. Step out. Wrists in. Wrists out'.

"Can you pull the ladder up, please?" Mia wraps her wet hair in a towel and turns the faucet on. She looks at the haze of soap on the glass and sets it back in the holder. She then spits a mouthful of water into the toilet and puts away her toothbrush. The small bucket under the sink makes her question the sink's working condition.

Bo pulls the ladder up and stumbles backward onto Mia's bed. He is surprised to discover that the bed has rollers on it as it coasts toward the wall.

"It's absurd that the only soap provided to us has to be used for our hands, our privates, and our faces." Mia tilts her head back and places a court-ordered pill on the back of her tongue.

"How long have you been taking those?"

She swallows down hard. "Since the British government labeled me as crazy."

"Do they help?"

"Without them it's like being awake in a nightmare." She feels about the sheets and looks up at Bo. "My bed has bars on it."

"It's a hospital bed." Bo walks over to his backpack and pulls down the zipper of the side compartment. He finds his logbook and writes in his entry for the day:

We have returned to the birthplace of Samantha Case, who has arranged for us to stay in a posh hotel. Posh it is not, and it is in the attic where we are staying.

Bo lifts his head in thought, while Mia flips through the television channels. "Sam is showing a strange interest in me; have you not noticed?"

"What?" Mia rolls her eyes. "Oh, I hope not."

"She had that long 'air-of-delight' on the train, and what about the kiss in front of the hotel?"

Mia turns up the television volume. "Sure would give me the creeps." Mia eventually becomes frustrated with nothing to watch and tosses the channel changer to the chair. "Don't get all committed to the idea. You're a Pisces, and she's a Sagittarius. Both of you will be waiting for the other to make the next move that will never happen."

"You believe in all that horoscope jaw, Mar?"

"It was Sam that pointed this out to me. I am an Aries, just to let you know, which explains why you and I can only tolerate each other. It is also why Sam and I bond so well."

"Is that why you had fun tormenting Peetrie?"

Mia climbs under her covers and reaches for the light switch. "We didn't know Peetrie was a Cancer until Sam got the truth out of him."

FEBRUARY 3rd: IT IS YOU AGAIN

High along the ceiling, where a glare of light breaks through a narrow slot in the roof, Mia opens her eyes to a pleasant aroma of coffee beans. She quickly wraps a towel around her head and releases the ladder to the floor. The source seems to be emanating from an opening in the hallway floor.

"Hello down there?" Mia calls and waits for a response.

"It is me down here!" She hears back.

Mia lays her bare feet down on the top step and sits down. "Who is me?"

"The day manager!"

"You don't sound like the person that checked me in?"

"No, I'm her great-great-grandson, Sen!"

A face from the cellar rises into the light, and Mia pushes her fingers into the man's cheeks. She then scrutinizes his dark eyes and facial features that might resemble those of the little lady. "I guess I see the common kin features. What's down there, if I might ask?"

"I'd be happy to show you."

"No, that's alright. I was looking for some tea and crumb cake."

"You won't find anything like that down there."

"No, I kind of understand that now. I thought I smelled other things, like maybe coffee beans?"

"Tools, pool equipment, and some old appliances. I found a few guests down there one time, but we don't advise it."

"Maybe if you kept the cellar door closed you might solve that problem. Well, while we are on strange topics, I do wish to inquire about the foldaway bars on my bed."

"This used to be a hospital in the nineteenth century. We kept the beds because they are still in good working condition."

"Wouldn't there possibly be some diseases embedded within the mattress fibers?"

"It wasn't that kind of a hospital. They were all mentally insane, not consumed with plague."

Mia slaps her knees. "Well, I have learned enough for the day. Keep in mind, day manager, tea and cakes would not be asking a lot for a $125 night stay."

The morning erupts with the noisy sounds from the street. Bo rolls over to hear the occasional car horn with a growing number of voices – the unmistakable soundtrack of a modern city. He rolls the other way on his bed to see Mia appearing before him. She is dressed in her walking attire: sweatshirt, black Lycra shorts, and training shoes. There is also a towel wrapped about her head that she is re-tightening. Bo stretches his arms and yawns, "What time is it, Mar? We missed breaky?"

"Don't make me any hungrier than I already am. Seems we need to go out again."

Bo stumbles out of bed and is immediately tackled to the floor by his own backpack. He slowly makes his way to the bathroom and turns the tap on the faucet. "We have a bathtub!"

"True!" Mia appears over his right shoulder in the mirror. "I recommend not going to bed with your hair wet though. It apparently gets very cold at night." Mia pulls off the towel to expose solid sticks of ice sparkling on one side of her head.

Bo chuckles and reaches into his backpack. He sniffs his pullover and looks it over. It is wrinkled, worn, and weathered, but he knows the unwholesome smell will go away in the open air.

"Should we go prom about town again?"

Mia follows Bo down the ladder, and soon they are both long stepping back into the streets. She runs past him with her energy a go! "Look, Bo! The Castilla de San Marcos. It was meant to protect the inhabitants from invading pirates."

"They're all over our country, Mar!"

Mia pulls out a guidebook and kneels in the grass. "So, this is St. Augustine. Says it was founded in 1565 by Pedro Menendez de Aviles." Mia pauses and looks about when she hears a childlike voice.

"You're pretty stupid if you have to read about that."

Mia suddenly feels the knees of a little girl bounce against her shoulder. She can't be more than nine years old with her hair in the shape of angel wings. She wears an old-style dress from forgotten times and shakes a styrofoam cup before Mia's face.

Mia pushes the little girl back and stands. "That's some appearance you have there."

"Thank you very much, kindly see." The girl dips with a curtsy. "If you haven't been to the Plaza de la Constitution, it once served as a marketplace. The statue of Ponce De Leon in the courtyard celebrates the first European explorer to Florida, and he arrived a half century before your so-called –'Pedro Menendez de Aviles'!"

Mia pushes Bo toward the other direction. "Forget her; the city gates are the other way."

The little girl shakes her styrofoam cup of coins while trailing closely behind. "After conquering South America in the early 1500s, the Spanish king wished to expand their religious faith in the northern lands. It is here where they ran into a French problem."

Mia grabs Bo's arm, "Let's go back and see the fort again."

The girl circles around with her cup shaking louder. "It took thirty years to build that fort. This city was intended to be a military colony and a base for colonization."

Mia redirects Bo back toward the city, but the little girl plops down before her steps and draws several lines in the dirt. "The two stone pillars before the city were joined by a stone wall. It served as a defense system to combat the English attacks in the early eighteenth century." The little girl points toward the fort. "Unfortunately, the fort's guns did little to stop the assailants from entering the city."

"And you were there?" Says an aggravated Mia.

"Well, I wasn't there at 'that' particular time." The little girl says while standing with her cup beneath Mia's nose.

"That is just what I thought." Mia brushes the girl aside and scrapes the markings in the dirt with her foot.

"Mar, she is just greeting us with some history. She's a salesgirl."

"You left out the part where she's intentionally annoying. You know what? I'm hungry. Let's go across the street."

Mia suddenly feels a slow drag on her footsteps. She reaches around to find the little girl pulling her backwards by her sweatshirt. "They came to escape the European wars, political freedom, and poverty! They came here for the promise of great economic wealth and free healthcare!"

Mia grabs ahold of the girl's shirt. "Free healthcare? You're just being ridiculous!"

"No, you're dickless!"

Mia stiff-arms the little girl while she swings her fists at her belly. "See this, Bo! She has nothing intelligent to say, and certainly, she can't go on talking with this nonsense."

"I would if I could, if I stood as I should." The girl slaps at Mia's arm while redoubling her kicking efforts. She suddenly stops when Mia begins pressing down on her hair. The girl then grabs Mia's hand and bites down hard, fleeing across the lawn in laughter.

"I was wondering how that was going to end. Forget the city. Let's go to the beach and then to Sam's."

"Sam's?"

"Yes, you do remember Sam, don't you?"

"Someone like her."

Mia claps her hands together. "Ah, the exhibition of doubt."

"I'm not doubting anything."

"I think it would be honorable if you would show her a little affection during our remaining days here."

"I hadn't noticed any affection from her in the past four months."

"Ever wonder why you are still single?"

Beatie is up early, sweeping the sand off the porch and pulling dust from her broom. She pours scalding fluid over some scraggly weeds and then returns to the house to wash her clothes. Her time in the morning is about her chores, but lately it's been more about falling back into the pages of her book.

She lowers herself onto the couch with another container of Mary Shiver's Coconut Sorbet. She has reached the part in the book that she finds most unconventional. Chapter Three expresses the dare to approach toward the men she could meet. The author makes this outlandish claim that Beatie is constantly defeated by internal worries that prevent her from interacting with the opposite sex. It is her 'loneliness' that is the root cause of this problem, and only with practice will she ever overcome her fears. The chapter then goes on to say that her inhibitions could be remedied with alcohol.

Beatie slams the book down and scoffs. This is the part she finds most absurd. Alcohol certainly didn't help Papa and Mamma when they first met – or did it? The book goes on to suggest that Papa drank in order to meet your mother, and then 'your papa' did this to 'your mamma' in order to create 'you.'

Beatie chuckles with a snort when the book also suggests several local bars in her area that she could attend. "Oh, sure, 'Mr. Gogster,' but you fail to mention the horrible things that do happen when meeting someone for the first time!" Beatie high-fives herself, thinking she has 'de-mastered' the 'master,' and then she looks down to see a response highlighted in red – 'alcohol can remedy this'.

"Oooh! This book is good! Setting me up for the old 'intro-conclusion, genitalia, symposium dilution.'" Beatie pushes the book aside with another scoff. She isn't so sure this book is thinking in her best interest. Alcohol just isn't at this juncture in her life right now, testifying to the fact that Papa was often loud and obnoxious whenever he was on fermented grapes. She steps out onto the porch for a moment, twisting her mouth from side to side in thought. She then rushes back to the book and flips to the last page. There it is on line twenty, inset by five spaces: *Never-ending happiness.*

Beatie walks back out onto the porch and looks up the street. The grog shops are only a fifteen-minute walk from her house. Her phone suddenly rings and she picks it up. "Tomorrow night?!"

The sidewalk glares in the noontime sun. The weather may seem cool to most Floridians, but after spending several weeks in the northern hemisphere, twenty-one degrees Celsius feels a bit much. Mia swivels her hips to keep a beach float from falling off her waist. She and Bo have covered quite a bit of distance, and her appearance has become that of an angry zombie. She walks with a flat-footed gait and a growling moan that is often attributed to the 'undead.' At the top of the bridge, she does see some relief on the boiling asphalt ahead. There, in the middle of the road, is an ice cream stand offering cherry-vanilla scoops at half price.

Bo lifts his arms to catch a strong breeze blowing off the river. The glue from his body has adhered to the fabric of his shirt, and it is making him feel like a wet rag. He stumbles backward and falls over his roommate. For reasons unknown, she is asleep in her float and holds a five-dollar bill to the air.

Bo drags Mia by the hood of her sweatshirt to a showerhead on the beach, and after drowning their dry mouths with water, they both find a place in the shade of a palm tree.

"Ah wanna go in da wah."

Bo nods his head. "A 'o irst!"

"Shrish Shree Shwish Shwah!"

Bo shrugs his shoulders. "O'tay."

Bo runs through the blistering sand, leaving Mia still trying to stand. He lumbers into the ocean and leaps above an oncoming wave. There is a strong pull on his feet and it isn't long before he finds himself washed upon the shore with an array of nature's products in his pants. He tilts his head and bangs the ocean out of his ears, looking around to find Mia chasing a ghost crab across the sand. There is also a little girl yelling words at Mia that she decides she should address with Bo. "It's another one of those Trouble-mites, Bo."

"You really don't like children, do you, Mar?"

"The proof is in their existence. Anyways, this one keeps pointing at my head and yelling Bumbee, like I'm supposed to understand 'bratty-little-barf' speech."

"Ignore her."

"Ignore her?"

"I'm sorry, Mar, but the beach didn't come with instructions."

Mia frowns at this and returns to chasing the crab – that is – until the little girl returns with cries of 'Bumbee' again.

"Well, I'm not your Bumbee, so knock it off!" It does not take long after the confrontation to see Mia in some sort of pain and the little girl crying. "You just said an awful, dreaded word!"

Mia, with tears of her own, responds, "I'm sorry, but it hurts."

Bo rushes to the scene and eventually comes to the understanding that two bumblebees had landed on either side of her head and stung her.

"Aye, Mar. Are you allergic to bee stings?"

"I don't know. I've never been stung before."

"Maybe we should head over to Sam's, fair game?"

Sam raises her eyes before the mirror and blushes. She is exploring the many Pantone colors in a makeup box and it is making her want to try new things. Something satin in the ingredients is making her face uncontrollably glow, and she feels like putting more on. After completely altering her appearance, she piles her breasts into a bucket bra and puts on a robe. Though she has never been forthright in saying so, she is hoping to keep Bo around through Valentine's, maybe longer if the stars remain aligned the way they are. Regrettably, she has been hiding her affections for Bo for too long now and can't help but put the blame on Mia for her inhibitions. If she had been coddled properly, she is sure she would have found this 'dare to be captivating' look a lot sooner.

Sam takes a deep breath and circles her arms several times in a counterclockwise motion. She is waiting for Mia and Bo to arrive, and with time remaining, she decides to clarify a misunderstanding she saw in this morning's horoscope. Nope, everything seems promising; the only part not mentioned is what to do about her hair. Sam drops the paper on the chair but quickly retrieves it when she notices a disparaging headline. 'Beastly varmints will ride the air, placing two discomforting horns in the line of her hair.' "How did I miss that?!"

Mia holds her hands to her head, groaning with the occasional cuss word she hasn't used yet.

"Mar, it isn't that far. I see Sam's house across the street."

Bo watches as Mia follows the extended chalk line down the middle of the road, slowly drifting to the other side without incident. He extracts the directions from her carrying bag and looks up. "Two-story, wood-frame home with a large oak tree and helicopter pods on the driveway."

Mia leads the way, lumbering ahead and up the porch steps. She knocks her forehead repeatedly on the doorframe, and is surprised to see Sam's hair in curlers and wearing a sheer robe. Her face is painted, and her lips are frosted, which also confuses Bo.

"You both are early!" Sam pulls her hair free from the curlers and shakes her head. She then walks toward the adjoining room like a penguin with cotton balls between her toes.

"Pardon Sam, Mia had an accident. She was stung by bees."

Sam stops in her tracks and bites her lip. "I thought this might happen. Go into the den and sit down. I left my shirt in the other room."

"You were expecting this, Sammy?" Mia groans.

"There was a special correction in this morning's horoscope. Apparently, there was a solar flare that caused a meteor to go off course in the Andromeda galaxy. Anyways, short story made longer, it was mistaken as a star and screwed up the predictions."

Sam returns shortly with a low-neck shirt sporting a lot of cleavage. She does a quick spin and takes a seat next to Bo.

Mia clears her throat. "Sammy, I'm over here."

Sam rolls her eyes and pulls Mia's chair closer to her. "I see two conical shapes on either side of your head, so what?"

Taking a deep breath, Mia feels two well-placed bumps and gasps, "Oh, my, they've grown."

"You may want to use some cortisone." Sam slides back next to Bo with her leg bouncing up and down. After a few moments of Mia's angry stare, Sam goes to the kitchen. Bo slides over to Mia and combs through her hair. "They are starting to look like horns, Mar?"

"Horns?!" Mia places her hands over her head. "Why does this have to happen to me?"

Sam returns and hands Bo the cortisone. She then sits back on the sofa, crossing her legs back and forth, while lighting a cigarette.

"Do you have ice too, Sam?" Bo asks of Sam.

"I'm making it." Sam recrosses her legs and blows out a long trail of smoke.

Bo looks curiously at Sam. "I didn't know you smoked."

"I don't. It just seems so interesting. It is like Mia's personality has finally caught up with her. I mean, there is no other way to explain why bee stings would create the shape of horns."

Mia lets out a sigh. "Valentine's Day is in two weeks. Who will want to look at me like this?" She buries her head in her hands and lets out a long drone.

Bo gives Sam a sympathetic look, and Sam frowns. She puts out her cigarette and claps her hands together. "The very reason you are here in St. Augustine, Mia. It just so happens there are a lot of men that like women with your condition."

"There are?"

"That's right, Mar! You know how you always complain about the normalization of men in London and their lack of intriguing fetishes."

Mia lowers her head with a louder moan.

Sam frowns at Bo again. "Mia, it should only be for a few days. We'll get some pills to take care of the growths. Meanwhile, you can wear my pullover. It has a hood."

Mia pulls the sweatshirt on and smiles. "It is comfortable. I like the color red. What is this writing, though? 'Sweetie, I ain't gotta pot to piss in.'"

It's a Southern thing, don't worry about it. It has an oversized, belly pouch so you can fit anything you want inside.

"I do like that."

Bo watches as the disparaging lines over Mia's face form a smile. "So, what about the cookout, Sam?"

Sam stands by the window curtain looking up at the sky, "Better wait until tomorrow. I need to see the paper's corrections on the new star alignment."

Under the yellowing sky, they watch the sun retreat behind the western horizon. There is a thoughtful moon placed high over the ocean that gives them a path back to the main road.

"Well, that's one off."

"It may be difficult to find a ride home at this time, Mar. You couldn't convince her to give us a ride?"

"Serious, Bo? You heard about the solar flare. She won't drive if there is a cloud cover."

"We never had any problems in Australia."

"That's because it never rains in Australia."

"She could have at least invited us to stay over."

"With her brother, Justin? No, thank you. Just wave."

It is a busy night with cars honking and brakes screeching. Ms. Weary turns and coughs her way into the parking lot before finding an open spot to sleep in. Beatie puts her dance shoes on in the car and looks up to see two girls she has never seen before. They are standing beneath a sign that reads: BON FESSEE NU FILLE DE SPECTACLE. Mimi is there too, but she is sitting against the wall with her hands over her face. Beatie can sense a nervousness in her that has her concerned. "What's wrong, Mimi?"

"Je n'aime pas ca! Je n'aime pas ca!"

"Pas ca? There's that word again. I guess you know what you're talking about, since it is your word."

"What's wrong with her?" say the two girls.

"I don't know, she's Mimi. That's pretty much all I can say about her."

Mimi starts trembling with her knees rocking back and forth, "Nu! Nu! Nu!"

"Yes, Mimi, we know. The club is new. The opening is tomorrow night."

Mimi looks up at Beatie with teary eyes, "Nu, tu ne comprends pas! Ecoute-moi! Fille de spectale!"

Beatie smirks, "I can't get any words out of her. It's this new language she keeps making up. I do like the word 'Pas Ca', though!"

Mimi buries her face in her hands. "Vous n'ecoutez pas! Vous n'ecoutez pas!"

"Well, let's check in," says one of the girls.

Beatie lifts Mimi by the arm. The sounds of the outside world quickly become absent with the closing of the door. They walk along a big stage that looks upon many rows of purplish plush seats. Ms. Malvenu's voice is soon present when she steps from behind a large curtain. "Alright ladies, put your shoes on!" On that introduction, Mimi is already hoofing it down the hallway and out the exit door. This deeply concerns Beatie, who turns her head toward the other two girls for understanding.

Ms. Malevnu claps her hands together. "I'm sure you have all listened and watched the tapes. Now, let's start with the first lesson: kick your right foot up, stretch out both arms, turn, and curtsy. Very good! Now, to the second lesson." Ms. Malvenu turns her finger on Beatie, who immediately stands on the tips of her toes.

"Beatrice, this is not ballet."

"Yes, Ms. Malvenu." Beatie then opens her arms wide and bows before the teacher. She hops forward onto her right foot, then leans back and hops onto her left foot; she then hops twice on her right foot, leaning back again and hopping onto her left. She repeats these exact movements five times across the floor until Ms. Malvenu finally loses her patience.

"STOP! Do you see why you get these assignments, Beatrice?"

"But Barfsleeve Berklemire says this is the latest dance everyone should be talking about."

"Barf who?"

"Barf Berkle – whatever I said – Sleeve. She is the lady who reporters are saying is the next Zhuzie Du Paw!"

"Beatrice! Stop this childish behavior right this minute! You don't see the other girls behaving this way, do you? Now, I have gone far out of my way to get you this position, because frankly, I thought it would help you grow.

Unfortunately, you only seem to be interested in acting like a four-year-old child!"

Beatie closes her eyes tightly. She does feel a little embarrassed about the name-dropping, but she would never have to lie if she felt the truth wouldn't hurt her.

"So, which of you girls listened to the tapes? Risky Salisky, alright; and you, Gentle Fleeburn? Very good. Hands on your hips; and Beatrice, you stand and watch."

Beatie sits on the floor and watches as they perform some very unique steps. It involves stepping up and stepping back, kicking to the left, and shaking their hands to the right. At times their toes are in, and at other times their heels are out, but they are always pointing their fingers, and adding that with a shout.

Beatie is finally called to step in, but she is having a hard time with her heel straps constantly coming loose. It causes her to fall, so much so that she has to improvise. Gathering a running start, she slides across the floor on her belly, and once she touches the control booth with her hand, she yells out, "Safe!"

Ms. Malvenue puts her hands over her face. "Beatrice, Beatrice. If you could ever try so hard. I know what we can do about you."

It is then that Beatie is made aware of Ms. Malevenu's quick substitution plan. She instructs Beatie to make a quick step off the stage and then a quick step back on when it's time for the finale.

"Ready for the finale, ladies? Now, shuffle forward, lean back, and lift up your dresses. Very good! Now, put your hands on your hips, shimmy your shoulders, and walk toward me. Excellent!! You will be performing right after the Great Groggy. She is a relic of this establishment, so you may want to ask her for advice. See you here tomorrow evening, and wear a smile if nothing else!"

Ms. Weary coughs and spits her way down the road, fighting a gust of wind coming up from the south. Beatie turns the bright lights on, not at all happy about having to return to the office so late, but she did lock Mr. Happiness out.

Beatie refocuses her eyes on two people standing at the next corner. She is a little concerned they might be trying to cross through the crosswalk. As she approaches, she notes that one of the figures has an oversized head with an urgent hand waving in her direction. The other just looks unreasonably tall. Beatie slows down to see what could be wrong with them, thinking they could be diseased in some way. She pulls close to the curbside and rolls down the window, suddenly shocked to see them get into the back of her car.

"The Hotel Hospitale, please!" says the hooded figure. Beatie watches her slap the other person's hand away while reaching into his pocket. The hooded figure then tosses several crumpled bills into the passenger seat and sits back with a huff.

"That's what I have been trying to tell you! Sam has been trying to get to know you the entire trip, and all you have done is ignore her advances!"

"Mar, her advances mimic avoidance; her demeanor is 'I already have a boyfriend'; and her conversations are 'You're not good enough to talk to me."

"Classic signs of a woman wanting someone."

"Seriously, Mar? And it's my thinking that has trouble finding a relationship?"

Beatie angles the mirror to get a better understanding of what is going on. They are apparently in discussion about something that can't be agreed upon. The hooded lady is quite intriguing, though, with her nifty words like 'Oye' and 'Ello', and 'Would you like some crumpets with your tea, mater?' Not that they make any sense to her; it's just how they sound. Thinking that they might be from the other side of the river; not sure.

"And how about that girl from Boston?! She thought she had found the perfect man."

"Mar, can you keep your voice down? Did we not discuss this already?"

"And have you been listening? Proof not!"

Beatie raises herself up in her seat, absolutely engaged in their conversation. They both seem so alien to her, particularly the lady in the hood. She is so forthcoming and so fierce, and her hands are so flighty. She also continually insults the other person until he speaks with a stutter.

"Hey, we're not moving! Hello! Miss!"

Uh-oh! The hooded lady is looking her way. Beatie checks her mirror for oncoming cars and then pulls out onto the road.

"She accepted your behavior only because she felt she had to. You gave her no choice!" The hooded lady then crosses her arms and shakes her head.

"How anyone could be in a relationship with you would only be possible if they were scared into it!"

Beatie's eyes and mouth go wide. 'Did she just say that to his face?" This woman is so forthright and so demeaning that it might be well to learn her trade. She starts with the finger pointing, then throws a few slaps across the wheel, feeling that this is what the lady would do next. Now for the silent meows and talon clawing.

"Hey!! What's going on up there?"

"Uh oh." Beatie freezes with her hands still in a clawing position.

"Lovely, you just passed our hotel"

Beatie slams on the brakes and begins backing up.

"You crazy bitch, you'll get us all killed!!"

Beatie stops the car and watches in horror as the lady reaches back into the front seat and takes a few dollars back. Without moving a single muscle, she continues to watch the lady in the rearview mirror while writing down her license plate number. After all is clear, she quietly pulls back onto the road. She doesn't know what just happened, but it still has her shaking with admiration.

FEBRUARY 4th: IGGIE'S

"We'll have the Platter-Splatter, thank you."

Mia leans forward to take a sip of her herbal tea. Her face still hiding within the shadows of her hood. After taking a long sip, she lowers her cup and turns toward Sam. "So! What if a rotting corpse is extracted from the ground – to no fault of his own, his chest plate is exposed, he stinks with decay, and in order to mesh with society, he has to support himself within the service industry."

"You still have to pay him minimum wage."

"But why should I hire a living-dead person if a living person is better suited for the same position?"

"You have to make it a requirement to give dead people proper training."

"What if the dead person turns rabid? They would have to be chained to the floor."

"Chain someone to the floor, Mia?"

"It would be an added cost, granted, but imagine the liability should he or she bite someone?"

"Then you require everyone carry insurance and take classes in anger management."

"They would still have to perform undesirable tasks."

"What about the film industry? That's a whole genre dedicated to dead people."

"That's a marvelous idea, Sammy! Fully agreed upon! Write up legislation!"

The waitress sets a pitcher of tea on the table along with glasses. Mia quickly pulls the container toward herself and fills her glass.

"It's really great how we can get together like this and solve the world's most unrealistic problems."

Sam hands Mia her glass to fill. "I'm sorry about yesterday, Mia. The horoscope did say flying beasties would attack you by air. Everything is looking good for today, though."

Mia 'tinks' the side of her glass with her spoon as the waitress approaches. "Food is here! We have eggs, sausage, muffins, strips of bacon, slices of steak, potato balls, carrots, peas, and cheese. All scattered about in clumps of jam, butter, and ketchup."

Bo leans forward and shovels a corner onto his plate. "So, what did the doctor say, Mar?"

"The horns will clear up in two weeks, but I have to stop taking my sanity pills."

"Are we talking about daytime nightmares?"

"The horns are already a daytime nightmare. Now it's about which of the two evils, horns or nightmares, I have to deal with."

Sam finishes her orange juice and lets out a satisfying gasp, "So what's on the agenda for the day?"

Bo takes a long look at Sam while she has the command of everyone's attention. She has taken a little extra time to look nice this morning. A few loose buttons on her shirt with her hair tossed in all the right directions. Now that she has made her intentions known, maybe he should make the next move.

"Bo, before you grab Sam's breast, I think you should allow us to decide upon the day's agenda."

"What?" Bo looks over at Sam, who is leaning away from him with discomfort. "No! I was going to tap her on the shoulder and give her my recommendation! The guide book recommends a pub called Iggie's! No breasts involved!"

Sam squints her eyes. "Well, I looked at your horoscope quickly this morning, and it says the Fountain of Youth would be a promising option."

"Oh, wouldn't it be great to be young again, even for a short time?"

"How young, Mar?"

"Not pigtail young, but maybe ten years younger than I am now."

Bo chuckles and smirks. "Do the stars say anything about Mia's rejuvenation, Samantha?"

Mia gives Bo a disturbed look. "That's awfully rude of you, Bo."

"What did I say?"

"Making fun of her horoscope. Sorry, Sam. I warned you."

Sam reaches into her pocketbook and gets up. "I'll get the car and meet you over there."

Mia's stuffs her mouth and smiles at Bo.

"That was rather an evil twist to my light humor, Mar."

Mia pushes the plate across the table and sucks on her fingers. "Ooh, look at this!" She reaches over to lift an unfinished cigarette from an ash tray. "I'll take this to go." Mia drums her hands across the counter, then points at Bo, "and you pay the bill!" Bo grumbles at Mia and looks at the piece of paper. He reaches into his pocket and places a few bills on the table."

It is a small city, but around the holidays it can easily be overrun by visitors. Mia has a plan, though; she has mapped out all the paths to the parks and all the back roads to the shops. All the restaurants that serve tea are highlighted in blue, and the entrances to the attractions she wants to visit are dotted in yellow. Not all that difficult really, since much of the area can be covered with a few tosses of a stone.

After leaving their fourth ice cream parlor, Mia hears a voice that causes her to cringe. One that has her looking to the heavens and asking, 'why?'

"Three centuries of war and disease! The Spanish were fighting the French, the French were fighting the British, and the British were fighting the Spanish. All of them fighting the Native Americans! OWWW!! What are you doing? Let go of me!"

"Mar, let her go! She's only selling historical information."

The little girl kicks and swats at Mia while she sits on top of the girl's back.

"I'm sorry, and you were saying? You will never bother us again, and you will be taking the next two weeks off?"

"Let me up!!"

"I don't understand you?"

"Mar, there are people staring."

"Yeh, okay."

The little girl turns over and brushes the dirt off her dress. She then fills her cup with earth and flings it at Mia. Mia chases the giggling girl to the next corner but eventually stops and walks back to Bo. "Now we're going to have to go a different way from now on."

"Because of a little girl?!"

"She's a deer fly, Bo! A pestiferous, airborne-afflicting midge!"

"You really don't like children, do you?"

"Do I need a reason?!"

Sam suddenly appears by Mia's side. "What did I miss?"

Oh, some little girl lifting a leg on me. I felt sprayed all over, Sammy! I really did!"

"The Fountain of Youth is across the street, ready?"

By way of a short paved road, beneath an archway of vines, they enter the historical Fountain of Youth. Cannons and clusters of magnolia trees freckle the landscape, as well as a reconstructed church and an indigenous village that could very well be the location where Ponce de Leon arrived over five hundred years ago.

"Race ya!" Flipping off their shoes, both Mia and Sam dart through the soft grass toward the percolating sounds of a spring. Sam pulls up early, claiming a calf strain, knowing too well that Mia has the speed she cannot match. She finds a soft mound of grass where she can look over the morning horoscope again. "'Pink and green and everything in between makes for a dandy appearance if you're early for Halloween." Sam looks up from the paper. "Why does this read differently now?"

Bo walks up behind Mia, sending her into a shiver. "How do you think it works, Mar?"

"I don't know. The cistern is unexpectedly big. I can even place my entire head inside." Mia turns to Bo with moisture on her face. "Can you believe this, Bo? The essence of youth and glow right here on my face? How could one not be tempted to hold its product?"

"I don't know, Mar. I'm thinking she's being kind of aloof again."

"Who are you talking about?"

"Samantha."

"Still? All you think about is a little 'rumpy-pumpy, hankie-panky,' while I'm looking to improve my outer self.

"I just feel I'm getting some mixed signals from her now."

"And the answers always lead back to the questions asked."

"Huh?"

"Maybe you should just be a little less anxious. Isn't that part of the scare factor we've been talking about?" Mia places her face over the largest of the vessels and sniffs the mysterious liquid. She places her hands on the rim and feels along the edges. "It's so big." She reaches her hand inside and gently stirs the water. "It's so cool and tingly to the touch." She places her fingers on her lips. "Ooh, and it stings too."

Bo watches Mia's head disappear into the big jug and shortly hears a splashing sound inside. "I can feel the water soaking into my pores. It kind of burns, but in a good way!"

It is Sam upon the hill that leaps from her resting place once she discovers the stars are no longer aligned with the sun. This occurrence is warning her that everything evil upon the earth is soon going to expose itself. Holding the paper like a baton, she races across the lawn, leaping over a few cannons on her way. She tosses the paper to Bo and pulls Mia's head from the cistern.

"I'm okay, Sam! I really am! It does tingle a bit, but ..." Mia touches her face with her probing fingers. "I can't explain what's going on. It feels like an exfoliator with an ever-increasing burning sensation that is trying to expose the inside back of my skull."

Samantha signals Bo to lift Mia into his arms. The people in the park are already stepping aside after witnessing the ever-evolving features of her face. Sam points toward a shelter. "In there! The mission church!"

It is a small room with wood beams holding up a thatched roof. There is a yellow light gleaming onto the center of the floor where they place Mia.

"I can't control my facial muscles, Sammy, but I'm guessing that's what the rejuvenation process is about."

Sam takes Mia's head gently in her fingers and turns her face from side to side. "There definitely is a disturbance. Bo, can you see how the one eyebrow is turning southward to connect with the west corner of her lip? And right here, see how her chin is more pronounced as it rises up toward her cheekbone?"

"I'm more concerned about her left eye twitching like it's trying to communicate in Morse code."

"Mia, may I have one of your cigarettes? So, this is the big picture I see. There is this faulty wiring going on in your face that is creating a color-coded texture best described as a carrot cream soup with bubbles of a fine broth."

Bo shakes Sam's arm. "Don't forget the odor of a tainted cider with rotten eggs and cyanide."

"I think she gets the point, Bo. How do you feel, Mia?"

Mia blinks her one good eye. "I'm not sure. It's like I have these odd cravings to be eating human head-pipes and tasty organ stuffings. Have you ever had those urges?"

"Mia, I don't think women in their second trimester have those kinds of cravings."

Bo surprises them both by re-entering the room holding the wrist of a lady wearing a Timucuan headdress. "I found someone who says she's a cosmetologist."

The lady greets Sam with a handshake. "As I told you before, I am a cosmologist!"

"What's the difference?"

"Origin and evolution. The fate of the universe. You must be desperate for conversation, am I right?" The lady suddenly screams and takes a few steps backwards. Mia is almost too bright to look upon, but using the spaces between her fingers, she can make out a structure that resembles a human head. "You might want to call an ambulance for this one!"

Mia sits up and holds one eye open with her fingers. "No, I'm fine. Besides, I don't have any insurance."

"I think with your looks you won't have any problem raising funds." The cosmologist raises her forefinger in circles about Mia's face. "I'll try a moisturizer." She opens up a wide jar from her carrying bag and sets it on the floor. Mia rolls over onto her stomach and places her face in the jar. She then lifts her head up with a crooked smile. "I can feel it sizzling."

The lady scratches her head and chuckles as she puts the lid back on the jar. "Let me help." She wipes Mia's face gently with a cloth and then opens her bag again. "Let's try something else."

After Mia's face is tenderized with all the natural ointments and creams, they all step out the door with the crowd applauding. Mia has a slight smile that is hard to decipher, but it is her fist pumping that seems to get the crowd cheering.

Beatie steers the mop across the floor, mechanically turning about the kitchen table like a quiet Zamboni. She reaches the open room with the music blaring in her earphones and starts her next routine. It's time for the bunny hug. She holds the mop with both hands and then taps the floor with each alternating foot. Next, she hops forward and hops back three times, repeating the motion until she is stopped by the flower table. She is as ready as she is ever going to be. There will be no shame in doing this; she is socializing and that is a good thing.

A quick appointment has been made with Parfie Der Barbeeb to have her hair set. Hydragew is a man well known for his familiarity with the lotions, potions, and the fabrics of the hair, and therefore, she trusts no other. Unfortunately, he also has a fascination with the 'unseen', which Beatie finds quite overplayed. She does not like to complain about things she cannot see and would rather complain about what she can see, that being Ms. Malvenu – that screech-worthy, bowl-moving succubus! No way can she not think Ms. Malvenu's comments were uncalled for, especially when her interpretive ballet should have called for a compliment.

The barber walks by habit with the air beneath his heels and a flap between his arms. Mrs. Giaguagua is there, and so must be Mrs. Birthspine – and she is; but so too is Simmy Lee Lamprey, known as 'The Eel'. This woman has the ability to slip in and out of a conversation without any notice, latching onto any compromising tidbit so it can be absorbed and spewed back later to her colony.

"Welcome, Bea'trie!" Calls out Hydragew. "Now ladies, I do say, if you need a place to pray, the edge of the cemetery is always your best location. Just do it before nightfall, or it turns into a séance."

Beatie finds an empty seat by the window and begins biting into her cotton scarf. She so desperately wants to talk about that stinky, sloth-breathing Ms. Malvenu, but she can't while the discussion is about the cemetery girl. Beatie would never be happy as a ghost, having to wear the same clothes every day – that, and gosh forbid if she were to be invited to the beach club and someone sits on her lap.

"So, Bea'trie, what brings you to the shop today? Were you not going to dance at the new theater?"

Beatie casually looks over to see the towel slipping off the sea lamprey's face. She can already feel that gangling, boneless, eel creature latching onto her mouth so she can no longer breathe!

"Bea'trie? Are you okay? Why are you suffocating yourself with your scarf?"

Beatie coughs the fabric into her hand. "Yes, sorry about that, Hydragew. I'm here for a Flamboo."

"Flamboo? You mean the 'flapper' hair style?"

"That sounds right." Beatie whispers through the side of her mouth. "It's tonight."

"It's when?"

Raising her hand to cover the side of her mouth, "Tonight." She isn't even sure she should be mentioning the name 'Ms. Mal-vaca-manuer' with all these stinky, intestinal Marburg worms listening in.

"Bea'trie?"

Beatie feels a tap on her shoulder, "Oh yes, sorry. What were you all talking about?"

"The previous residents of the city? Wouldn't you like to know where they go at night?"

"Ghosts? Still? Isn't it just the usual way of going about listening to things that don't really exist?"

"Bea'trie, I've lived here my whole life, and I've never seen a ghost, I've never been accosted by a ghost, and I've never had a ghost serve me any dressing, if you know what I mean."

"Not really."

"But times as hard as they were back then; it's hard not to believe. You know that child seen scampering about the cemetery digging up arms for her little basket? Does she not worry you at night?"

"Because she's lonely? I'm reading this book that says this happens."

Hydragew accidentally drops his scissors causing Beatie to freeze. She can see the 'Eel' has left several green algae skins on her chair and is headed toward the door with her walker. The 'Eel' has probably latched onto enough discriminating information so she can regurgitated back to "Ms. Mal-vaca-manuer! That two-faced, bowl-exploding, beetle bladder!"

"Bea'trie?!"

"Oh yes. Sorry, Hydragew. What were we talking about?"

"You said something about Ms. Mal-vaca-manuer's bladder?"

"Mal-vaca-manuer? I thought I came to get my hair done."

"You did. You also said something about Ms. Mal-vaca-manuer."

"I did?" Beatie waits patiently as 'The Eel' untraps her arthritic foot from the door plate. "Well, sure I did!! That stinky, putrid, barf, puking, blood sucking, poison-pussing, assassin bug! Stabbing people with her proboscis and injecting venom into their skulls! She even chased my second-best friend in the whole world out of the class yesterday! You being the first-best friend, Hydragew. Anyways, angry I was! Even shocked to the innermost layer of my epidermis! Can you imagine that? To be humiliated by that crusty, corn dog eating, grass-nipping, vomit bug!! It was just so ... so discrupable!"

"Discrupable?"

"Yes, discrupable: unbelievable without reason. Largely incoherent, as well."

"Oh, you are talking about Ms. Malvenu."

"Could there possibly be another?"

"I hope not." Hydragew begins combing the hair on the back of her neck, which sets her at ease.

"I'm not so sure about this, Bea'trie. There is some secrecy to this woman that you should not be talking about."

"I know! Like what?"

"Like, she's been seen with this man who opened a showgirl spectacle downtown."

"That's them!"

"The man also runs a séance club at the local cemetery. He is looking to expand, you know. We're talking about connecting with dead people from graves all around the world. I'm said to be the chosen hairdresser for all their hair requests."

"You're working with dead people now, Hydragew?! You don't think my new hairstyle will attract ghosts, do you?"

"HaHaHa. No, Bea'trie. Ghosts have their own hairstyle."

"By the way, how's my Flamboo coming?"

"It's all done. And you can borrow this headpiece; everyone was wearing them at the time."

Beatie looks carefully at the ornament. "It's shiny and very erect."

"It was a time of promiscuity."

"Promiscuity? Ooh, I do so like that word. It has that word 'promise' in it, and that's a good thing, right?"

"I guess so. It depends on what you want to find in your bed the next morning."

"Usually stuffed animals."

"Better than spiders, right, Bea'trie?

"Hahaha. Good one, Hydragew. Spiders! I like that."

Mia walks flat-footed into the Zoological Park, refusing to compromise her mood now that she has been told her skin condition won't improve for the next two weeks. Add that the new pills, along with the horn pills, are making her even more loopy than the pills she has to take for her sanity. All three together have turned her into an entirely different person. But despite her intolerable behavior, Sam still believes a visit to see a few spoonbills, ospreys, sloths, and alligators could not possibly go awry.

Mia walks directly to the lavatory and shuts the door. The sounds of lock-clicks, bolt-sliding, and chain-rattling are all promises she is not coming out. In fact, it would take a line of angry women and a fireman with a double-bit lumber axe to finally extract her. Mia then decides she would rather sulk alone by a reflection pool than spend time with Bo and Sam at the sloth display.

The response from the staff would go unheard, however, when Mia begins dangling skinned chickens between her toes above the dark water. It would then take the splashes from an albino alligator, along with the confiscation of her feeding rights, to finally decide her sulking would be best served elsewhere. Unfortunately, shortly after that, she is asked to leave the zoo while using her hands to imitate a mouse at the snake enclosure.

There, at the crosswalk; under the glare of a treetop shine, Mia would see a familiar face holding a stick over his shoulder with a blanket tied to its end.

"Catalan! It's you! You're a bindlestiff."

"Ah, yes! Missing in Action. Great to see you again, but why the long hood?"

"I am afraid of all those who might judge me."

"Only if you let them." Catalan surprises Mia by pulling her hood back, much to her disliking, but she quickly finds that he is not dismayed with her looks at all.

"This, Missing in Action, is the true beauty in you. Triumph over pain. Pragmatism over half-baked."

Mia slips back under the hood. "Thank you, but please call me Mia. Missing in Action just seems so, well, you know, formal."

"As you wish, Mia. Truly, you are very much like the beautiful Valide Sultan."

"Ooh, the Valide Sultan. I would very much like to be a 'mother' of something one day."

"And if you do, it will make followers of us all."

Mia lets out a soft squeal right before the discomfort of a bologna sandwich hits her on the side of the head, followed by a pickle and a drink carton. "Get out of the road, you red-hooded wombat!"

Catalan brushes the debris off her hood and smiles, "Don't let the actions of a few angry people set you back, my dearest one. The almighty causes them to do this only to make you a better being."

Mia looks at Catalan with a tear in her eye. "What a wonderful thing for you to say to me."

The nonstop honking along with the whistles from the traffic monitors, pressure the two to move out of the crosswalk. Catalan then takes Mia by both hands, "L'altevue would like to meet with you as soon as it can be arranged."

"L'altevue?"

"He speaks to us all."

"Is he like you?"

"There are no labels on this one. No birthright. No face of recognition. He does, however, accept horns and facial quirks." Catalan parts her hair and presses his scruffy face into her forehead. "Como yo."

Mia sighs and looks into his admiring eyes, "Como yo, to you too."

Catalan takes several slow steps backward and disappears into the glare of the light. It is at that moment Mia realizes that she needs to help those who live without shelter. Sam and Bo both dodge the traffic to reach Mia. "Are you okay, Mar?"

"I want to help the helpless."

"Of course you do, just not in the middle of the road."

Darkness settles over the ocean and makes its way toward the western horizon. There is barely a hint of daylight over the city, and only the red-light district remains active. Beatie shimmers as she walks beneath the lights, ignoring the catcalls that are coming from across the street. Cheapening herself with less clothing was obviously the demand of Ms. Malvenu. Her instructions about how to wear the attire couldn't be more pointless, since the garment itself demonstrates how it works.

Mimi, so far, is a no-show. Her whereabouts are uncertain. She won't answer her phone and she refuses to make up any new words. This troubles Beatie, because Mimi is her most trusted friend and she really had high hopes she would attend. She is also the only one Beatie can count on to perform worse than her.

Beatie looks up to see Ms. Malvenu standing by the curtain, pointing to her watch.

"Ms. Malvenu! Ms. Malvenu! I don't think Mimi is coming!"

"Beatie, go to the dressing room and finish getting dressed."

"Finish getting dressed? So, what I'm wearing is just the underwear?"

"Beatie, go now."

Beatie hurries down the hallway looking for the room she is supposed to be in. She is feeling a lot of tension from Ms. Malvenu, and is worried nothing is going to go right this evening.

The air is fragrant with two parts perspiration and one part cologne. There are many people with unusually large busts and wide hips in the hallway; again, a quality very important to Ms. Malevenu. Something else about the people in room forty-two. They all have bright, shiny colors applied to their faces, and feathery turbans projecting from their skulls. Their shoes, too, seem to have a life of their own. Kind of like, 'Come follow me and I'll show you an exhausting time,' kind of shoe.

As Beatie ventures further, this is when her curiosity becomes her mistake, and this is because of the ladies in room forty-seven. They have very large hands and their feet make them look twice everyone's height. Beatie stumbles back against the wall when a partially dressed woman with large breast prostheses approaches her.

"You're in the wrong theater, dolly." She says with a deep voice.

"I generally don't go to these kinds of movies."

"I've never heard that one before." The lady gives Beatie a comforting smile and directs her back to where she came from.

Beatie runs as fast as she can with her heels clopping like horses in a panicky stampede. She finally comes to a stop before Ms. Malvenu and bows with a breathless panic.

"Beatrice, I thought I told you..."

"But Ms. Malvenu! Ms. Malvenu! I saw it! I truly did! There were these ladies down there wearing these Manly Bunyon Critter Boots with enormously large, bulbous crotch regions!!"

"Beatrice, there are other theaters in this building. You just went a little too far."

"But the idea just seemed so unusually loud!"

"Beatrice, I need you to calm down." Beatie's face suddenly feels the hands of Ms. Malvenu pressing into her cheeks.

"But Ms. Malvenu, you have the ang-lie shape of your fingers in my face."

"I don't want you to say anything more to me. Am I clear on this?"

Beatie's eyes shift from side to side, soon realizing her mouth is being held closed on purpose.

"I said, am I clear?"

Beatie nods her head and rapidly blinks. Ms. Malvenu releases her with a smile and smooths away her face wrinkles. "Very good. Now go back down the hall and go into the first room on the left."

Beatie enters the dressing room, where her two cohorts are welcoming her back. She is happy with their excitement but a bit confused by the dirty hand imprints on their butt cheeks. She picks up two small pasties with tassels and starts play fighting with them. One of the girls, seeing Beatie's misunderstanding, grabs the pasties from her hands and turns her body the other way. When she turns back, she is shimmying her arms with the tassels twirling around her nipples, "Wah, Wah, Wah!"

"No way!" Beatie lets out a snort. "They can't be serious? All this makeup, skimpy outfits, and these milk-making toys. Don't you feel differentiated and malnourished?"

"Beatie, there can never be loneliness when looking good."

Suddenly, Larvely Falarly, the club's assistant manager, enters the room and begins clapping her hands in earnest. "Let's be pretty ladies, shall we? Just like the way you practiced in the recital."

As soon as the ladies are all gussied up in their garb of promiscuity, Ms. Falarly leads the nervous girls to the curtain. All three are very worried about the possibility of a mishap, having been given only one day to practice.

Beatie peers through the curtain divide and sees the seats are full, and rightfully so, the 'Moistured Groggy' is set to make her comeback appearance. At the age of seventy-two, she is still quite the delight to all those who saw her fifty years ago. Beatie knows this is a big deal, because the 'Grog' has been the delight of the club since the recital, and she is thinking it might be worth learning her trade.

There she goes – the 'moist one' – quickly strutting her prowess across the stage, hardly missing a step in that geriatric kind of way. Her fingers too, so stiffly poised in a claw, accomplished only by the miracles of arthritis.

Shortly into her routine, however, Beatie sees her performance as anything but delightful, and rightfully disgusting on all levels. Every lift of her leg and every squat over the chair, has her audience tugging at their pant pockets and clapping their hands like babies without discretion. This is someone's grandmother for their kid's sake! Next, the crowd calls for the 'Moist One' to take her top off, and she doesn't disappoint, following that up with lifting her skirt and performing a full frontal spread across the floor! Just appalling to see the expressions on both the young and old with an uncontrollable ejaculation of penile proportions. Fair to say, Beatie will not be following in the interests of the Great Groggy.

Beatie plucks at her outfit and looks down at her tasteless shoes. Ms. Falarly is still holding the curtain rope while the other girls are getting into position. "Alright, ladies! What do we say in this business?!"

"I'm butt perfect and if you like butts!" The three girls slap their behinds in unison. "You'll like me."

"Absolutely disgusting, ladies; just why I hate this business. Places, please!!"

"Attendez! Ecoutez-moi! Ecoutez-moi!"

Beatie spins about, amazed to see Mimi holding onto her waist. "Mimi, why aren't you dressed?"

"C'est une mauvaise danse!"

"A mauve dance is right. You sure have a great perspective on things, Mimi."

"Quoi? Nu, pas ca, pas ca!"

"Mimi, you can't just go around saying 'Pas ca' all the time; you'll wear out its usage."

Mimi starts stamping up and down. "Mauvaise! Mauvaise! Le meme que, Cookie Peacock!"

"Cookie Peacock? Ooh, yes, I do so hate Cokie Poocock." Beatie suddenly stands proud. "Now I see what you're trying to tell me. No matter how disgustingly silly I appear in front of others, never shall I ever let Cokie Poocock get the better of me. Hey, check this out, Mimi. I bet 'Poopy Do-peacock' can't do this!"

Beatie rolls her shoulders to get the tassels spinning on her nipples and then looks up to see Mimi is gone.

"Ready, ladies!" Ms. Falarly calls out.

Beatie lifts her head high and takes in a deep breath.

"Dames! Pretes!!" Beatie hears, and then she closes her eyes and prays. It seems to take forever for the curtain to go up, but once it does, Beatie is swaying and kicking, just as she had practiced at home. It doesn't really matter that she's dancing out of turn, confirmed by all the increased occupation of male genitalia before her, but Beatie does her best to make a smile of it. Still, after too much pocket-pulling, she can't take it any longer and decides to leave the stage.

"Beatrice, get back out there this instant!"

"But Ms. Falarly, I'm not fully moisturized!"

"Beatrice! You are not going to screw this up! Now do as you are told!!"

Beatie looks down at the exit sign. The same one Mimi took. She is reluctant to return to a crowd that has lecherous desires on their minds, but she also fears the retribution from Ms. Malvenu. Without speaking another word, Beatie drops her left wrist and places her right palm beneath her chin. When the curtain goes up, the girls remove the fabric over their breasts and let their tassels do the twirling. And here in the auditorium of the sparsely elected, they too got what they wished for.

Beatie sits in her car heaving a deep sigh. Her face crinkling and sniffling with indignity. She realizes that the sentiments of optimism and nicety have not prepared her well for a wolf's life. There is no support group to rely on, no playmates to learn from, and no one to show her how to run with the pack. The word 'lonely' in Lucifer Goggy's book is defined by a common line drawn between the people she knows and those listed as a percentage that don't care about her. "I'm going to die alone, and no one will ever know it."

Beatie slips Ms. Weary into gear and lumbers down the street, coughing three times, before climbing back up over the bridge. They are both heading home.

FEBRUARY 5th: SUPERSTITIOUS CHARMS

Bo wakes to a static sound playing in his ear. The radio is a slight touch away from an actual station. He pulls out his logbook and quickly jots down the prior events of the day. A voice can be heard coming from the crawl space, and through the circular window, he sees by the positioning of the sun that he has slept in. Mia is glistening by the pool's edge, wearing a wide-brimmed hat that covers most of her face. Sam is lying in the pool before her on a deflated raft with her promontories keeping her afloat. She is a much paler version of Mia, but her overflowing breasts in a white bikini top is what really highlights the difference between the two.

Mia tosses a plastic tube into the center of the pool and waits for the ripples to reach her feet. She could indulge in this unproductive habit for the rest of her life if she could find a way to do so, but after a long, motionless minute with her face to the sun, she finally returns to a large plastic chair where a newspaper awaits her.

"Get a load of this, Sammy! Marbaline Shmelby wins the British Globe for her portrayal of an elderly woman in 'Sometimes I Die Tomorrow.' Lovely, but wouldn't it have been more deserving if she had portrayed the roll of the twelve-year-old boy?"

Bo bursts through the open gate bearing off with his shirt, "Suns oot!! Take yer taps off!" He steps before a sign that reads 'Please shower before entering the pool' and then drops his drawers. He rinses his body beneath the showerhead and turns slightly to face the girls. He then walks across the diving board and stares down at the pool's surface. It certainly appears deep enough, but if there is any time to make an impression, it has to be now. Soon the water engulfs his flailing mass and while looking up at the distorted surface, he watches with interest as the many broken pieces of the pool try to become whole again. Amazing how serene and weightless it all feels.

Mia rolls onto her back, chuckling to herself after hearing a loud smack. "Haven't we seen this behavior in him before? All for what – our attention?" Mia licks her fingers and turns the page of the paper. "Will you look at this, Sammy! It will be seventy-two degrees today. What's that in Celsius?"

"I just subtract thirty and divide by two. Mia, has Bo ever learned to swim?"

Mia sets the paper down and grimaces. She approaches the pool's edge and looks at a distorted vision of Bo in the deep end. "Hey, Sammy! What's the record for holding one's breath?!" Mia doesn't wait for a response and lunges into the water. Within a short moment, her head pops up with Bo thrashing upon the pool's surface.

Bo's tiptoes reach the shallow end and he sees Sam still ignoring his act of bravery. He is going to have to do better. "Whit ye-ye doing, Mar?!"

"I'm saving your life?"

"I don't need ma-ma life to be saved. I was enjoying the p-p-peace and tranquility of the wa-wa-water."

"It looked to me like you were drowning."

"I wa-wasn't drooning, I-I-I ..."

"I can't wait for this." Mia throws up her hands and lifts herself out of the water. She quickly marches back to her paper, semi-aware that Bo has drifted back toward the deep end of the pool. Sam's disappointed face tells her all she needs to know.

"Oh, Blimey." Mia dives back into the pool, and this time, she grabs Bo by the hand and drags him to the railing of the stairs. She returns to her chair and kicks up her feet, ignoring her recent rescue attempt that interrupted their conversation.

"But Sammy, he said 'como yo'!"

"I know, you said that already. So, did you get his number?"

"Better than that! He gave me his address. He lives over on Cordova Street!"

"Really? Cordova? You know what I'm thinking? You may have found a winner here!" The two girls scream.

"Oh, Sammy, he is so fit. He's maybe thirteen stone with really broad shoulders and strong hands. He also has this rugged look you just don't see on faces anymore."

"What does he do for a living?"

"I'm not sure. He said he has been working in New Smyrna on an indigo farm."

"New Smyrna? That's like seventy miles from here. There used to be a plantation down there; that's all I know. Maybe he's financing one of those archeological digs."

"No, I think he's more of a laborer. He had this rugged look and blue dye all over his clothing."

"Mia, no one has worked on that indigo plantation in over 250 years. Maybe he is a supervisor or a quality inspector, unless ..."

"What is it, Sammy?!"

"What if you are interested in a rotting corpse, extracted from the ground, through no fault of his own?"

"HaHaHaHa!!!" They both laugh.

"Mar, you are talking about the homeless bloke we met in the park, right?"

"Free Society Explorer!!"

"What?"

"You keep referring to them as homeless!" Mia turns away from Bo and addresses Sam, "He said he can arrange a meeting with their leader."

"Mar, homeless people don't have a leader. They live a solitary existence."

"Free Society Explorers!!" Both Mia and Sam yell again. "Poor Bo! You're just jealous, admit it! Now that I have someone and you don't – to no one's fault but your own! HaHaHa!!" Mia flips over onto her back. "Besides, Bo, I'm not like you. I don't have to pretend to like someone to get to know them. Always trying to breed with anyone willing to breed with you!"

Sam lowers her head, suddenly feeling an awkwardness in her own love life. She gathers her items and quickly leaves.

"Oh, wait, Sam, I didn't mean ..." They watch Samantha scurry off toward her car, stopping on occasion to pick up a few dropped items. "Well, there you've gone and done it again, Bo. A perfectly good conversation about my happiness suddenly turned into a useless sales pitch about yourself." Mia leans back and opens the paper. "Hey, there is a ghost tour tonight!"

"No! You can't treat me like that you ... Crappy Corn Crusty Cairn Barbie!!!" Beatie wakes with shivering sweats and hears a loud banging noise. She slides out of bed and shuts her door, soon aware that the knocking is coming from her window. She does have a door to her room, but it seems the intoxication of her two roommates offers them different privileges.

They are Olivia and Nikki, both tall and lithe with an appearance about them that is expensively detailed. Their faces are colored to perfection; their clothes never miss a sparkle; they have hair that cannot miss a part; and even the air about them is forty percent moisture and sixty percent shine. What else can she say about them? They are both wealthy and posh and have very high expectations for the people they are seen with. They also measure men and their money in the same way – is there enough to buy them happiness? Unfortunately, both always fall short of expectations.

Beatie holds no resentment toward their privileges, she just wishes they were a little friendlier. They are not all shrugs and kisses, and there is never any call for a meaningful compliment. Even while interviewing for the roommate position, Beatie was required to fix them hors d'oeuvres, and afterward, they made her take a two-week cooking class.

Anyways, they are knocking on her window. Apparently, their parents have arranged a lavish gathering that requires them to invite a loser as a measurement for a hierarchical order in an otherwise perverse society. This is really not about getting to know Beatie at all, but rather about how they appear around a lower class of human form. Accepting their invitation is probably not in her best interest, but it is a repulsive society where she feels she belongs. Plus, Beatie likes getting all gussied up for that someone special – namely Parker Ken. They met only briefly when he stopped by the local shops to say he was purchasing the city block. He was so intoxicated at the time that the local employees took it upon themselves to pull his underwear through his open zipper. It was that look on his face of a bug hitting a windshield that had her most captivated.

"Beatie, you'll need to dress nicely!" The girls laughed while drunkenly falling over the hedges.

"I know how to do that." Beatie replies.

"And you'll need to speak properly," giggled the girls somewhere beneath her window. "You probably have no idea what we are talking about, but it's called etiquette."

"You mean that undefinable way about the two of you?" Beatie closes the curtain and twirls away from the window. She runs to her closet and sifts through all the possible outfits she could wear. She knows very well that the wrong selection could cause her to fade into oblivion, but unfortunately, her best dresses are kept at her mother's house.

Beatie parks her car under the empty carport. She had lived with her parents for twenty-three years before realizing it was time for her to discover a life on her own. A hard decision to make, but she had grown tired of sitting with her stuffed animals and closet full of memories. Now that she has settled into a new residence and stable job, she is hoping to regularize her visits. It's just too hard to tell her mother she doesn't need her anymore, particularly when it was her mother that had always helped her with her independence. Now more than ever, she needs to return the favor because there is something else Beatie isn't telling you. The past few years her mother has been very forgetful, not just missing car keys in her hands or leaving a room she can't find her way back to, but at times, just looking into her mother's eyes and seeing someone entirely different. No one knows just how it started. A queer choice of a mistaken identity when her mother introduced the nine-year old boy down the street as her husband. In any case, it has caused Beatie to try and convince herself that she is not the one at fault – except this may not be entirely true. At the age of four, Beatie flushed her stuffed animals down the toilet, thinking it was the best way to get them clean, and then a year later, the kitchen caught on fire because she thought burning the trash would reduce landfills. It's not hard to imagine those incidents didn't have some effect on her mother's well-being.

Beatie calls for her mother and turns to hear the soft sounds of steps approaching. Mrs. Backlebond is holding a cake on a platter that has been tenderized with a fork.

"Let me take this from you, Momma. We'll set it on the table, okay?"

A shrugging mother gives Beatie a hug and presents her with an invitation. "We'll be having a fine cotton-mouth spritzer on the morning porch this evening. I left an invitation for the animals across the street." Beatie nods her head and turns the television on for her.

The shades are drawn in her room, but everything remains as she had left it. Always there are the stuffed animals and the Polly Pocket toys, but there is no time for pleasantries; she is here for a dress. Beatie walks into her closet and turns on the light. It doesn't take her long to find the one dress that attracts her the most. It is surrounded in a thick plastic, tamper-resistant cardboard box that used to hang in her mother's closet. Now it is in her room, so it is fair game.

Taking a deep breath, Beatie unzips the box and almost faints. She wasn't expecting something so 'red'. There is even a manual with instructions: How to behave in a strapless mermaid gown. Beatie spins about when she is startled to see her mother now brandishing a garden tool. She is probably concerned to find a thief among her clothes. Beatie waits patiently as her mother closes the door and pretends to lock her in. Fortunately, there is a mirror behind the door.

Beatie holds the dress up, amazed at how it just cascades down over her body and spreads across the floor. There is only one problem, and it has more to do with her narrow shoulders and shapely waist. She has always thought her shape was normal for a blossoming young girl, but apparently, the dress doesn't think so.

The door flies open again, and this time Beatie's smile reminds her mother that this is no intruder. She sets the garden tool on the floor and then embraces her daughter once again. Beatie holds the dress before her body. "Momma, I need another body."

"Charlie Bop doesn't think so."

"The nine-year old boy down the street?"

"Remember what he said to you in your graduation gown?"

"Yeah, he wanted to know if I was naked under my clothes."

"In years to come, he will say that with great conviction."

Beatie reaches back into the rack of clothes and pulls out another dress. "Wow, Momma, you have a dress with a sash belt?"

"But that dress is for the evening!"

"Yes, I know, and I'm going to a special party with Olivia and Nikki."

"And their special needs are...?"

Beatie looks at her backside in the mirror. "I'm not sure."

"And you think this dress will find you the right man? A man that will comfort you for the rest of your life? Tell you he loves you every night before bed? Runs to you whenever you've been apart for too long?"

"At best!"

"No, Beatie, that dress is not for you."

"But it's perfect, and look what I found!" Beatie opens a box of low heels.

"You can't take my Mary Janes with titanium heels and kitten paw straps!"

"But Momma!"

"No! You're not old enough to wear those shoes." Mrs. Backlebond snatches the shoes from her hands. "These are my sexy shoes; they're not for a little girl!"

"But Momma, you never wear them!" Beatie's fingers slowly creep back to the shoes.

"But they're mine!" Mrs. Backlebond snatches them back. "I wore them the night I met your father. Who knows when I'll need them again?"

Beatie looks at her mother confused.

"I don't want you to find a man wearing these kinds of shoes, so I offer you a replacement!" Mrs. Backlebond slides past Beatie and unzips a bulky bag on the floor. "Ta da!!"

"Dad's Army boots?!"

"They won me over!"

Beatie lets out a deep sigh. "Momma, you are just being mulish."

"Now, would you like some spam?"

"No, Momma, spam won't help. It's too salty, and if you haven't heard, salt can dry you out from within. They don't have lotions for that yet."

Beatie pats her mother on the shoulder and reaches for some boxes to carry to the car. Mrs. Backlebond follows in silence, while Beatie returns for her mother's musical discs.

"Mom, I won't be stopping by tomorrow night because of the party."

"But what about the spritzer? The animals will be disappointed."

"Maybe another time."

Mrs. Backlebond frowns, "If you are going to go, then do so, but don't tell me crickets can't sing the Carmen Ohio on the back of a white-tailed deer!"

"Yes, Momma." Beatie tosses her mother's disks onto the front seat and then leads her mother back to the couch. She changes the channel to something she can enjoy and gives her a kiss. "When is Papa due back?"

"I didn't know he was gone."

"He left a note. It reads he has gone hunting for Mothmen and Skunk Apes. Be back when he finds one."

"I'll be watching and waiting!"

Beatie twists her mouth and wonders if there is anything else she should take. She sneaks back to her mother's closet and finds the shoes, stuffing them in a laundry bag and hurrying toward the door. She pauses to look back at her mother staring at the television. "I'll check on you later, okay?" She waits for a response, but her mother doesn't make a sound. Her mother was a child once and now she's a child once again. If not for the face of her daughter, her memory would be entirely lost. Papa is going to have to step up. She cannot do this on her own.

With the afternoon lowering into the western horizon, the city begins a magnificent transformation into a maroon shadow of itself. The time is not quite lights-out, but the thought of ghosts occupying the city is already on the mind of many of its residents. Empty houses are of special interest to the tour guides who believe this is where the ghosts are still said to be found. Whether it be in the spaces beneath the staircases, the passageways behind the walls, or the closets in uninhabited rooms, these tend to be the play sites where ghosts take their comfort.

Mia leaps back to the edge of the zebra crossing and holds up her middle finger at a passing car. "Did you see that, Bo?!"

"Mar, the lady didn't mean to do it."

"The lessons will never be learned if they don't raise the standards of the people living here."

"That's kind of harsh."

"Harsh! It's about societal softness. If we let them drive through crosswalks, next they'll say stop signs are just a suggestion."

"Okay, Mar. I think you made your point."

It is off the busy streets and west into a suburban silence where Mia and Bo find their first haunted house. It is a chilly evening, and Bo wears his bomber cap, while Mia hides beneath the hood of her sweatshirt. She does not want to leave the suggestion that her bee stings resemble anything like a demonic entity. Despite her insecurity, the choice of a ghost tour seems rather unusual, considering Mia, herself, does not believe in celestial inhabitants roaming the hallways of an uninhabited household. Add to that, this is a woman who requires an explanation for everything – spelled out, signed, and most likely notarized. She will also demand an admission of fraud and the promise of extensive "rest cure" therapy, which will likely include shock treatment. That all being said, the only reason Mia could possibly be attending a ghost tour would have something to do with her evil nature.

The house they have selected supports these intentions, for it is one that has seen way too many visits. A dimly lit porch that cannot hide the weight of a thousand steps; the creaks in the boards that cannot hide the few remaining nails left to hold it together; and if one-directional scuff marks suggests a ghostly presence, it doesn't hide the fact the house is more frequented by living tourists than by those that have passed on.

"My name is Norba Hebe!" Shouts a lady, standing four feet, nine inches on the stems of her ten-inch heels. She is a death counselor and tells the story of the lives long past. She is dressed in gold from the top of her wasp-nest hair down to the tips of her sparkling boots, and the dome-shaped farthingale most likely suggests she is trying to confuse both the living and the dead.

"I am here to tell you that ghosts do live a sexually gratifying existence, kept quiet only by the street noise outside," continues the guide.

"Not much of a queue." Mia pulls on her hood strings after looking around to count eight people.

"Silence!" The guide yells. "These people came to admire what they cannot see and what they wish they could hear!" The counselor then raises her hands and closes her eyes. "Their nymphomaniac assemblage recently appeared here in the garden. Take note of the disturbed earth before my feet and the outline of their enjoyment." The enchanter rolls her eyes to the back of her head and then kicks out a left foot. "They were inflamed by a disease, and now with two hundred years of celibacy, they are beyond horny." The guide then circles her hand and waves the group forward into the house. "Remember, ghosts do not appreciate change, so please do not touch anything inside that does not belong to you." The guide pauses and turns to smile at the crowd. "Courtesy of Beaver Hole Bootles, for all your special hygiene needs."

The group passes through the Janus room and into the empty house, where the rooms have been built to the dimensions of people half their size. Bo is the first to bang his head on a dusty door jamb, sending Mia into an uncontrollable sneeze.

The guide leans down to pick a prophylactic off the floor. "These are not violent ghosts, but they do like to torment the psychics." She then chuckles, "a whimsical additive to keep tourists engaged."

The guests roll their eyes in laughter and Mia nudges Bo, "What a Gerschmeel."

"The crowd does like her, Mar."

"Common sense is a gift; stupidity is inherent, Bo."

"Mar."

"What? Ten years of outstanding service to the deceased, and to this day, no one has ever asked me if I've ever witnessed a resident get up and leave their resting place!"

The guide floats through the rooms on the first floor with the muted sound of her heels beneath her gown. "Does anyone know the significance of the chimney? Anyone?"

Mia brushes up against Bo. "I got this." Mia steps forward and waves her hand. "It means the homeowner was wealthy."

"No, to keep you warm at night. It gets very cold in the winter."

The group nods in agreement, and Mia swats Bo on the shoulder. "Did you see that? She disagreed with me on purpose."

"Mia, let it go."

The group follows the host up the steps to the second floor and through the remaining maze of little rooms. They are in awe every time Ms. Hebe swings open a door and advises them the ghosts were recently engaged in a lewd indecency there. Mia quickly becomes annoyed with the guide when she initiates an after-sex soreness walk and demands everyone imitate her. "'Pop and glide everybody! See, you can all do this!"

Mia elbows Bo in the ribs. "This is absolutely corny. We shouldn't have to be asked to do this."

The guide finally shepherds the group into a chamber room with a large bed that is held up by four tall posts. There is a mantel case and three large eighteenth-century paintings on the walls that give the room an antique look.

"Shh, everyone, if you stand quietly, sometimes we can see the chair by the window rock back and forth." She then raises her head. "Some spirits remain to protect the living from the not so friendly. They watch to ensure the peace. Peace is all we can ask from the non-living." The guide then stretches her arms out, "Is there not segregation between the Neadrathals and the Jingle Peppers? Where does this all end?!"

Mia pulls her hood slightly back and looks about. "What the bloody hell are Jingle Peppers? She's making this up, Bo." Mia looks about, suddenly attuned to something odd. "Did you all hear that?" She takes several steps back and circles the group, sensing a strange sound coming from somewhere inside the room. She returns to Bo, and, again, hears the same strange sound that nobody else is taking interest in. "Listen everybody! Just shut up for a moment! Can you not hear that?!"

The group is shocked by Mia's outburst but excited too.

"Yes, I hear it." Says one attendee. "It's not even coming from a spot where one would expect to hear a noise." "Maybe it's a cat." "Maybe, it's a Jingle Pepper!"

Ms. Hebe raises her hands, hoping to incite the group. "Oh, okay, this is the part where you all are supposed to get scared."

A tall, thin woman with white cotton hair suddenly lets out a scream. The guide, sensing the tension, soon corrals the group into a circle. "Are these not strange occurrences happening right before our very eyes?"

"It's like a rushing wind with a slight whistle sound to it." Mia then spins toward Bo with her hand to her ear, "Bo, do you hear it?" Mia looks at Bo with his lips making the same sound she hears. "It's you!!" Mia shoves Bo against the wall, causing the room to shake. The guide then contorts her face and raises her hands to a quiver. "I feel an angry presence coming."

"Yeh, my foot up Bo's arse."

The guide swings about with her finger pointing toward the rocking chair, then toward a sound of footsteps rushing behind the wall. The candlelight flares to five times its length, and the group watches in horror as several twisted shadows rise up along the wall.

Bo leans down to Mia, "This is staged."

"Are you sure about this?"

Bo nods his head, and a devilish grin comes across Mia's face.

Ms. Hebe raises her arms and spreads them wide and apart as the bed begins to shake. "Rise up you old lascivious concubine. Come forth so we may visualize your sexual habits once again!" The guide looks at the group and winks. "That make her mad."

The lights again flicker, and there are soon abrupt calls to make the bed shaking stop. "Ms. Hebe, it is getting hot in here!" "Now the room is getting colder!" "We need to sacrifice something!"

"Control yourselves, people! We are not sacrificing anyone!" Ms. Hebe strikes a match, only to be outdone by Mia flipping on a light switch and clapping her hands.

"Yeh, yeh, Blah. Blah. Blah. A beautiful story told by sloppy reading. It seems this relic we have entrusted our time with has gone too far without a proper challenge."

Ms. Hebe grinds her teeth and steps forward to address the crowd. "Did you not see the bed shake? We should be thankful that there are a few among us that will try to make peace with the dead."

Mia walks up behind the guide and places her hands on her shoulders. "Yes, but Mrs. MacNeil, the problem with your daughter is not her bed; it's her brain (ii)." Mia turns to the crowd. "You see, people, it's not she you need to understand; it is what you need to understand about yourselves. Your belief in the paranormal, the light-reflecting apparitions, the naturally occurring drafts, and the planned furniture movements – all manipulations of the mind to expose exactly how gullible, and mostly stupid, all of you really are. This truly highlights the expectation of the human race, and so far, it's not looking good for procreation."

Ms. Hebe closes her eyes and presses her finger against her temples in a gesture of pain.

"But I get why you do this, Ms. Hebe, I really do. I mean, what other line of work would possibly accept you at your age?" Mia continues to walk about the group and then back to the guide. "That being said, I do have a few cemetery plots back home available for those feeling a little short on time."

"Mar!"

"Too much?"

The room is silent, but after a moment of reflection, the cotton-haired lady steps forward. "Thank you for all of this, Ms. Hebe, we do understand the paranormal activity taking place here tonight."

Stepping forward, another lady offers a somber take, "Yes, Ms. Hebe; it's not your fault."

Mia finally claps her hands. "Excellent confession by the few sane among us."

A man steps forward and rests his hand on the guide's shoulder. "I'd be mad too if someone walked in on my sexual activities." "Yeh, so true!" "Thank you for your services, Ms. Hebe."

Mia's eyes suddenly go wide. "What?!"

There is a cry out with several applauses, for which Bo even lets out a whistle.

"Haha, you all funny! Good crowd! Best ever! I'm sure the ghosts have all gotten to know each one of you a bit better now, if you know what I mean. Wink. Wink."

Mia throws up her hands feeling foiled, "Well, that's a dry, bloody sneeze! What is wrong with you people?! Aren't you all afraid of being seen the way others see you?"

Ms. Hebe waves everyone toward the stairs. “Thank you much for coming. The ghosts have a tip jar at the door. No coins, please, they are too heavy for them to pick up.”

Mia steps slowly down the house steps before the gathering of the group. “Well, that was disappointing.” She says to them.

“You ruined our experience.” Says an angry attendee.

Mia takes several steps back up the porch steps. “Come now. I thought I was addressing a rational crowd. I thought you might thank me for uncovering these fraudulent claims of grandeur.”

The group steps closer to Mia with their hands on their hips.

“Okay, yes, I'll pay for the tour.” Mia reaches into Bo's pockets. “And here's a little extra for inflation.”

Beatie spent the day at work going over the chances she might meet someone at the party tomorrow night. By late afternoon, she had met someone who agreed that all indications look promising. More luck came to her side when the little sales girl outside the door said it would be someone she would least expect. “Parker Ken!!” They both scream. The little girl then hands Beatie a half-priced brochure for further encouragement. Beatie loves to think about how her pleasant thoughts might work in her favor. The warm pleasure of cuddling with something other than a stuffed animal is always on her mind.

With the departure time set at 5:30pm, it definitely sets a damp squid on her plans to leave early, even on a slow Sunday evening. The party is tomorrow night, and she still has a lot of dreaming to accomplish. Apparently, her boss doesn't understand how women operate.

“Mr. Happiness, I have to be somewhere tonight.” Beatie grabs her coat from the rack and walks toward the door. She turns the knob until a click can be heard, hoping to hear anything but an empty response. Rolling her eyes in silence, Beatie returns to her desk and watches the fading light. There is another option – leave without notice. No, not if she wants to avoid another speech. Beatie walks within a few feet of his office and waves repeatedly, but he doesn't acknowledge her plea. Rolling her eyes again, she returns to her desk with the decision to leave a note. With little thought to the words, Beatie scribbles: 'I'm going to meet with a family from Papua New Guinea. I will see you in two days.' She puts the seal of the letter to her sparkling lips and slaps it to his door. After stepping in and out of the office several times and slamming the door for a response, she finally retrieves the letter and tosses it into the garbage. She then sits at her desk and begins folding the second batch of brochures.

FEBRUARY 6th: HOW ABOUT A FAIR AND A TALE

Beatie had woken early and has not left her bed yet. She is busy reading with one hand circling the air and the other following the lines of her book. It excites her to speak the words on the pages, as if they might become her own:

"You are never too old to start something new, and you are never too young to start something old"

"Okay, I guess that can be true."

"You want to belong to what you can't see, and what you can see, you don't want to belong to."

"I have no idea what that means, but I can go along with that."

In fact, Beatie isn't sure what most of the words mean, but she does like the way they roll off her tongue. The book slides between her knees and onto the floor. She rolls out of bed and goes to her closet. A big day is planned, and she has little time to prepare for what is truly to come. She places her mother's sash-belt dress on the bed and then lifts the lid off the shoes. Suddenly, she is filled with a tormenting skepticism. Oftentimes, she finds herself at odds with the very clothes she accepts, simply because they don't have her best interest in mind. That's what mannequins are all about. She has never been seen in this outfit before, and how she will be perceived at the party will most likely be determined by what her shoes have to say about the dress.

Beatie peeks out her door and looks down the hallway, wondering what the gossip is regarding Olivia's outfit. Dresses do have secrets of their own, and what her closet full of clothes might have done in confidentiality is often told by the shoes sitting on the rack. Beatie stops before Olivia's door. It is closed, but she finds it is also willing to be opened. "Olivia, are you in there?"

Beatie steps forward into a large room arranged with several couches and a wet bar. She is absolutely astonished, and a bit perplexed too. It's as if she has walked into an entirely different household. The listing on the house states a two thousand square foot, single-family residence with a gable-style rooftop – so where does the mansion come from?

She follows a corridor past three closed doors, four closets, and a large alcove, and soon arrives to an entertainment studio with a dance floor and an observatory deck. The floor plan on a kiosk shows there is another hallway that enters into a small gymnasium, and it is there where she finds herself in the land of 'Boo-yah!' – and yards of it! Not just pieces of clothing, but whole matching outfits. And what she thought were going to be bleachers filled with spectators are really silver mannequin heads wearing hats from many different parts of the world. And not just hats, but also scarves, tippets and visards; cockades and bustles, feathers and ruffs; almost anything that can be adorned to one's head and neck – she has it.

Beatie hears a splash and takes a quiet step between two Julia Cummings satin-laced gowns. She now finds herself inside a large bathing room filled with wall-to-wall mirrors and slip-resistant tiles. It is here too that she finds her roommate – Olivia Davelport, nourishing her long legs in the froth of a saltwater aquarium. At first, her roommate's nakedness makes her feel ashamed, but soon she realizes her head will not turn in any other way. It would seem impossible that she could oil her legs anymore, but she does, lifting yet another jug to make them even shinier.

Beatie retreats to her room and lifts up her mother's dress. "It will work just fine," she says to herself, slipping it on over her head and rearranging the shoulder pads. She paws at the mirror and lets out a squeaky giggle. "Stop that, you dirty vixen. Are you always like this?" She then stretches her foot over a chair and pretends to bathe her legs in a shiny, viscous oil, just as Olivia did. It is while reaching toward her toes, however, that the sash belt falls from her waist and a boob pops out. Then while reaching for the belt that had fallen to the floor, her other boob pop out too.

Beatie sinks to the floor in dismay; presenting herself at the party like this will certainly create some confusion down the road. Fortunately, she has taken the day off from work and isn't required to be anywhere important.

The door to Meeshman's flies open, and Beatie hurries toward the window, pausing only briefly when Mrs. Bookafleely smirks. There is no time for pleasantries; her sight is on the dress in the window. She is certain that this is the dress she should always be wearing; the only problem is, it's missing!! How could this happen on such short notice?! Her only alternative is 'The Farmer's Flee Furry Goat Smock with imitation 'Bah' footwear' – but it's gone too!! Ooooh, that Meeshman! She is most certainly behind all of this!

Beatie storms to the front counter. "I've been noticing that someone in this store is always missing!"

"No one is missing, Beatrice."

"I'm talking about the best salesperson Meeshman has ever had, DC Kiebler!"

"We had to let her go."

"We had to let her go?! That's a lot of 'Hoddy-Doddy-Picky-Poo-Paw!' May I ask why?!"

"She wasn't selling anything."

"But she was my friend and my confidante! She and her face-grooming dog, Paco Daublie! They know all the dresses I want to buy! The very reason I come back every week!"

"And the very reason she wasn't selling anything."

"But I'm the customer here, and you are going to blame this firing on me?!"

"Beatrice, this is going nowhere. Like I said, find someone who can pay for all this clothing, and then you can have any dress you want."

"Well, I do have someone, and when he finds out you have been firing female employees with emotional support animals, you'll be forced to sell all of your dresses – for at least half off."

Mrs. Bookafleely raises an eyebrow. "Boyfriend?"

"It's true! He has these scanty-rimmed glasses and emotionally styled hair, and he's going to fire everyone I don't like!"

"Emotionally styled hair? You're lying to me, aren't you?"

Beatie droops her shoulders. "Only because it feels good."

"Like I said, find someone who can pay for all this."

"But I'm trying to work that out, Mrs. Bookafleely. I found two ladies who are tony-sharp and kicky-suave, and they just invited me to a lavish party at the Gummy Baba! You should see all the dresses they like to wear!"

"Beatie, clothing is just a distortion for what we cannot see. Trust me, I know about those people and their parties. They don't care about the people you see every day; they only care about how they are perceived by those most important to them. You are not going to find the right friends there, only a lot of disappointment."

Beatie pulls a camise tightly over her head; she doesn't want to listen to Mrs. Bookafleely anymore. Just because Mrs. Meeshman says she can't afford to be a lady doesn't mean she isn't capable of being one.

The door flies open again, but this time it is the six enthusiastic assistants, all dressed in Meeshman's Flim Flam nap-dresses. Except for the one very tall assistant, they are exactly the same height. "We can assist you, Miss!!"

Mrs. Bookafleely turns around and laughs, "Now ladies, you have no idea what you are getting yourselves into."

"Nonsense, Irma. Auntie Bolivia will be quite thrilled to hear you are not willing to help one of her regular customers." The tall girl leans toward Beatie with a pleading look. "You are a regular customer, aren't you?"

"Every day at one time or another."

Mrs. Bookafleely sits down with her sandwich and chuckles, "Fine, you nieces go right ahead and indulge yourselves."

Quickly two of the girls take Beatie by the arm and rush her into the racks. She is absolutely ecstatic to have this much help! Instead of one thought, there are now six thoughts to her one, and of course, the consequence of finding one perfect dress always leads to the discovery of another! This also means the dress in 'holding' for 'Miss Poodle Moth' – the lady in the fluffy white coat that buys everything Beatie has an eye on – now becomes available!! It really is the only dress with the right color.

While scurrying toward the wall where most of the expensive dresses are, Beatie accidentally knocks over a solid object that falls to the floor. She is angry at first because it is one of those mannequins, but it is also pointing at her as if saying, 'Look at me now and wear me later'.

"Hmm! I haven't seen the likes of this dress before." Beatie knows all the dresses that pass through the store, so why has she not noticed this one? She looks for a tag but can't find one.

"What did you find, Miss Beatie?" Shouts one of the girls.

Beatie lifts up the dress and twists her mouth, wondering if it might be invalid for her to wear. It has a style to it that she has never seen before. It also has an artistic pattern that uses a surface shine that she really likes too. Beatie begins circling the mannequin, pulling on its dress tails. Obviously, there must be a name to it or it would not have been made. She finds a label on the floor that says it's a Fermian Particle Dress. It is also available with food stamps. Happy wow!! Beatie pulls a sleeve around her body, hoping to draw in the aroma, and that's when something lavender and suede enters her nostrils. Beatie lets out a soft squeal and nearly faints. A life in this dress would certainly be different than any life she has in her closet.

"Hey, I don't see a manual!" Beatie yells back to the girls who are still searching for other dresses. Beatie strips the dress from the mannequin and apologizes for leaving it naked. She then holds the dress before the mirror and twists her body from side to side.

Five of the assistants finally arrive and make a plea for her to select one of the dresses they had found.

"I know, and I thank you, but this one is dearest to my heart."

Beatie twirls about the floor, imagining how she might appear before the guests at the party –thinking it might even lead to – a kiss! The girls scream!!

Beatie loads an armful of clothes onto the table before Mrs. Bookafleely, and then spins around with the Fermian Particle dress before her body. "What do you think, Irma?"

Mrs. Bookafleely gives her an evil look. Only her husband addresses her by her first name, much to her disliking, and will even correct Ms. Meeshman whenever she makes the same mistake.

"You know what, Beatrice? The image in the mirror so rarely reflects the true self, doesn't it? One should always be judged from the perspective of variety, am I right." Mrs. Bookafleely grins.

Beatie claps her hands together. "Absolutely right! We don't want to get this wrong, do we, girls? How about several more dresses!"

"Yeh!!!" scream the girls.

Mrs. Bookafleely sits back down before the television and chuckles. Beatie resumes her gathering of clothes, and when she feels she has finally collected enough, she returns to the front window all giddy with confidence. "Hello, 'Ebullient!' You didn't think I would forget about you, did you?!"

Arm in arm with the assistants, Beatie skips her way to the checkout counter, where Mrs. Bookafleely looks up with a smile, "Yes, Beatrice?"

"Now, I would like to put all of these dresses on layaway!"

The six assistants suddenly drop their shoulders and sigh.

Mrs. Bookafleely snickers, "We don't have a lay-away plan, Beatrice."

"When did you stop that?"

"When you first brought it up three years ago, and then every visit after that."

Mrs. Bookafleely pushes the mountain of clothes toward the assistants, "Sorry girls, and make sure these dresses are returned to their proper location. Your auntie will be quite displeased if anything is out of place."

Beatie closes the door behind her and leans back against the building wall. "Life isn't just about dresses," she tells herself, "... but it sure is close." She feels a tap on her shoulder and looks up with surprise. It is Hope Durbrie, the tall assistant with a smile on her face, and she is holding something behind her back.

"Don't tell anyone; just pay for it when you have enough stamps."

"The Fermian Particle Dress?!" Beatie gives her an eye-closing, body squeeze. "Oh, thank you. I won't ever forget this moment." Beatie says with a tear in her eye.

Mia splashes her face with the water from the tap and looks for a towel. There are no clean towels, and this angers her. Now she has to stare into the mirror and watch the water sizzle and pop off her face. The incidents over the past few days are firmly entrenched in her mind. It was only three days ago, a young, delicate-faced, free-spirit woman stepped off a train and frolicked before the city lights. Now her blemished face and altered skull structure are all that remain of that once jovial and optimistically driven woman.

Bo watches while Mia takes a seat at the kitchen table with her head hanging over a teacup. She resumes the eating of her peas and mashed potatoes and pauses only to pop a few pills into her mouth. Half past six has arrived and her lifeless appearance is still hanging over a teacup. Finally, she looks over at Bo and shakes an empty vial. "I could use more of this!"

"How about we go out tonight!"

Mia rinses her mouth and spits back into the cup. "I feel ridiculous. My face hasn't improved, and if there is any change to my horns, they are at least a bit wider!"

"Remember that place called Iggie's? They have live music there. Your guidebook also says it is a place for demented folk."

Mia suddenly raises her head, "That could be promising." She rushes to her backpack and pulls out what little she has clean. She then pulls on her ankle-boots and ties a multi-colored, tri-corner, bridal babushka around her head.

"Before we go, Mar? A photo opportunity? Smile! Maybe not smile that much." <SNAP>

The house appears silent, but it is Olivia's expensive car beneath the carport that lets Beatie know they are still here. She creeps through the front room where her roommates are still putting on their evening touches. Olivia is dusting her decollete in the hallway bathroom. Her long legs are toned in a caramel extract. Nikki is in her own room dressed in a long-sleeve, chiffon gown with her legs hosed in silk. It's just amazing to see all that beauty, and neither one is nervous to look that way.

Beatie's dress slips on nicely, sliding over her shapely body like a cashmere glove. She puts on her mother's heels and brushes her hair back with her hand. It is time to show her two roommates that she can appear just as pretty as they can.

"You're going to wear that dress?" "Do you even know its name?" "You probably haven't read the instructions, have you?"

Beatie sinks along the wall and crawls back to her room; and just like that, the joy of getting dressed comes to a halt. She finds a small booklet on the floor and quickly opens it up.

"Instruction One: 'Please stand, put your hand on your hips, and cross your legs. Are you a pretzel or a pear?'" Beatie stands, and after falling to the floor, she looks about to see her body is all contorted.

"Instruction Two: 'After you have fallen to the floor, roll about in a ball and what do you see?'" Beatie follows the instructions, and quickly finds parts of her body poking through the dress seams.

"Instruction Three: 'Stand, lean forward and then lean back, and what do you see?'" Watching her butt cheeks go flat, she is even more disheartened when she leans the other way and her boobs pop out. "Just great, what does this dress have to say about me?" Beatie flips to the last page: "Conclusion: 'You are a 'Won Ton, Fu Ton, loosely dressed whore.'"

Beatie's eyes go crooked and she slumps back to the floor. For some reason the dress looked better on the mannequin than it does on her! But isn't that how it always is?

Beatie steps out of the dress and walks into her closet. There is another dress she has not forgotten about, and it is the blue opal dress with a neon yellow waistband. She wore it to a high school dance once, and it gives both shine to her luminous chest and shape to her robust derriere.

After wrestling into the outfit for ten minutes, she pauses and exhales. With a little more effort and crowbar leverage, she finally, with the help of a doorstop, stretches the dress just enough to cover both her areolas and thigh cleavage. "Booyah! Now the dress is more about chance than a free ticket to ride."

Beatie lifts her head to hear the sounds of giggling from the hallway. "Is that mothballs I smell in there?" Shutting the door with her foot, she returns to her bedside. She slides her shiny nylons up over her thighs, and then rushes into her closet for her gold metallic, four-inch-heeled booties. After running a lightly scented perfume along her neck and wrists, she is finally ready for a showing.

"Is that how you want to look? A dress looking for a good time? Where do you buy your clothes anyways? Meeshman's?" The two girls laugh in unison.

Beatie finds a cloth to pull around her neck. The nights in Northeast Florida can get a little chilly in February, so she grabs a jacket and tosses it into the back seat. She closes the car door and pauses. Whenever she gets nervously excited like this, she has to listen to some music. She pops in one of her mother's musical discs, and after several tries to get the car into start, the music finally comes on: "Yes, tonight, Josephine. Yip Yip (iii)!"

Beatie drives with her eyes fixed on the road and her hands gripping hard on the wheel. Olivia and Nikki were rather vague in their directions: Turn right before the beach, left at Mumfries, and go past the Christmas Mimosa tree. What is a Christmas Mimosa tree anyways? Are they even serious about her making an appearance? And why does she have to introduce herself as the hired help?

"This must be the place!" Beatie tilts her head to see several expensive accessories walk into a luxury hotel. Slamming her car into reverse to an outcry of screams, Beatie turns the wheel inward, and thrusts the parking brake into hold. She stumbles across a lawn through a curtain of bugs and rushes up the steps to the waiting attendee. Tapping her chest, she coughs out a wing and a foreleg onto his guest sheet. "Sir, you may find me under the name 'Olivia and Nikki's Assistant."

"Oh, yes! The ladies did mention a maid that would be arriving shortly. Here is your broom and trash collector. Use the side entrance to the right, please." Beatie smirks when the attendant steps aside to let her open the door for herself.

The voluminous lobby appears perfectly nice: the marble floor, the walls of Eden, and the window of Eutychus. It is the celestial ceiling that has her spinning about in paradise – that is, until the attendant taps her on the shoulder. "Ma'am, you take a left at the kitchen and walk straight to the storage closet."

Shortly after the kitchen, Beatie changes her direction toward the enchanting voices coming from the end of the hallway. There she lets out a soft squeal. It is just how she envisioned the room – the tall tables, the angled furniture, and the big plates of sandwiches. There are pots with golden lids and baked hors d'oeuvres that she is sure to have chocolate-cherry sauce in them, and get this, the trays of caviar are being served by people displayed in tailored outfits!

Beatie sashays over to one of the tables to see the names on the plaques, and of course, there is no one here she knows. Still, she is sure this is the room where everyone wants to be. Brandi Baily and Burly Brindebar are here, and so are Cleona Leona and Jeta Burley. The host of the party is Beezy Bumay, whose friend Loungie Carler knows Garcy Graskiglio. At least that is what she overheard Prindy Reeshmen of Ghost City News say to Gurty Foulweather. Beatie pinches herself, could all these socialites, with their fine clothing and glittering jewelry, possibly know people like her even exist?!

The clink of an empty wine glass, and soon a stylish lady appears before a microphone. She is introduced as a delegate from The World Order of Nobs and Toffs and wishes to deliver a very spirited announcement about the bug's digestive tract and how it might be used to feed the common people. Complex as it sounds, it is the complexity of her outfit that has Beatie most captivated. All the puffs and angles in shades of black and blue are so ominous; the dress is sure to culminate into a fierce storm if she doesn't get what she wants. The lady is well-spoken and speaks of pestilence and decimation. She also believes that if everyone opens up their wallets, what wonderful things could be eradicated in the years to come. The speech is so invigorating, in fact, Beatie herself can't help but be the first to clap – and then the next to be tapped on the shoulder. Apparently, a slab of Kobe beef had fallen to the floor in aisle seven, and it is Cricky Goondabar that is asking her to clean it up. She couldn't be more insulting when she tells Beatie her outfit smells like mothballs.

It is later, while changing the air filters in the ceiling, that Beatie first notices Mr. Happiness entering the room. He is holding hands with Miss Nikki, which is most intriguing, because on the other side of the room, Olivia is holding hands with Meanburn Furvery. Sir Furvery is the city's tax collector who is investigating Mr. Happiness for underestimating the value of his business – and his girlfriends. Olivia is apparently playing with the wrong partner, and even for her that seems a bit gutsy, considering she too has been seen with Mr. Happiness.

Beatie leaves a cleaning bucket under the dessert table and lingers back to the party. She cannot help but be drawn to all the gentility and how they might accept her into a tournament of opposing thoughts. Her first stop is with the group of stuffy, old business owners. The hot topic is about pleasure and pride over those who are deprived. Following a few gasps and several scrutinizing glares, she then listens to another discussion of wealth and foreclosures, a more appropriate transaction between the minds. After hearing their arguments, however, she soon realizes their numbers are adding up, but their sentences don't equate to very much.

Beatie needs to find a topic less analytical and more socially accepting. She gravitates toward the women kissing the spaces beside their ears. There she finds the mayor and the city planner discussing a new high-rise being built for affordable housing. This is absolutely the perfect opportunity for Beatie to provide a clever anecdote. "Well, if you can judge its height and determine its length, you better be ready for the day it falls!"

Beatie shuffles back to the kitchen behind a dapper old man. The servants pass the plates, the food is readily absorbed, more food is rushed out, and even more plates are returned. Beatie looks at the dirty dishes in the sink and decides to let them soak. She grabs a glass of wine and scurries over to an empty table with plates of unfinished food. She is caught by surprise to see the one and only 'Moistured Groggy' sitting alone at the table's end. Her hair is tied in a bundle with a red scarf draped around her neck. Her lips are plentiful, covered in a thick gloss, and she is still loosely dressed, but her manner is much more reserved.

"Moistured Groggy! I saw you perform at the club downtown."

"Please, my name is Dagmar."

"Okay, Dagmar Groggy with Moisturizer. That was some performance you put on."

"Dear, can you help me with my necklace? It seems to have come loose again." Ms. Groggy brushes her hair aside to expose the many folds down the back of her neck. "It must have fallen down there somewhere; can you retrieve it for me?"

Beatie reaches down the back of her dress, over her lumpy back of greasy vanilla extracts. The chain had fallen all the way down into her brown cleavage of emollients when her fingers finally reach the necklace. Beatie wipes an oily liquid along with some tangled pubic hair on the tablecloth and then hands her the necklace.

Beatie is having a miserable time, and at some point in the evening, she had joined the staff full-time. She does not deserve this. The accident of attending a party of well to do socialites, only to be voluntarily put in charge of cleanup. If it could get any more demeaning, it would have something to do with the staff giving her the chores they don't want to do themselves. Sadly, while emptying a cigarette tray into a Fiddle Tree bucket, the captain tells her she's fired. He even promises to dock her pay. Really! What pay?!

It did go on; the party, that is. Late into the evening, whether she would partake in it or not. The word from the attendees on the comment cards was she spoke with a gentle voice from a primitive mind. That made her feel even more unwanted, but she took the advice kindly. After all, they do have experience in these matters.

Beatie sits at an empty table before an unfinished plate of risotto. It has Alba truffle sprouts over a gourmet sauce, which she likes. Rolling it around on the back of her fork, she looks to see her appearance is attracting the attention of the older men. They seem to be engaged by her youthfulness, silky skin, shiny opal dress, and plucky bosoms. She doesn't care that they are horny; she is hungry. That's when she sees Parker Ken. The man that had made the embarrassing appearance at her workplace last week. He is rotating around in a swivel chair, firing off his fingers at his friends. Need he be any more engaging? He has that character of likeness that make people want to share him. Beatie blinks several times in succession, thinking she is sure he will remember her, but he doesn't. In fact, he even turns his head away after she cups her hands over her breasts and licks her lips.

Beatie's shoulders droop, and her frame becomes much smaller than her dress, much to the delight of the older men.

"Beatrice Backlebond. I thought I recognized your concupiscent presence!"

Beatie drops her fork and sits at attention. She knows that voice. It is that queasy, 'I-just-swallowed-my-own-vomit' kind of voice, and it can easily liquefy the innards of any stomach with a full plate of risotto. But who could possibly create such a bubbling, bowl-exploding flow of dysentery? You guessed it: Cairn Barbie from Australia.

Samantha pushes open the car door for Mia, who then slips into the passenger seat. Sam is wearing a long black coat and knee-high leather boots. This does raise some suspicion as to where they might be going, add that her hair is shaped like a tarpon fin with blue and black stripes, and her eyeliner is thick and dark like a raccoon.

"Sammy, don't forget to Ka-clunk-a-clink."

"You are referring to the seat belt, Mia?"

"I am amazed that after all your time on the British Isles, you still don't know our idioms, nor have you developed an urge to drive on the other side of the road. I also find it interesting that you chose not to invite your brother."

"I figure he scares people."

"Oh, that he does."

The car rolls over the bridge and turns north. In forty-five minutes, the eyes of the city open to all those who appear before its lights. The travel book describes Iggie's as a place where delectable girls get all dolled up with glistening, gilded faces and display themselves with an anti-puritanical proposition that is heightened with their stimulating clothing.

Sam pulls along the curb side to get a look at all the high heels and short dresses. The air is frosty, and long pants could not be more appropriate. Sam finds a parking spot in an unlikely place, where low-lying bushes are not sturdy enough to prevent her from parking there. At the club door, a man whose height and length challenges any prehistoric monster takes his time reviewing the credentials of each patron. "Give me your IDs."

"What for, Mar?"

"I'm going to get us in for free."

Bo motions with reluctance until Sam convinces him to give her a try. "Mia is good at this, Bo. She has a three-step process: first is the flirt; second is the shoulder massage; third, she lifts up her shirt, and if that doesn't work, it gets awkward."

Bo watches with curiosity to see what Sam means by 'awkward,' and Mia doesn't disappoint. She leaps onto the man with flailing arms, and while he struggles to get her off, she begins yelling 'help' in a very loud and effective voice. After a well-practiced tumble backwards, Mia next yells out, "I'm hurt!" Naturally, to prevent the attention from getting any worse, the bouncer relents, with Mia hobbling forward. "I'm going to need help. My foot is strained," waving her fingers at Bo and Sam.

"Yes, go on through," is all the man can say. "The first drink is on the house." Mia steps through the doors with a big smile on her face and the doorman's stolen wallet.

The club is dark, except for the recessed lighting above the bar. There is ample space between the booths and standalone tables, and at the back of the establishment there is a wide staircase leading to an open dance floor. It is not overly busy on a Monday night, but there are plenty of adverts regarding a band playing. At the large oval bar, Mia unfolds a roll of cash and waves over a bartender.

"Two Mojitos, please, with tonic water, crushed ice, triple the rum, and make it a tall glass." Mia sticks her tongue out at Bo and pushes the wallet towards him. "You get what you want."

"Can I have my ID back, Mar?"

"What's your rush?" Mia points to a girl standing next to him. "Go ahead. Chat her up. It's on me."

"What should I say?"

"Tell her one of your crappy tales."

"Aye, a tale would be nice, but maybe some information first." Bo turns toward the lady and leans on the bar. "I'm Bo Fox from Scotland. What's the crack on the street?" Her eyes briefly on Bo before she abruptly turns the other way. He taps her on the shoulder again, "The clavers, ye know, the clavers!"

Bo turns back toward Mia with a wet face. "That was a waste of a good beer." Mia smiles and pats him on the shoulder. "You'll suss it all out. We're going to the lavatory. Watch our drinks, and don't talk to any more women."

Bo sips Mia's drink and then sips Sam's while waiting. He looks about the bar and then down at his watch. The atmosphere in the room has suddenly changed to a lot more men and a lot less women. When Sam and Mia return, Mia is swatting her clothes like she is covered in ants.

"What's wrong, Mar?"

"The bathroom was absolutely disgusting! Water was all over the floor, hair was in the sink, and someone left a squidgy in the loo." Mia looks about the bar. "And where are our drinks?"

Bo rubs his chin, and Mia sends an elbow into his midsection. Sam quickly interrupts, "Wow, look at all these men, Mia."

Mia's eyes soon pop open wide. She quickly adjusts her babushka and shakes her hands out. "Sam, what does the horoscope say about tonight, and Bo, how do I look?"

"You look fine; you only smell like toilet paper."

Sam unfolds the paper and nudges Mia. "It says here – the smell of scented paper will signal to others you have cleaned your dirties."

"Oh, that's just lovely!"

"Mar, calm down, no one will notice."

"The smell is in every household! How can one not notice?"

Sam stuffs the newspaper back in her bag. "Mia, just rub your skin down with alcohol. You'll mix in perfectly fine."

Mia gives Sam an angry look.

"Well, I don't know, Mia. Most people take up cigarettes."

Beatie looks about the room and notices there are more attendees gathering around her than necessary. It obviously has to do with the woman sipping a glass of Drambuie with an orange wedge clasped to its rim. She is a local celebrity of sorts, Cairn Barbie, or whatever her name was before her trip to Australia. Happiness and tranquility do not exist for this woman. She was once said to have been seen with a smile and then had it surgically removed.

It is always the game of Ms. Barbie to ruin the lives of others, using degrading claims to demoralize her opponents into a quiet submission. Oh, how the witch trials would have gone her way, so cunning and hawkish, fruitfully using false testimonies, visions, and social biases to prove others are at fault for their own existence. For someone to have that much hatred boiling inside of them can only be a blessing from hell.

"My, oh my. Beatrice Backlebond. Somehow you found your way into our party, but I guess being an unwanted bug, like yourself, you will always find a way into a room that abhors you. Such is the nature of bugs; am I right?"

Beatie clasps her hands together. "Well, I'm glad you thought that through. I'll be going now."

"Did I say we were finished, bug-crawler?! How will we ever rid of you unless your presence is once and for all extinguished?"

Beatie looks around at all the attendees now crowding her in. Abuse toward another is always the highlight of their evening.

"I'm really just trying to extract the truth about who you really are, Darly. You are very silky, your legs are well shined, and your neck perfumed. Add that you have the tongue of an aardvark and the thighs of a kangaroo, but let us not leave out the arrangement of your attire, for it is meant to attract a different kind of prey – the girl every man's penis wants to know?"

Beatie runs a drum roll across the table and smiles, "Well, if nothing else will do!" A gasp follows from the crowd, and Ms. Barbie's face quickly turns into a wanted glower.

Those would be the last words Beatie would speak at the party. From there, Ms. Barbie mocks Beatie, and not just about her appearance, but about how her mother's mind is the result of her unrefined upbringing. How could Beatie deny her? It is her fault that her mother can't think for herself. She did this to her as a child.

Ms. Barbie continues to pick Beatie a part until there is nothing left to make her whole again. Then after one large assortment of well-chosen insults, Beatie finally melts into the grooves of the Lux Touch glass floor and drains out into the hotel lobby. It is there where she reviews the image of herself before a dark window, and what she sees is what she has always seen, a very proper woman just looking for companionship, and she can't help but wonder why there should be so much anger directed her way.

Beatie wipes her eyes as she crosses back through a running sprinkler system. She came to this party with the hopes and aspirations that made her cling to a society that would never accept her. Now she must accept that her desire to be someone she is not, means she will have to find out who she is supposed to be.

The night is not over yet! Chapter Three says, "Seek and you will find." Beatie puts the car in reverse and drives back over the median to the screams of locals and the sound of blaring music: "Well, everybody's heard about the bird, B-b-b bird, bird, bird, the b-bird is the word... (iv)"

Beatie drives about the town with the thought of getting out, but the behavior of the people she sees is very inconsistent with what she sees in her own daily life, starting with their failure to walk a straight line on an otherwise perfectly flat road. Then there is their need to water bushes with projectile vomit and genital explosions. Is this not what a home bathroom is for?

Beatie flips on her turn signal and turns the next corner. The book says there are nightclubs this way that promise 'never-ending happiness.' But is this the kind of happiness she is looking for? The evening activities are definitely inconsistent with her own activity of waiting in her bedroom for the night to come to an end.

Before the four stores opened, the area was five lots to be weeded. It now has a strip mall, a gas station, and a dog park to be seeded. Iggie's? The men in there are obnoxious, uncouth, intolerable, and sexist at best, which is absolutely appalling, but at least she knows what she's getting into. Beatie parks the car, grabs her purse, and shuffles toward the nightclub door. She wishes she had brought her coat, because she has a bit more skin and a lot less dress than she wants to show. She has never gone into a bar before; not that there are any laws saying she can't, it's just not the sort of thing she does.

With hesitating steps, Beatie approaches a large man with frightening eyes. He looks so mean, and he is so inhumanly large. It's likely he'll devour her skull if he's hungry. "I'd like to get inside, please, but I don't know the password."

"Five bucks will do it."

"Oh, that's easy – five bucks." Beatie crosses her arms and waits, but nothing changes. "Am I saying it wrong?"

"It will cost you five dollars to get in."

"Oh, so the password is five bucks, and then you pay five dollars," looking into her purse. "Rats. I only have a ten, and that's too much."

"You want to leave, don't you?"

"I think so."

"Then ten dollars will cover that too."

"Oh, okay. That I have."

Beatie is certainly pleased with her courage but ultimately disappointed with what she finds inside. She has never seen the male species so repulsively riddled with mistakes before. Their drab clothing, shoeless toes, exposed bellies, and unshaven faces are so undesirable that a mere glance in her direction makes her want to vomit.

Beatie finds an inconspicuous seat behind the bar and asks the bartender to clear off the counter. She looks about the room to see what her own species is drinking and quickly places an order. "I'll have what they are drinking."

The bartender reaches for a tall fancy bottle with a red liquid inside. Beatie pulls the drink closer to her and sniffs the glass. "That's fermented sugar! My papa drinks that. Is there a chance you might have something else?"

"That's what the ladies around here are drinking."

Beatie does remember the book suggesting alcohol. "Interesting. It does kind of make me feel warm."

"Ten dollars will do it, ma'am."

"So, it costs ten dollars to come and go, and then ten dollars to get something to drink? Does the owner know what's going on here?"

"Would you like to start a tab?"

"You are suggesting I have more than one? How many drinks am I supposed to have?!"

"Until someone in the room starts looking good to you?"

"Interesting, and you guarantee this stuff will do that?"

The bartender shrugs her shoulders. Beatie downs the glass, takes a series of short breaths, and then looks about the room.

"Maybe you are right! That man over there is starting to look interesting to me. Ooh, and will you look at that wrong head on the right body? Now, let me see, if you take his 'buku' chest and put it on that tight "butt-wad' over there... Wow! This is fun!"

"Now, you are getting it, ma'am."

Beatie drinks down the glass and sets it carefully on the counter. "Here is more money. I'll have another." Stroking the shaft of her glass, Beatie spins about the bar, eager to see another patron. Her eyes lock onto a man with his hair arranged as a directional post and his belt strapped around his forehead. She can't help but blink in disbelief when he raises his glass and smiles at her. Swiveling back around to the bartender, she slaps her hand down on the counter with a chuckle and a snort.

"Are you enjoying your time here, ma'am?"

"This isn't at all what I thought it would be."

"Would you like another refill?"

"It feels perfectly nice. Yes, please."

Beatie drinks half the glass and then analyzes everyone around the bar. Obviously, sorting out the right man is going to be a challenge. She doesn't even know how to react to the man wearing a gym suit and holding barbells. She certainly wants to avoid the embarrassment of low standards.

After another refill, Beatie becomes overwhelmed with the selection of men entering the bar, expecting maybe less variety of one and wanting more of the same for another. The book did say that her first choice has to be correct, or it will be awkward if someone better shows up later.

That is when she catches her first glimpse of him. His head is tilted back and his mouth is guzzling a tall drink. It's as if he is trying to extinguish a fire down his throat, not with just one drink, but with several in succession. Afterward, he shakes his head, and crinkles his mouth with the most amusing expression on his face. Well, obviously, he spends a lot of time outdoors with that rustic appearance and unbelted waist. Even his feet are encased in unbuckled boots that make that annoying sound when he walks, and if there is anything that would remotely suggest a comb might improve his appearance, he was not informed of it.

"And there he goes again, slamming down yet another one of those intoxicating drinks. This man is absolutely low-grade, rancid cheese butter! I'm amazed his mother didn't spank him every morning before he left the house."

Well, nothing is going to make her get up and admire this man, but gaze at him she will. Beatie's pocket phone suddenly lights up. It's Papa. "Uggg!!! Where to listen?"

The bathroom is horrendous and the smell is drowning her clothes in putrid fumes. There is also no sustainable air that would possibly allow her to survive a lasting conversation, save the few breaths that she might retrieve from beneath the hand dryer. "No, Papa, I'm not using the vacuum. What?! No, I'm pretty sure we are not being invaded by space aliens! Dinner?! I'll need to text you back!!" Beatie races back out the door, gasping for clean air. She then responds to her father by text: 'Not tonight.'

It does not take long to find him again; his presence is known without her having to look up, and the more she does, the more he is liquefying the fire in his throat. There is absolutely no reading material that can define this man in a positive way. He is unrefined, uncouth, and undeniably uncivilized – and yet – for some terrifying reason, she feels drawn to him. Maybe it is the entertainment he provides to the others, or maybe it's that awkwardness in his face and the embodiment of all things unnatural in a flawed smile.

"Excuse me, Ma'am!" Beatie waves to the bartender. "That one over there looks interesting. I admit, he looks a bit unsure of himself, but I guess I'll have him. Will ten dollars cover it?"

"Miss, if you are interested in a man, you need to go up and ask him if he would like some company."

Beatie gasps, "Ask him?! Please! I gave you four of these ten-dollar bills for some giggle juice, and you are telling me I have to go to him?!" Beatie chuckles and snorts; she knows herself way too well to do anything like that. "Okay, one more drink and that's it!"

Beatie holds the stem of the glass and looks down into the dark contents. She is wondering if she, too, can drink as fast as he can. "Ready! Set! Go! Go! Go!" Beatie downs the drink and lets out a loud burp. She then quickly slaps a hand over her mouth and awkwardly smiles back at the bartender. The alcohol is definitely taking effect, and after she tosses the glass into a soap tray, the bartender signals to the other bartenders that she is cut off.

"One more, please!" Slapping her hands down with a drum roll across the counter.

"No, Ma'am."

"How's come? Oh, I see, because that's a twenty-dollar bill I set down. Well, I don't seem to have another ten, so I guess I'll just have to..." Beatie tears the bill in half, "and here you go, ten dollars."

"Sorry, Ma'am."

The expressionless stare from the bartender tells Beatie what she needs to know. She decides to move to another stool, behind a support beam where she can imagine herself hooking up with him. Maybe hoping that at any moment, her reluctant self might break through. Unfortunately, banging her head on the support beam is only giving her a headache.

Throughout the evening, Beatie takes up several different positions around the bar. At times, she is within touching distance of him, and at other times, she is forced to turn away because their eyes meet. In either incident, it is the usual thoughts that prevent her from going any further – that, and the unusual nature of another woman. The same woman who has been encouraging the man to drink until his face permanently deforms. Odd, how she wears a tricorn babushka commonly seen in 1970s commercials, and too, how her hands continually toss about the air as if they want to slap him silly. They seem to make good on their promise, because right now, she is slamming his head upon the bar.

Beatie watches the man slip away for a moment while Miss Babushka orders another drink. This is the moment her book tells her to act, and so she does, quickly intercepting the babushka-wearing sadist holding the man's ID in her fingertips.

"I'll take this!" Beatie says to the lady while racing ahead up the steps to the dance floor. She stops only briefly when an absurd-looking performer dressed as Dracula demands that a group of ladies, dressed in parochial outfits, march back and forth to a song he is singing. Beatie, herself, can't help but get caught up in the hoopla, and too, begins stepping back and forth with a twirl, that is, until she remembers what she came for.

Bo stands alone on the outline of the crowd, looking awkward and out of place. Something soft and continuous quickly approaches him, and his eyes soon meet with a smiling and glowing face. "It's me!" she says.

"It is?"

Beatie reaches forward and lays her forearms over his shoulders, rolling her eyes, "Like you already knew."

"I did?"

"It's in the book everyone is reading: Change by Way of Means by Lucifer Goggy?"

Beatie feels a tap on her arm and looks up to see the babushka lady with her arms crossed. "Bo can't dance!"

Bo smirks, "This is Mia."

"It is?" Beatie replies.

Mia pushes Beatie's arms off of Bo. "Thought I'd save you the smile." She gives Beatie a scowl and then pulls Bo forward, kissing him on the lips. "Let's go, Bo!"

Beatie's eyes look worried and confused. "This is not how it is supposed to work."

"Sure can, and it will! That's how I work!" Mia clasps her hand under Bo's arm and pulls him toward the steps.

Beatie watches while he looks over his shoulder with a lost look on his face. The book suggests that when he does this, she should take something that belongs to him, and in return, she must give him something that belongs to her. She follows Bo to the bottom of the steps and reaches into his back pocket, while reaching into her own pocket to find something of hers.

"This is for you." Bo spins around and looks at a napkin placed in his palm.

"It has my number on it." Beatie replies.

Bo continues to walk backwards with Mia pulling on his arm. Rather than follow him, Beatie just sits on the bottom step and watches him leave, thinking that he could pull away if he wanted to, but he doesn't, at least not for now.

After the bar closes for the night and no one else is left to be scrutinized, she exits the club. Crossing the street to her car, she pauses to look at the match booklet in her hand. "Qui Qua's?"

FEBRUARY 7th: DANCE OF THE AUGGIE'S

Bo's eyes open wide to his surroundings. He remembers breakfast, and he remembers sightseeing, but he does not remember why he should be sitting on the sidewalk before a telephone pole with his nose in pain. He looks up to see Mia on her phone.

"Not that one, Sammy! She was wearing those 1950s, red winklepicker opera shoes, worth about fifty-five dollars on a shopping spree. I don't know, they were engaged in some sort of dance the locals like to do here. One moment: Bo, are you going to call her? Sammy says the horoscope says you should!"

Bo stands up and uncrooks his nose.

"Sammy, I'll have to call you back. Bo is still not responding to anything I say. [CLICK] What is wrong with you, Bo? We've been walking around for the past hour and you haven't said a word. In fact, I became so bored I had to call Sammy for company."

"I'm confused."

"I am too. You just walked right into that telephone pole, like it wasn't even there! Kind of like at the intersection, when you fell on your face?"

"I fell on my face?"

"Well, not on your own, I helped."

"Why would you do that?"

"Same reason two blocks ago when you had to brush the dirt off your pants. That was me that pushed you over the stone wall."

"Mar?"

"Because of this theory that I can do anything to you that I want to while you are in some sort of a LaLa Land. So, let's get back to reality. The girl at the club gave you a phone number?"

Bo reaches into his pocket and rubs his fingers through the napkin. "Aye, will ye 'looky' here. It's all smudged."

Mia grabs the napkin from his hand and unravels it. "Lovely, it's all wet! Wait, I can make out a number." Mia opens up her phone, pokes at some numbers, and waits. "Shhh! Someone is answering. Hello, is this the girl at the night club? It's Mia. What? You were drunk and it was all a terrible mistake? That makes sense." Mia hangs up the phone and tosses the napkin at Bo. "I can't make out any of the numbers anyways."

"Mar, I don't even know her name, and I probably wouldn't recognize her if she walked right into me."

"You know something, Bo? One really doesn't need a lot of information to form an opinion about you." Mia points across the street, "Half past noon and we haven't been to a fort yet."

"As I said before, they are all over the British Isles, Mar."

"Romance! I need romance, Bo! I read there were a lot of adulterous affairs that caused men to be chained to the walls there."

They spoke nothing of the party the next morning; Nikki and Olivia, that is. Both just going about their own lives shadowed in secrecy. In fact, Nikki, at this very moment, is sneaking through the side door, while Olivia is preparing to meet the same man for lunch. Both pretending to be somebody else's nobody. Beatie cannot help but snicker at this. They'll have to figure Mr. Happiness out on their own. She has her own complicated admiration for someone she met, and just like them, it's for someone she hardly knows.

It is still early, and she doesn't have to be at work for a few more hours. She pulls into her mother's driveway with the music blaring from the cassette player: "If I knew you were comin' I'd've baked a cake" (v).

She walks through the front door to see her mother still sitting in the same position she was in two days ago. Picking up the remote, Beatie turns off the television and watches her mother fall to one side. There is a note that falls from her hand revealing a present is available for her in her bedroom.

The door is locked with her training bras, but she finds a pair of scissors willing to cut through the elastic. She is delighted to see a package waiting for her with a note that reads, 'Happy Gastric Frog Juice Day!' Although her mother is forgetful, she never does miss a holiday. Of course, the dates are often mixed up, but that doesn't put a damper on Beatie's spirit. She doesn't mind receiving a Christmas stocking for her birthday, Valentine flowers on Halloween, maybe a birthday cake for Thanksgiving, or even a carved pumpkin under the Christmas tree. It's just the comfort in knowing that her mother still thinks of her.

Beatie sits on the floor with the package between her knees. She hears a scurrying sound from within and quickly sets the package down. After pushing it away with her foot and tossing a stuffed animal at it, she eventually retrieves a rake from her closet. Her mental curiosity tells her to lift the lid very slowly, so when she does this, two motionless eyes peer right back at her.

Beatie quickly shuts the lid. “Momma!!” She walks to the backyard, removes the lid, and then runs back into the lanai. Her mother soon appears with dry leaves on her clothes. “How were you able to convince a baby squirrel to get in a box?”

“Chickle Putz! It's their favorite. It requires five of those bags, you know, and with prices doubling these days.”

Beatie begins brushing the leaves from her hair. “I thought you were on the couch.”

“I thought I was in the garden.”

Are your friends stopping by to play Scrabble today?”

Mrs. Backlebond shrugs.

“They seem to show up without notice now, don't they?”

“All this Ficus Tree Rabble stuff – what's a spider to do?”

Beatie walks hurriedly around the house to see if there is anything unusual since her last visit. Sometimes she finds the little Mossley Guber girl from down the street, taped inside a box in the closet. She is supposed to be replacing Beatie while she's gone. No one is in there, though. Beatie next looks for the little black droppings on the counter, finding only a small trail of ants. The four oranges on the counter are okay, but the two potatoes with several small bites in them raise a concern.

"Momma, have you noticed any mice? I'm going to have to call the exterminator tomorrow. Will you be out for any reason?"

Her mother slowly lifts her head from the couch with blank eyes. Beatie sits down and hugs her mother as if she were the mother herself. "Thank you for the present, but I'm expecting a call at home. I've made a sandwich. What do you think of peanut butter and jelly?"

"Gobble, gobble."

Beatie smiles and walks out the front door, locking it with the key. It was a hard decision for Beatie to leave, but it was a strong recommendation from her very own mother two years ago.

Beatie returns home to her bed and flips over onto her back. She looks up at the ceiling and immediately begins outlining Bo's features with her finger. There, she imagines him dressed in a suit with Italian shoes. His hair is trimmed and brushed to perfection, and he is tall, but not all mus-cul-lee with aggression. What else? Maybe he has a Romanesque nose with a square jaw and thick eyebrows. This part she can draw with her thumb. Now it is time to draw that two-story home. Beatie looks down at the phone but sees there are no messages. It's probably too early for him to call anyways; besides, it's a good time to revisit the fifth chapter of her book: "What to Expect After the Date." Beatie grabs a pencil because there are a series of questions that require thoughtful answers.

'What did the clothes tell you about the person at the bar?'

"There was definitely a rustic appearance about him that made me want to flee."

'Is he a man in a suit or a court jester with a flute?'

"Well, there were many things that appeared country, but flutes?"

'How was your attempt to connect with the man? Were you able to initiate a response?'

"I think he looked at me first."

'When the evening wore off, were there any regrets?'

"I'm still thinking about him, aren't I?"

'Has he awakened you with a morning call or kept you up with a late-night brawl?'

Beatie quickly looks back down at the empty messages on the phone. This question does kind of bother her. She hasn't heard from him in the last twelve hours and wonders if this is even allowed.

'Do any of these words describe you? Kind, gentle, and caring.'

"Why yes, I'm so sure I am all of these words."

'Then that's probably why he hasn't called.'

"That Guber Pasting Male Feces!" Beatie throws a stuffed animal across the room, then races around the house until her anger is exhausted. She leaps back onto her bed and begins searching the book for an answer. "What should I do, Mr. Goggy?"

Beatie finds the response. "Please call our sponsor." She immediately begins dialing the given number: 1800LOVESME. Maybe she hasn't been following the book's instructions closely enough, referring to the comment in Chapter Four: "Hello, is there anybody out there?"

"Yes. Hello? Oh good, thank you. So, I met this guy discussed in Chapter 5 and it says he is supposed to call. Well, that's just the thing – he hasn't. No, I found him first! Yes, of course. No, I'm sure he was the right one! Well, because I walked around the bar and found no one better. What's that? You suggest that I show up at his place with flowers? Listen, pally, I'm the girl here! No, I'm not yelling!! Okay, I'm calm and listening. You recommend I go back to the club? Do you think he would be there? No, I'm not naive! Yes, I heard you! There are men who want to be with you, and there are also men who want to be inside you, and you are trying to warn me about the latter. What kind of advice is that?! Is there anyone else I can talk to? No, I won't do that to myself! Because there isn't the remote possibility it would fit! Hello? Hello?! Oh, no. The line is disconnected again! The phone service around here is so unreliable."

Beatie rolls off her bed. She really doesn't want to spend time looking for him, and the book does suggest starting over. It's half past ten; which is more important, work or starting over?

She wears the same clothes she wore last night, knowing that they worked before. The day is a little chillier, though, so she grabs her long coat and gloves. It is not a far drive, only two corners past the Jambalaya Hut, and the town has a pleasant appeal in daylight, which makes her smile. It's more civilized and the bushes aren't being assaulted. She raises herself up in the seat and leans forward. "That's it! Iggie's!"

The bar smells the same as it looked last night, only with more empty booths. Beatie sets her coat and gloves on the bar and waves to the bartender. He is the same large male who allowed her entry last night. She reaches into her pocketbook and finds a ten-dollar bill.

"I would be interested in meeting the man I met here last night."

"We don't offer those services, ma'am."

"You don't remember me?"

"I see lots of people, lady."

"Faithfully true, but you could at least remember those that are most important to you."

"You are absolutely right. Let me guess. You would like a chardonnay?"

"Ooh! So far, so right." Beatie reaches out and grasps the glass by its stem, smiling as he fills it halfway. "I don't normally come into places like this. It usually involves meeting people at the city gate and circling back to the old cemetery." Beatie is disappointed to see the bartender raise an eyebrow and walk away. No matter. She isn't here for him anyways.

Tapping her foot with great anticipation, she watches and waits. She really does hope he will return, because there are so few options to choose from: two men wearing the same clothing with different faces. A perfect example of what the book calls a 'double conclusion.'

Beatie finishes her drink and gives the glass a sour expression. The bartender leans across the counter. "Would you like a refill?"

"No, thank you. It doesn't seem to have the same effect without anyone to look at." Beatie pushes the glass away and reaches for her coat and gloves. "I'd like to see the upstairs now?"

The bartender grins and makes a hand gesture toward the stairs. Beatie smirks. "So, Mr. Large Animal Beef, I'm just wondering if you could tell me, where do all the better people hang out?"

Beatie closes the door behind her and returns to her car. The bartender didn't have to be so rude. Possibly a mistake in her own thinking when she agreed to this 'dating project.'

She sits in her car wondering what to do next. What she achieved last night did nothing to reassure her further revisits would yield better results.

However, to do nothing is to return to loneliness again. Her worry for lack of companionship has her thinking she should reassert her claim for the man she has already found. But how? He certainly is a mystery. Chapter Six states a mystery is best written as a puzzle where the reader has to put the pieces together in order to solve it. It suggests 'tracking' someone in order to achieve her desires for 'eternal happiness.' Beatie frowns at this; she is not at all happy about tracking someone, particularly when her normal interest would take her to the downtown bootery.

She pulls into an empty lot and tosses her heels into the back seat. It is a novelty shop for country folks. She feels he should always be in a place like this; the only problem is he isn't, despite there being several close replicates. Next is a retention pond, followed by an abandoned construction site, and still, his whereabouts are unknown. Already, it is mid-afternoon, and it is cold enough to start a fire. Beatie reaches into her pocket and pulls out a match booklet along with an identification card: Beauregard Heathan Fox and Qui Qua's. "Both do sound country."

There is a small neglected parking lot trending toward fire ants and sock burrs. Qui Qua's, as seen through a warthog path, looks like a building that had fallen out of the sky and landed on top of its roof. When Beatie gently knocks on the window, it suddenly flings open with a loud bang against the wall. She follows the steps down to the floor and calls out the name on the counter plaque. "Cornelius Bumpkin, please!" Beatie grins. It sounds like a stable food crop.

A man of short stature with a red bow tie and white hair curled above his ears approaches with a wide-open smile.

"I want your cooperation." Beatie takes the matchbox out of her pocket and sets it before him. "But first, may I call you Fun Bobby? It just sounds so much better than Cornelius Pumpkin Head."

The man smirks.

"These matches are yours, aren't they?"

"They are."

"Okay, good." Beatie pulls out a photo ID and places the card on the counter. "I'm tracking this man."

The storekeeper picks up the ID and holds it before his eyes. "Sure, I guess so."

"Anything more in detail about this?"

"He said he is staying at the Hotel 'Ho-spee-tal.'"

Beatie looks at the man with a puzzled look. The only name she remembers even close to that one is the abandoned hospital, and there is no way anyone would want to stay there. She places the ID in her pocket and twists her mouth. "Anything else?"

"He had a lady with him."

Beatie puts a scowl on her face.

"They appeared to be rooming together, and she said she would prefer to be on a lake."

"Hmmm, more interesting."

"That's not all. The lady bought a lot of seasonal food."

"Wait! There's a statement in a book I'm reading that says: If a reptilian man says, 'I'm hungry for lakeshore food, where would the alligators hang out?'"

The owner lifts his head, "The Alligator Farm?"

"Oh, my! Fun Bobby, just so super! So that's what I'll do then." Beatie races back up the steps and briefly turns back to the attendant. "Fun Bobby? You seem like a very nice man. May I ask you – why do you work here? I mean really, this place serves animal food, germ-filled bottles of slimy drinks, and roach-squashed grapes."

The man leans forward with his hands on the counter, "I own this place."

"Well, then! That's probably why." Beatie turns on her heels and steps outside. The window-door slams shut, causing the support beams to fall and the ceiling to cave in.

Beatie parks with a view of the alligator farm. She has booked tours at this place before but has never actually been inside. Animals being fed other animals just isn't her thing. Beatie stands at a distance before the gate, tapping her foot while waiting to be received. It's taking unusually long for someone who shouldn't want to stay in there all night, but he must come out; a woman in need means a man must heed. It states so in the book.

By late afternoon, Beatie is wringing her hands, worried that he might never come out. Another thought is the exhibit could be closed. Sure, people work on Tuesdays, but maybe animals don't. Impulsively, she starts dialing the tour office to get the exhibit's hours, soon realizing her mistake. Mr.

Happiness recognizes her voice, and despite her many attempts to say she is someone else, he still demands she return to the office. "Do you hear me, Beatrice?!"

Beatie starts wheezing and making abundant ambulance sounds, pretending not to hear him correctly.

"Yes, Mr. Happiness. That's what I'll do. I'll stay away from the office until the spread of the disease has passed!" < Click>. Taking the rest of the day off seems the right thing to do anyways, since she is in limerence.

There he is, walking toward the motels. She is relieved to see him but saddened too to see him wearing the same clothes. "Doesn't he have a need to change?"

Beatie starts to follow, but realizes he is with someone that has a very abundant shape to its head. It could be the babushka lady from last night. Maybe she contracted some sort of a disease. Not sure.

Mia finishes her tumbling exercises and rests her elbows on the floor. "I was watching the weirdest show while you were sleeping. It was called Koljack, the Night Stalker; it scared the crap out of me."

Bo lies back on his bed with his eyes focused on the rafters. He can't help but reminisce about the girl he met at the club. She was so full of enthusiasm and promise and had that certainty about her that had been lacking in other ladies.

Mia draws back her hood and puts her hair in two large pegs. She then pushes her bangs together and blows upward.

"Your horns are gone, Mar."

"Not entirely. I still feel them. Anyways, I have been thinking, if you are not planning on seeing that girl at the club again..."

"I don't know if I will, Mar. It's complicated like that."

Mia smirks and loosens her shirt from the waistband. "I know what you were hoping to see; remember these?" She raises her shirt, exposing her naked chest, then quickly pulls her shirt back down in embarrassment. "Just lovely, may I help you?"

Bo turns about to see a pretty young girl with a glowing face standing on the top step of the ladder. She is staring at him with unblinking eyes, then looks away with a shifty-eyed shyness. "Hello, I remember you; would you like to remember me?"

At first, there is no recollection of the girl he had met at the club, but the dialect in her speech soon jogs his memory. "You're the girl at the nightclub."

Beatie scurries before Bo and spins about on one leg. "I wasn't certain I'd find you in a hotel that I didn't know still existed."

"Aye, we had heard it once was a day care center."

"Pretty much worse than that, but that's okay. I thought something might be wrong, and I wanted to give you your matchbook back. Oh, and here is your ID card too."

Mia watches as the peculiar girl takes several spinning moves around Bo with her bosoms flopping up and down. She looks down at her own breasts, lifting her shirt and then quickly pulling it back down. "Pardon, Bo, may I speak with you." Bo slowly steps away from the girl and follows Mia towards the kitchen, "Hiya, love."

"Hello, Mar."

"Do you recognize anything unusual here, because we have been through this before? Oh, yes, we have. That wanton display of getting your attention." Snapping her fingers in thought, "Who am I thinking of... Keira from Perth?"

"Keira from Perth does not have this girl's bosoms, Mar. Just look how they ..."

"Bo!" Mia swats his arm and lowers her voice. "You're dancing with the Auggies here, not the Sawnies."

Beatie watches in fascination as Bo's roommate is getting all bent out of shape. Her hands are twirling in circles about her head, then her arms are tossing up and down by her sides. It reminds her of the lady she picked up by the side of the road earlier.

Mia looks over Bo's shoulder to see the girl pretending to roll doll in her hands, tossing it to the air, and then reaching down as if accidently dropping it. "Excuse me? What are you doing?"

"Uh, oh." Beatie tightens her arms by her side. "Nothing, I'm just waiting for you to finish."

Mia squints her eyes and turns back to Bo. "It's like I said about this 'Lilly-nilly, slouching-silly, poodle-piddling, wanking-willy.'" Mia stops and looks over Bo's shoulder again to see the girl now flapping her arms up and down, walking in a circle, and pecking at the ground. Mia smacks her hands together. "I see what you are doing! You're making fun of me!"

Beatie freezes. "No, I'm not! Nothing! I'm not doing anything!"

Bo looks back to see Beatie with a childish pucker on her face. "Mar, she's not doing anything. You're just making her nervous."

"Serious, Bo, that girl is bare crazy!" Mia looks again to see Beatie grabbing her head and shaking it, as if she is having a massive migraine attack.

"My brain hurts!"

"That does it!"

"Mommy!!" Beatie yells, cowering against the wall.

Bo quickly grabs onto Mia while she tries to bull rush the girl. "Mar, will you slow down?"

"She started it!!" Mia suddenly stops. "Where did she go?"

A notepad sails up through the stairs and lands before their feet. Bo picks up the pad and reads the inscription, "Do you like gourmet food and tasty desserts?"

Bo writes on the pad and tosses it back down the staircase. Moments later the pad flips back up onto the floor. "Good, I'll pick you up around 11:00am."

Bo walks to the ladder and turns back to Mia. "There's no one down there."

"Hard to imagine a reality where there ever was."

FEBRUARY 8th: BARSTOOL CONCLUSIONS

She puts on a dress she normally wears for the holidays, hesitant with a stick of lip gloss that might add too much shine to her looks. She tilts her head back and forth and makes four quick swipes, next lifting a perfume bottle for a light sniff, "Lilac. This will work."

She dampens and tugs on the ends of her hair to get as much length as possible. Nothing overly special, since she will be wearing a cloche hat. She puts her hands on her hips and practices a few kisses before the mirror, thinking perhaps this date might lead to... "No, not going to happen! It's way too early to be thinking about barstool conclusions."

Beatie turns down the main road, looking at the hotel from a distance. She has never really noticed it on her way to work before, sensing it to be very unloved and neglected. Dirty, crusted windows with green mold growing without stagnation just isn't her thing.

She pulls into the far end of the parking lot and honks her horn twice. She had spent the entire morning working on a slight modification to her giggle, a suggestion the book thought might improve upon her maturity. It's a bit boisterous, though, since it involves using more of her throat muscles with an open mouth. "Bahaha!"

Except for the low rumbling noise of the water pipes, the sounds of the street are light on a Wednesday morning. Bo crosses his hands behind his head and looks up toward the rafters. He is startled by a loud thump and quickly puts his feet to the floor. Mia is lying awkwardly next to her bed and appears to need assistance.

<SLAP> "What are you doing, you squat puppet, fleece-coddler!?" Mia rolls out of his arms, pulling Bo to the floor with her.

"You're welcome, Mar. Maybe you should put the bars up on the bed." Bo staggers toward the bathroom.

"You want to be of help? Have a cuppa ready for me when I wake up in the morning!"

Bo pops his head out of the bathroom. "It's alright to be gentle once in a while, Mar. Isn't that what you always used to say?"

Mia breaks into a slow smile. She climbs back into bed and pulls her knees to her chest. "It's always cold in here. Doesn't the heat work in this place?"

Bo pokes his head out of the bathroom again. "I see what you mean by an indoor pool. Toilets are backed up."

"So, why do the pipes always rattle up here?"

"It's a water heating system."

Mia wraps herself in a blanket and crosses the floor, placing her hand onto the iron coils. "They're cold!" She returns to her bed and watches Bo extract some clothing out of his backpack."

"Are you going somewhere? I thought we'd go clothes shopping."

"I have what I need."

"You need a bathing suit."

"Another time, maybe."

"What about today?"

"You were here, Mar. You heard what I was planning."

"You're off your trolley if you believe she's actually going to show up! That whole scene yesterday was an unsubstantiated, uncorroborated, and impossibly conceived appearance that never took place!"

Bo senses Mia's tension and knows she just needs a little spoiling to get her smiling again. He turns the heat on the water and places a tea bag in a cup. "How about that cuppa?"

"Thank you. You know I'm not in agreement with this arrangement. You just met her and already you're planning dates."

"It always has to start with some beginning."

"She was annoying, rude, and inconsiderate! She barged right into our attic while I was undressing." Mia takes a few more sips of her tea and stares into the cup. "You need more control in your life, not this free-spirited, rumpy, bumpy, pumpy attitude whenever you meet a woman."

"I'm under the impression you don't like her?"

Mia throws a pillow at the heating pipes. "She just seems misled in some way."

"Dinnae fash yersel, Mar. You don't even know her."

"You don't have to know people to like them, Bo."

"That's very human of you."

Bo looks at his shirt and grimaces. He reaches into his backpack and fingers through each clothing item, finding they are all wrinkled and faded.

"Just wear the shirt I bought you. It's hanging in the closet."

"It's awfully blue. Is there a tie that can go with it?"

Mia watches Bo put on the shirt and goes to her own backpack for a tie, "PTA."

"PTA?"

"Please turn around." Mia places the tie about his neck and straightens out his collar. "Too bad you don't have a nice pair of shoes. Myself, I always look at a man's footwear to tell me who I'm dealing with. I hear honking! Do you know what you are going to say?"

"Aye, I will tell her a fine tale from the Misty Thloethum. The story about the little girl planting herself in the unspoiled soil so her roots will grow far and wide."

"Cut the tale crap! You're always on about telling crappy tales. Remember – courteous, mindful, and respectful. Be these things!"

"Aye, I can do that too, Mar."

"Ask for her name too; that's generally respected."

The wind blows a powdery green filth onto the windshield of her car. How revolting to be covered with this poisonous pollen on what is supposed to be a palatial setting for a promising date. "What is taking him so long? Does he not know the sun will eventually have to set?" Beatie steps out of her car and waves her cream-colored hat over the dusty glass. She tilts the mirror to one side and reviews her smile. She really is looking forward to this date. It was Mr. Happiness' idea to schedule the luncheon at his social club, with the understanding, of course, that she returns to the office afterward. She knows the importance of a first date and the need to make the right impression. The club is also the place Ms. Barbie describes as a place she will never get into; all the more reason for her to attend.

Beatie sits back in her seat and lowers her hat over her eyes. She can already imagine the food that will be served there: lobster tails, shrimp salad, and scallops in butter milk. It's exactly the food she wants to be served on a first date. And the conversation – with all those 'upstarts' waving to her for the latest gossip. "How sagacious and prodigious you are today, Ms. Backlebond. Well, Pas Ca to you, Mr. Cloverweeds. Would you like some Grey Poupon with your Bull Frog Squeech?"

Beatie leans forward and honks her horn twice again, watching an oversized handbag fall from a roof window and into the dumpster below. She chuckles and snorts while a few garments drift slowly into the trash bin.

She is also looking forward to seeing him more in a true light, not in that casual attire he's been wearing the past two visits. How nice it would be to see him wearing a cashmere suit with a paisley tie, and maybe Italian shoes with a pocket scarf.

Bo suddenly appears around the corner, and Beatie immediately puts the car in reverse. "Not this again!" His ungainly approach is not only cringe-worthy, but dry heaves and aching constipation would be better to cope with than having to regurgitate a bucket full of stomach chyme. All because of his choice to wear pleated corduroys, barnyard shoes, and an awful, wintry blue shirt that has her shivering with constipation. And what is that around his neck – a bolo tie?! The sole purpose of a new outfit is to look better in a higher social structure, not to fit in with a group of backwoods cadavers on a pig hunt!

She would have gotten away too, if it were not for Ms. Weary running aground in a security wall of buttonbushes. The least he could do is appreciate the better half of the engagement, but he doesn't.

Bo too is confused. He isn't so sure this is the same woman he had met before. He was expecting someone a bit more trampy and not so conservatively dressed. "And you are again?"

"Beatrice Backlebond, but most call me Beatie."

Bo looks over the back seat. "I've seen this car before."

"Why would you have seen this car before?"

"I'm not sure."

Beatie starts up the car. "My baby does the hanky panky (vi)," and quickly shuts off the music. She is already starting to feel uncomfortable. True, she liked him at the club, but that's when the alcohol was dressing him as a better man. There is no way the social club will let him in like this.

The drive is silent, with both looking at each other with the occasional smile. Neither is sure what to say to the other. She looks over the seat for a blanket, suddenly feeling a draft coming from his shirt. "You sound funny today; are you trying to talk that way?"

"Not that I am aware of. I'm from Scotland."

"Is that on the west side? I'm afraid I don't cross the ditch very often."

"It's more like across the ocean."

"Bahaha!"

After a long drive through an ocean preserve, the traffic picks up along the main road. A few turns of the wheel and they arrive at an ocean club. Beatie leans forward over the dashboard to see a doorman holding the door for some very wealthy people. "This is it!" She slams the car door and rushes to get in behind the money couple, leaving Bo still buckled in his seat.

Bo approaches the restaurant, trying to make sense of Beatie mouthing words from behind the glass.

"The restaurant is full! Please wait in the car, and I'll come and get you in an hour," seems to be what she is saying to him.

As the attendee moves her aside and opens the door for the next lavish couple, Bo quickly follows in behind and salutes Beatie. After squinting her eyes and twisting her mouth to one side, she takes in a deep breath and approaches the maitre'd. "I have a one-time coupon. See on the back? It's for life."

"Yes, Ma'am. It's based on availability though, and unfortunately, everyone just came off the golf course."

Beatie holds the ticket to the man's face. "Do you know who the owner of this ticket is?"

"Yes, ma'am, I recognize the name, but ... I have an idea."

The maitre'd grabs two fold away chairs and a small table. He then leads them towards the back of the dining room and places the makeshift furniture against the wall.

Beatie takes a seat and looks about at all the old people with their fluffed hair and gilded faces. Even more eye-catching are the plates of poultry and the bowls of porridge, right next to the cakes of cheese and dishes of drippy desserts.

Bo looks at the menu with discarded prices. He can hardly pronounce any of the dish names, let alone guess their prices. He lowers the menu and smiles at Beatie, who has a premade smile of her own.

"So why are you here?"

"I'm on a two-week stop over before going home."

"Is that Brunswick, Georgia?"

"Scotland."

"I've only visited places around here, but it all seems much the same. People and more people."

"Aye, the area where I live only has eight people per square mile."

"I could never live in a place 'that' remote. I'd have to give up my parents and the beaches too."

"We have unspoiled beaches and beautiful cliffs where I live."

"Our beaches are swept of debris and don't require a rope to access them."

"On a beautiful day you can watch the dolphins swim."

Beatie frowns, feeling a competitive spirit from her date that she is not liking. "Well, we have diversity in our ocean life – porpoise, great whites, and swordfish!"

"We have the dramatic views of landscape on the Isle of Skye."

Beatie slaps her hand down on the table. "And we have the calm waters of Talbot Island!!"

"I like the sounds of Talbot Island. I'd like to go there one day."

"... and maybe, you will find someone to take you." Beatie lifts the menu before her face.

Bo feels her uncomfortable response and lifts the menu before his own face. Silent and imaginary interruptions continue while they wait for the waitress. Beatie leaves her hand adrift in the air, trying to think of a song to keep her busy. She casually glances up at Bo and feels a shiver, "Is it cold in here, or is it just your shirt?"

"Pardon?"

Beatie looks up at the waitress that quickly passes them by, "Oh, Miss! Miss?! I'd like to order. Darn! Now we have to wait in agony until she returns."

Bo doesn't want to make a comment, but he is already wishing he were somewhere else. He looks for an exit and begins to think of a reason to leave. The waitress reaches over and fills Bo's empty glass. She then takes the glass out of Beatie's hand while she has it held over one eye. "May I start you off with anything to drink and possibly an appetizer?"

"I'll have the lobster, the steamed mussels, and corn on the cob."

"Okay, and you, sir?"

"Do you have any haggis or spotted dick?"

Beatie fans her face. "Sorry, ma'am, he's from Georgia."

"Sounds like he's from Scotland. 'De a bheir thu gu Ameireagaidh.'"

"Tha mi an seo gus boireannaich Ameiraganach a dheanamh nas reidh."

Bo smiles and looks down at the menu. "I'll have the lobster macaroni and cheese. Can I save money by removing the lobster?"

The waitress smiles. "I'll see what I can do."

Beatie shoots a glare at Bo. "What was that, some, 'Georgian Swamp People Talk?'"

"I told you. I'm from Scotland."

Beatie stands up and looks about. She has made an awful, horrible mistake getting involved with a man from across the river. She needs to get out of this situation and looks about to see a set of swinging doors. It is over by the large industrial gas burner where she pulls out her phone and begins dialing. "Hydragew, it's me. How do I get out of here? No, I'm at the club. No, not at that bulbous-crotch-stroking club! I'm at the country club near the beach. Yes, I'm in the kitchen, and my accidental date is sitting by the door. Okay, I'm listening. True, I can't see him, but I can still hear his voice. Again, true, I understand there are many things that can be felt but not entirely seen. Hydragew?! Ghosts?! No, I need to get away from my date! No, he's from Georgia! I agree. Yes, there's a ladder by the air duct. So, I just push up on the ceiling panel and I'm free? No, I have to go! Yes, if I see one, I'll call you. Very good."

Beatie climbs into the ceiling and crawls along the rafters. She remains cautious, but halfway through her climb, she finds that her heels are causing her a serious problem. When reaching back to remove them, she soon discovers her mistake. She punches through one of the rafters and loses her balance. It isn't a long drop, just one she wishes weren't over a lobster tank. Climbing out of the water with lobsters clinging to her arms, she falls to the floor. She ignores the silent snickers and quickly retrieves her heel from a stubborn lobster before scurrying off toward an exit.

It is an outdoor patio, surrounded by expensive flowers with many different fragrances. She sneezes and falls back into a table, knocking over a water pitcher. "Crap!"

"Well, well, well. What unpleasant words do you have for us today, my dear?"

Beatie is suddenly attuned to a growing number of hearing aids being turned up. She is also aware she is among people who are forced to give up who they are, just so they can become people everybody hates.

"We have had this talk before, haven't we? But I gather you are never listening, for if you had, you would not be here today."

"Yes, Miss Barbie, I know I shouldn't be here, but..."

"It's a bit late for that, isn't it?"

"Yes, Ms. Barbie, but I really do need to be going. I'm here with someone and ..."

"I heard you danced."

"Danced?"

"You danced. It was said to have been a prurient display of affection that only a mating peacock spider like yourself could have performed."

"A mating peacock spider?"

"It was Ms. Malvenu that came to your defense, however. Apparently, she said we are in need of entertainers like yourself."

Beatie has never heard Ms. Barbie ever mention Ms. Malvenu's name before. Never knew there was a likable alliance between the two.

"Ironic, isn't it?" continues Ms. Barbie. "How you are always complaining about the way things are, and yet, you continue to do the things the way they are."

"And that would be my fault, Queen Mother!"

Everyone's eyes suddenly shift toward a man standing at the patio door. Ms. Barbie lowers her glasses and observes Bo as he approaches. "And you are?"

"I'm her foreign advisor."

Beatie turns her head toward Bo and gasps.

"A foreign advisor?" Asks a puzzled Ms. Barbie. "What, pray tell, can you advise on this one?"

"I am on a student exchange program, and one of my assignments is to find an anomaly within a higher structural order and help that person adapt with proper education."

"Like reprogramming?" Ms. Barbie looks to a nodding crowd. "Interesting."

"My apologies, I thought the golf club might be the best starting ground for her. It would give her something to reach for."

Ms. Barbie raises an eyebrow. "We have been in discussion about what to do with this one. Of course, we thought it best to run her out of town, but we are reasonable people. Maybe education should be provided to our misguided ones." Ms. Barbie looks at Beatie and glowers. "I still believe this one is incorrigible, but that being mentioned, I will assist you in your endeavors, young man. I give you this number for her to call. It will ensure she is properly reprogrammed."

Bo smiles and takes the card from Ms. Barbie, then hands it to Beatie.

"And what is your name, young man?"

"Baueregard Heathan Fox, madam."

"Well, so be it. Here is two hundred dollars to assist you with some proper clothing. One should always look smart when providing guidance to those less desirable, don't you agree?"

Beatie approaches Ms. Barbie for the money and smiles at her surly appearance.

"Let the crooked smile not dismay you, troubled one. For with the proper results, it can be made to bend in the right direction.

"Well, the sooner we are able to cover up your defects as a human being, the better our community will coexist without deterioration. I do hope the next time we meet it will be under better circumstances. If not, shall we never meet again?" Ms. Barbie releases the two with a gesture of her hand, and then with a low bow, Beatie and Bo both back their way out of the club.

The ride back to the city is silent, but with all smiles. Beatie's face blushes with admiration as she thinks of him as her foreign advisor. He still has little taste, but how much taste does he really need when he can score two hundred dollars and appease the doppelganging, Frankenstein. Beatie pulls into the hotel parking lot with the car running. "Well, good night."

"Good night? The sun has hardly heated the pavement."

"Yes, but it's getting late all the same. I do have work to go back to." She motions Bo away and then puts her car into gear. Bo quickly knocks on her window. "Maybe I could stop by your workplace."

Beatie puts her foot on the brake and rolls down the window. "True, there is still much to learn, isn't there? I work at *The Happy to Book with You Tour Shop*. Is that enough?"

Bo watches Beatie pull out of the parking lot. He shuffles toward the hotel, pausing to see several articles of his clothing hanging over the side of the dumpster. After retrieving several pieces of his garment, he looks in to see his backpack in a shallow puddle of rusty water.

Mia is missing and the room is no longer in disarray. His pants are pressed and hanging over the chair. The food, however, is missing and there are coins scattered about the floor. She is getting sloppy or she just doesn't care. Bo drags his backpack over to the kitchen table and sets it on its side. He goes through all the compartments and finds all his pockets empty of change. Further inspection of his pants reveals the robbery is a bit more extensive. All his pockets have been robbed of the bigger notes. Bo smirks. He thought he had admonished this behavior in Mia with promises of parting, but now the threat no longer matters.

Bo finds a unicycle in the lobby. It seems fairly simple to utilize; the only uncertainty is whether the bike goes forward or backwards. After twirling about for several minutes, he finally has the hang of it.

It does not take him long to find Mia getting onto a bus headed out of the city. He pedals with a breathless agitation just to keep up with the route, but once over the bridge, he finds a hold on a bus advert and steers his way into town. Bo watches Mia exit a convenience store and follows her into a neighboring park. She approaches a fountain where she tosses treats to a flock of pigeons. As Bo approaches, it is not long before a dirty-faced man in soiled clothing appears carrying a bundle over his shoulder.

"Catalan, it must be hard finding work dressed like that."

"Take me wisely, Missing in Action, and borrow my words for thought. No matter what you hear of me, I am not the half-witted pillicock you see before you."

Mia lightly pushes Catalan. "Oh, Catalan, you're not a 'pillicock', whatever that is."

"Then listen to this; there will be a rendezvous Saturday morning in the town park. The Alteveu will be there. He will be most interested in meeting with you." Catalan grabs Mia's arm, "for he is hungry like I am."

"Hungry? For change and a better society?!" Mia rises on her toes.

"Sure, and bring some food."

"Yes, of course. This is great news, Catalan. Long have I wished to hear the ones that struggle to see the light. Will you be there?"

"If you bring that soup with the salt-free crackers."

Bo keeps at a distance but follows them out of the park until midway across the street when Mia turns abruptly, causing Bo to swerve down an adjoining road. His lack of practice sends him crashing over a metal railing and down into a ditch of shallow water. He sits in the water for a moment, moving his jaw from side to side until he realizes he is not hurt. After returning to the road, he jumps up and down on the bike frame. It's not perfectly straight and it wobbles when he pedals, but it will get him to where he needs to go.

Samantha corners her cat against the bedpost and carries the little rascal into the soaking room. The devilish feline with a twitchy tail had knocked her cosmetics off the vanity and was having a good time of it. Sam pulls the cat hairs from her cream-soaked face and is soon startled to hear the front door ring. Wiping her face down with a towel, she presses her cheek against the window to see who it could be. There's no car she can see, and she can only assume that someone must have wandered onto her property. She gives a quick look at herself in the mirror and combs some curls into her hair.

The musky odor of the river once she opens the door forces Sam back into the house. She motions Bo to step away from the door and into the lawn. "How's come you stink?"

"I'm sorry, Sam. I had a bit of an accident."

"You and Mia are getting good at this."

"Mar is out with that jakey she's been talking about."

"In English, please."

"The displaced person we saw in the park. The one Mia sees as a potential Valentine's date."

"You're referring to the man that Mia refers to as Catalan?"

"I can't help but think she's taking this out on me. Anyway, the reason I'm here is that it is a fair walk back to the hotel on a broken bike. May I stay here tonight?"

All afternoon, Beatie has been drifting in and out of a dream before a confused group of tourists. It is the dream about going into a clothing rack and finding a suit for Bo.

Mr. Happiness storms into the office, not at all thrilled to find his employee standing on her desk and having a conversation with somebody no one can see.

"Come to me he will, in a Jefferies Gweneer smoking suit with slim-footed bobble shoes. Ask not where he got his tie, for it is said to have made his shirt look cold."

"Miss Backlebond!" Mr. Happiness calls out. "Not only did you fail to wear the required outfit for Wednesday, but ..."

"Shhh. Mr. Happiness, will you please keep it down or come back a little later? I'm working on some poetry."

"How about you come to my back office so we can discuss your barstool behavior?"

"No, that's not a good idea." Beatie raises her hand and flips the page of her notepad. "I want to be able to touch you with my eyes, warm you with my cheeks, and scent you with my skunk juice. Only then will you be forever mine."

"Beatrice Backlebond!"

"You know what is wrong here, boss-man? It's the shoppers, isn't it? They're getting on your nerves too, aren't they?"

"Beatie, what are you up to?"

Beatie strides to the window, fanning her face before going into a dramatic reading. "Woe is my life that a ravaging disease should cause hemarthrosis to my arthritic bunions and spray liquids between my orifices!"

Mr. Happiness watches in shock as the group outside scatters. "Beatie, those could have been potential customers."

"The next ones are always better, Mr. Happiness."

"Beatie! If you don't get those customers back here right this minute...!"

"What's that, Mr. Happiness? Is that the phone I hear? Could it be Mrs. Happiness wondering why her husband hasn't been home every night to feed his five children?"

"Beatrice!" growls her employer.

Beatie grabs her coat and steps past Mr. Happiness, "Let's do this again next week, shall we?!"

If the car had failed to start up, Beatie was not aware of it. If Ms. Weary had failed to initiate a blaring horn at the crosswalk, she was not alert to it. If there was a news report about a crazy lady creating thirteen accidents during rush hour, she was not familiar with it. Beatie walks into her room happy to get her clothes off, face shined up, and under the warmth of her covers for the next chapter of her book. "There you are, Mr. Lucifer Goggy. What fine words do you have for me tonight? Chapter Eight: 'Fun with Words.'" Beatie bursts out in laughter. "Mony a mickle maks a muckle?" She tosses a stuffed animal into the air and catches it. She is having so much fun reading about the silly phrases she can use on their next date. "'You're the wee hen that never laid away.' Bahaha!!" Beatie slaps her hand over her mouth after she burps. "Stop it, silly! Am I usually this way?"

Beatie flips the page and finds a list of pet names to be used as a form of endearment. She thinks Max and Rex would be good names, since they were names of her favorite dog and favorite turtle. Kipper, too, the cockroach that always scared her mother. Beatie rolls onto her back, smiling about how everything is progressing up to now. She is ready to be something besides her normal self and this excites her.

FEBRUARY 9th: WHAT IS IN IT FOR TALBOT

Mia places a pillow over her head to shelter out the noise in the room. After changing her position a dozen times, she finally sits up and punches her pillow. It is that unpleasant clanking of the pipes again that has her beating up her bedding. It is time to settle this disturbance once and for all. Mia covers her body in sheets and stumbles her way down the hallway, reaching the front desk dreary-eyed and yawning. She collapses head-down on the counter and then begins to mumble.

The day manager looks into the dark spaces between the sheet and taps his pencil where her head should be. "Miss Pearl, am I right?"

An arm thrusts forward from within the folds and grabs onto his shirt collar. After banging his head repeatedly on the counter several times, she finally replies in a low, growling tone, "Pipes on the third floor. Do something about it?"

"I don't know how I can," removing Mia's fingers and rubbing his forehead. "We don't have a third floor. We have a basement, a first floor, and an attic. A third floor just doesn't exist in this hotel."

"Semantics." Mia's hand retreats back into her blanket and shortly returns with her finger tapping on a room map.

"Yes, I see. You are pointing toward a storage space. It does not hold guests though."

Mia points her finger upward to the attic, and then back toward the blanket, signaling to herself.

"If I may continue, floor space is the measurable area used to assess the value of a property. All partitions, such as attics, basements, and storage facilities, can be used to calculate the overall square footage as a way to determine the taxable value of the structure."

Mia's hand sways back and forth several times in an apathetic manner before raising a middle finger.

"That being said," the day manager smirks, "the space is not listed as a floor because it lacks the necessities for one to live there in comfort."

Mia reaches out and grabs the assistant manager's collar again, pulling him close enough that he can feel her warm breath. "There is a space above us and below us," growls Mia. "I reside in one of these spaces, that for which has annoying water pipes."

"Well, yes. Of course! All floors and spaces have water pipes!"

Mia tightens her grip. "How about silencing those pipes?"

With a gasp and shortness of breath, the assistant manager croaks out a response, "I will not be held liable for shutting off the water while there are still guests in the hotel." The day manager feels his collar tighten even further. "However, I will show you where you can turn the water off yourself." Mia releases her grip and pats him on the head.

She trails behind him, still hidden from head to foot within the sheets. Sen suddenly stops at the attic's ladder to her room. "What makes you so sure the noise is coming from the pipes anyways? No doubt you have heard the cries of the phantom air?" The day manager lifts up a rug and pulls up a floor door to the basement. "No one can really say what is the matter with this city. For two centuries the ghosts have wandered in anger and seclusion, unable to affect the current affairs of the city. Some just moved on, which is thought to be the reason for their exodus into the suburbs."

"The Phantom Air does this?"

"The Phantom Air is that which consumes the air around us with their presence." The day manager points down into the dark opening. "The pipe valve is in the basement."

Mia feels the cold, wet air permeate the blankets around her and steps back. "You expect me to follow you down into that dark, damp hole?"

"You want the pipes shut off, true?"

Mia shakes her head and tightens the blankets around her body. The steps creak as she follows the day manager down into the basement, and once her foot touches down into a frigid puddle, she yells out a line of profanities.

The day manager lights a fiery torch exposing a line of wooden planks. "The knob is in the corner."

Along the walkway, she notices water lines on the support beams as high as her knees. Below her are the sounds of sucking beneath the planks. She is regretting this already, but she has no choice if she wants to get any proper sleep.

The day manager steps up onto a wooden platform and pulls on a string to a light bulb. Mia sees several large shelves filled with appliance parts, paint buckets, pesticides, and various jars of green liquids. Without a doubt, they belong to a family of maintenance equipment. She approaches a decaying box on one of the shelves and lifts up a book, "Change by Way of Means by Lucifer Goggy?"

"It was his last book, following his first book of a different name."

Mia reaches into the box again and lifts out another book beneath it, "The Illuminator of Foggy Pants?"

The day manager lifts his hand in prayer and recites a line: 'To end darkness is to turn on the light so that we may reveal the true nature of what we thought we once saw.'

"A bit periphrastic, don't you think, Day Manager?"

"As wordy as the words may sound, they still have meaning today."

Mia opens the book to see many drawings. "He certainly uses a remarkable description from imagination. Is this the same lighthouse seen on the river? Its beacon is shining down on a group of boats in distress. It looks like the occupants aren't going to make it."

"They were the teacher's minions, attached to a cause for which they could not see. To obtain their safety, they had to agree to help him first." Mia looks at Sen tapping the side of his head with his forefinger. "To control the mind is to control the spirit, but some were not willing to be controlled."

"Who is this man calling from the top of the lighthouse?"

"That is their savior, or by any other name, the Alteveu. Rumor has it, he has once again returned to the streets with his band of cadavers."

"Ghosts being raised from the dead?"

"There is a reluctance to disclose what they are really about, but it is told that their purpose is not friendly."

“Ah, the haters. Who is this man on the shore assisting the boat occupants?”

“The Catalonian. Not too much is known about him. He was said to have been enslaved on a nearby plantation, eventually becoming the Alteveu's primary assistant.”

“Catalonian? The story sounds familiar. So, Day Manager, you were going to show me the turnoff knob?”

“There are many things out there that are beyond our understanding.”

Mia snaps her fingers, “Day Manager, let’s take care of the pipes, please? I'm tired.”

“It's before you. You only have to turn the knob clockwise, but only after eleven in the evening please! Then turn it back on before six the next morning. The guests are sure to complain if you don’t.”

“Hard to imagine you have other guests.”

The day manager takes the book from her hand, “Maybe you would like to see the town from the perspective of a local. That being myself?”

Mia takes the book back and places it tightly under her arm. “I don't know you well enough, Day Manager.”

“My name is Sen Lin Khan, what else is there to know?”

“Oh, the usual things: Do you casually dine, do you eat with your hands, do you read picture-dominated material, and what else? Do you live with your great-great-grandmother? Things that are important to the modern-day woman.”

“Can't these questions be discussed over lunch?”

“You are a very intriguing man, Day Manager, but for now, I think I will just take the book for entertainment.” Mia follows the planks back to the stairwell and rushes up the steps. Once in her room, she leaps onto her bed and rolls about until she feels the warmth settle around her body. She places the book under her pillow and closes her eyes, happy to have some reading material for the days of boredom.

Beatie pulls on the blinds to fill her room with the morning light. She is disappointed by the day’s appearance. It is going to be a wet hairnet, overly moisturized, clammy-skin, kind of day, not at all what she was hoping for.

She walks about her room, picking the clothes up off the floor, noticing she has never had to do this before. A clean room has always been the staple of her daily life, thinking she must have picked this bad habit up from somewhere. Drifting back and forth from one end of the house to the other, she discovers there is nothing left to do with plenty of hours to waste. Maybe she'll pass the time sleeping. She lands on her bed and flips onto her back, remembering there is something she has to do. It's the reprogramming lessons requested by Ms. Barbie. Beatie reaches for the music player and pops in a lesson disk: "It's what you always want and expect from your own kitchen."

Beatie grunts and repeats the line. There are several tapes she has to listen to; all of which are programmed responses whenever a socialite speaks to her.

Beatie sits up abruptly and shuts off the tape. A large trash bin can be heard rolling across the lawn. It is followed by another loud slam coming from the front door. Beatie rolls out of bed and peers down the hallway. It is Nikki and she is fixing herself a strong drink.

It's the same story, really; she caught him breeding again. Not by actual observations, but based on vague expressions of sincerity from a man proficient at defending his absences. Cruel suspicions leading to betrayal and mistrust. When they first met, he was very uxorious, bowing to her needs and making her feel as if there could never be another, but while exaggerating their romance to 'so-called' friends, it became obvious she could only be significant to him for a short period of time. Sadly, these matters are always discussed at the same parties with the same ladies that think no differently than the thoughts of her own. That fixes nothing, since these are the same ladies involved with the same men who are already married to someone else. Now dependent on the relationship, the natural process of wilting begins.

After tossing several glasses of an amber liquid down her throat, Nikki noticeably walks unsteadily down the hallway. Beatie does not wish to be involved with this lady's psychotic episodes, particularly because she knows the man she is involved with. She dives beneath her bed and quickly rolls to the wall, trying to drown out any sound that may be Nikkie's.

"I'm in here, Beatie!"

"Uggh!" Beatie shoves the earplugs into her ears and turns up the sound on the reprogramming tape: What would compel this lady to bother her anyways? She hasn't done anything wrong. Think about it; it's always the same discussion with Nikki. It starts out with her being the victim, and then eventually she releases her anger on less respected people. Typical socialite.

"Beatrice! Yahooey!!"

Beatie rolls out from beneath her bed and closes the door with her foot. She then rolls back against the wall, and for the longest smiling moment, she relaxes. That is until Nikki storms into her bedroom with those bulging, red eyes and thunderbolt forehead veins; while of course, looking stunning in a black sequin evening gown. She then grabs Beatie by the toe of her bunny slipper and forcibly drags her across the hallway into her own bedroom. Her head hitting the doorframe is when she blacks out.

Beatie awakens to find herself seated before a vanity mirror under the care and warmth of a hairbrush and a bright light. She has never been in Nikki's room before, and she is quite intrigued with the luxurious decor of coffee tables, antique chairs, Persian rugs, and abstract paintings.

"Where should I begin?" Is how Nikki starts her story in a very cultured and somber tone. "He had a very compelling but guarded truth, and for the sake of the prior, I trusted no other."

Beatie, inwardly, rolls her eyes. 'Seriously Nikki,' Beatie says to herself, 'you are imprisoning your roommate, so you can explain the role of the victim you have been forced to play!' Nikki then goes on to say that equally important to her are the facts that he is incapable of considering another and that she is still sure of his innocence. 'UGGHHH!! You questioned him before. What told you you were wrong?! This paramour of yours is a man who had found love before and is still legally bound to it in marriage! How is that working out for you?' When he locked her out, it made no sense to her – not accustomed to being locked out before, so now she has to imply that no one could ever do this to her.

"Don't you agree in his innocence, Beatrice?" Nikki inquires.

When the relationship began, it was her most trusted friend, Olivia, that told her it would never blossom and that it was only through suspicious kindness did she acquire him. Unfortunately, Olivia was right about his conniving ways. In fact, everyone who knows this man knows to avoid him, except Nikki – and Olivia, who ironically found him cordial at a dinner party that Nikki, herself, was throwing! Do you not know the people you associate with, Nikki?! Or does she not know that Olivia, herself, is the orchestrator of conniving wickedness?

"Beatrice? I asked you a question."

"Oh, yes! Your door knockers look like real pepper shakers."

Nikki quickly covers her mouth to avoid a whimper. "I never let him think it is about his money, so why would he think my love for him is truly fleeting?!"

'Really, Nikki? You say you know this man? Have you not met his wife? This isn't your game to play. Yes, he has the money, and lots of it, but it's not for you. This is the new strength in a civilized but unsociable man! This is their virility: one minute you are playing with his childishness and the next regretting it.'

"Can you believe this, Beatrice? That he could do this to me?"

"I think I would like to discover my sexuality elsewhere."

"There I was, dining in a quaint restaurant, before all those that would admire me, brushing my shoulder at the mere price of a meal, and then you know what he says to me? 'Oh, my dear Nikki, my money is tied up in the business this week. We will have to use your credit card tonight.' So, you know what I told him? No lips, no hips, no pointy little ..." Nikki grabs the end of her nipples through the fabric of her shirt. "How do you like that response?"

"I think bushes grow for a reason and not just so you can trim them."

"Oh, Beatrice, how so naive."

"Yes, ma'am." Beatie knows not to say anything more than what is said on tape. The repercussions could be worse than dish cleaning. Besides, there would be little to offer her in the way of comfort anyways. She is talking about the same man who made the same gestures toward her when he first hired her. It's not just a coincidence that he behaves this way.

Beatie raises her hand, "Nikki, I have a question."

"Oh, what is it, Beatrice? Is this about your new boyfriend?"

"My new boyfriend?"

"He was explained to me by concerning minds. I heard that you hired a him as a consultant."

Beatie squeezes her knees together. Time to abort, Beatie! You said it yourself, Nikki plays the victim and then takes her anger out on less respected people. Do you actually believe this woman is going to take interest in your well-being?!

"Beatrice, I want to know what your involvement with your new boyfriend is!"

Beatie blinks her eyes rapidly. This is a direct question, not one for the practice lessons. "I guess I like him. He seems nice. He behaves much older than most adolescents my age."

"Like the men at the party? 'Those kind of men?' The kind that will get you pregnant and leave you to do the cooking and cleaning, then off with their mates to fornicate with any woman ready to bend over a kitchen table?!"

"Premarital sex? I heard about that."

"Yes, premarital sex, Beatrice." Nikki drains the bottom of her rum glass. "Maybe I should talk to this boyfriend of yours."

That's not going to happen. True, Beatie is open to whatever people might say in general about relationships, but in no way can she trust Nikki to handle the interviews of her potential boyfriends.

Beatie walks back to her room after Nikki throws herself onto her bed in a flood of tears. She is a wreck from whichever angle you look at her. She pulls on a robe and leaps back onto her own bed. The next hour is about dropping her head into the pages of her book, which now is about her acceptance into the exclusive society called 'Love!' How wonderful does that sound?

Beatie lies back on her pillow and turns the page. "Ooh, this sounds exciting: 'Dreams are made for the success of one, but should also be about the success for another.' That sounds promising."

Time passes quickly, and she knows she needs to get ready for work, but she also feels excessively glued to the pages of her book. It's just so delightful reading about the promises of forever happiness – that is, until she turns the page to Chapter 9: "Dealing with the Man in the Barn: 'The comfortable attraction to a captivating person can many times lend itself to finding comfort in one who is not.'" Maybe this is about the raggedy clothes he extracts from a garbage bin? Beatie chuckles to herself. "No way! He has a closet in his room. Every closet has better clothes waiting inside for them."

Beatie stares into space, but what if he doesn't have better clothes? True, she is not from a wealthy background herself, but if he is in charge, would he have her dress like him? He hadn't suggested he would, but would she have to buy a backpack and sleep in hotels too? And how does she feel about this? Does she really want to look like his roommate? A hooded head with a possible disease growing inside of it?' Beatie stuffs the book back under her pillow and shakes her head. This is Nikki's doing. It is her comments that are giving her these conflicting thoughts.

She looks at her clock and realizes she has forgotten something. "Burning Piss Blanket! I forgot about work!"

Beatie rushes into her Wednesday outfit, even though it's Thursday. It's Mr. Happiness' fault that he can't understand women. She stamps her foot repeatedly on the gas pedal to resuscitate Ms. Weary, and once she gets her to turn over, there is a sudden rap on her window. "He's a cheat! He's a cheat!"

Beatie looks at Ms. Nikki's witchy face pressed upon the glass. She slowly rolls down the window, careful not to disturb her features, and then smirks. "I'm sure it's not like that."

"No? Then I'll tell you a different story. One with a far worse ending!"

Beatie puts her hands in her lap and lets out a deep breath. "Okay, go ahead."

"Your boyfriend has other thoughts on his mind. More corporeal with extreme sensual arousals in his loins. He uses that part of the brain because the animal inside his pants makes the decisions. What do you think of that?!"

"Well, it sounds like I don't like that."

"Good, there's more you should know. He foolishly hooks up with any enamored woman he doesn't care to know. He also won't keep his promises, because he doesn't have to. He is not from here, and when he does leave town, you will be a forgotten amoeba!"

"Amoeba?!" Beatie is mortified to hear the sound of that word. It sounds so small, so simple, and so easy to lose.

Beatie pushes the car into gear and watches Nikki fall to the ground with Ms. Weary puffing smoke on her. "Why doesn't he call you, Beatrice?!! Why?!! Tit Willow! Cough! Tit Willow! Cough!"

Beatie shifts into a higher gear to get away as fast as she can. "Enough of these 'Kak Cams' from Ms. Nikki. That woman talks specifically about Bo, as the atypical male, who just likes to participate in immoral activities. Duh, what male doesn't? Well, Ms. Nikki, you may be sympathetic with your eyes, but your ears are never listening! Manipulative, imperious, and condescending – that is the game you and Olivia like to play!"

Beatie reaches the quiet part through the preserve and suddenly has to slam on the brakes for a flashing light. She watches as several family members make their way across the crosswalk, then she continues her rant. "Foolishly hooking up with anyone so they become amoebas. Isn't that what Nikki just said?! Her comments should be more about minding her own business!"

Beatie suddenly looks up to see a man kicking Ms. Weary and yelling, "Watch where you're going, you barking pregnant tree spider!"

Beatie is absolutely shocked to see the man acting out this way, even while holding a toddler. And for what? Something that wasn't even Ms. Weary's fault? What's wrong with the Suburbians these days?!

Beatie waits until he reaches the other side of the street and thinks about the words he used. In fact, it was the same word that Nikki used earlier. What if it is true? What if the man she is dating is only interested in getting people pregnant? Is this not who he is?!

Beatie suddenly slams the brakes on again when she hears another scream. "I'm sorry, is that your pet? I'll get you a new one."

When the door to the tourist office opens for the first visitor, Mr. Happiness quickly pushes his glasses to the crook in his nose. He is a tall, lanky boy with a quirky smile and unbuckled boots. He appears to be looking for someone in particular.

"You are here for one of our tours, yes?'" The proud business owner inquires.

"Well, in fact, I'm looking for someone. A wee lass that I met a few days earlier."

There is a loud clambering at the door behind him and the falling of a coat stand. "Sorry, I'm late, Mr. Happiness. People, cars, crosswalks, and more people; it kind of makes for the usual ride here." Beatie lowers her head, expecting a scolding, but instead, is surprised to see her boss' merriment.

"Nonsense, Beatrice, you are just in time for our first customer!"

Beatie's eyes go wide, caught off guard when she sees who the customer is. She is also a bit angry too. It seems her questionable boyfriend, who does not like to call anytime soon, only appears when he is ready to get her pregnant. Naturally, she needs to reject him and maybe too, toss him to the street like the garbage he's been behaving!

But there is something else too that has her most confused; like she is relieved to see him again and wants to pull the skin off his face and wear it as her own. It's hard to explain; it's a girl thing.

"Oh, it's you." Beatie quips.

"I was wondering if we could go for a walk and pick up from where we left off?"

"Well, I don't know; I'm rather shocked right now. Maybe come back when I'm not ovulating." Beatie turns away and bites down on her hand. How so confusing this all is and how so dramatically close she is to making her first mistake. Remember what the book said about going slow, or he might have the impression you're interested.

"Well, I did make a promise that I would come to see you. Maybe we could take a walk on the beach?"

Mr. Happiness steps from the back office. "Is there something the matter, Beatrice?"

"Ugg. No Mr. Happiness." She picks up one of the brochures from her desk. "So, have you been to the Fountain of Youth?"

"I have; it didn't go so well."

"It didn't?"

"Apparently, the water in the cistern has a harmful reaction when applied to the face."

"That's nice." Beatie watches as Mr. Happiness retreats to the back office, leaving his door slightly ajar. "Well, thank you for stopping by, but I'm sure you have other women to molest."

"Pardon? No! I was just hoping to spend a little more time getting to know you."

"That's sweet, but I can't meet with you right now; I have errands to run and other men to seduce."

"Well, okay, bring them along. How about lunch? You have a lunch break, don't you?"

"Lunch? How much lunch can we have?!"

"But I thought you enjoyed our lunch."

"Sure, but we had lunch yesterday; other people have to eat, you know!" Beatie takes a few steps away and turns with a soft squeal. Oh, how the sound of his enthusiastic voice puts a spell on her. It makes her want to brush her hair aside so he can caress her shoulders.

"Okay, so we don't have to eat lunch, but how about if we go window shopping? Women like to shop, don't they?"

"What's that have to do with anything? You can't just come to a woman's place of business, go shopping, and then expect to pay for it! I think you better leave. My acquaintance, BoBo Highbrow, is on his way, and he doesn't like people who can't pay for everything."

"Bobo Highbrow?"

"Yes, you probably met him. He was the tollbooth at the nightclub the other night."

Bo slumps his shoulders and turns toward the door. "Okay, my mistake. I won't bother you anymore."

Beatie watches him leave, painfully indecisive about what to do. She would leave her hand in his pockets if she knew there weren't any spiders in them. Again, a woman thing.

"Beatrice?!" Calls out Mr. Happiness. "You'll need to stay late in case we have 'after-hour' walk-ins! We are starting to see a lot more visitors! Valentine's isn't just a day for flowers; it's also about spending money on tours." The phone rings and Mr. Happiness answers it. "Hold on please. Beatrice there's a party of ten asking about the Goombash Gorge Tour... Beatrice?"

Beatie is amazed by Ms. Weary's friendly behavior, thinking that maybe her car knows more about this mystery man than she does. Oddly, too, how the nodding heads of roadside flowers are showing their full acceptance of him as well.

They travel over the bridge between the calm river and the drifting clouds. Beatie is in full tour mode, and she cannot help but go into great detail about how body parts were found outside the historic hospital. It is at this moment she refers to Chapter Four: "Hello, is there anybody out there?" ... where she makes an emotional plea in order to obtain a nurturing response. "Sob, sob... It was awful! And the bones are still there!" She stops at a light and leans into Bo for comfort, but unfortunately, he fails to react. That was something the book did not have an answer for.

When they arrive at the restaurant, Beatie immediately has to restrain herself from screaming through her eyelids! Not only does the man she is dating lack empathy, but his choice in fine dining has its glaring faults too! The parking lot is filled with grass turds; the walkway has leaves that move with critter bugs; and at the front door, she has to leap over a pygmy snake just to get to the maitre'd! But nothing at all compares to what she sees inside. There is not a single living entity in that restaurant that can remotely be classified as human, taking note that her blood would probably be essential and fresh. The shirtless men with their slipper shoes and the women who think clothing should be optional. Add to that the loud burps of food consumption and the lack of dining utensils that can only be attributed to people with a hematophagous ancestry.

Beatie takes a hard look at the pygmy snake and then back into the restaurant, trying to ascertain which of the two evils to attend to. Unfortunately, her date has already made a decision, proving to her that the clothes worn by the people inside are equal to his own.

Beatie quickly reaches out to a server, "Excuse me, miss? Do you have any seating arrangements where we can put our heads out the window?"

The young attendant looks at Beatie's work attire and gives her a quirky smile. She then leads them through the restaurant, stepping around stacks of plates and buckets filled with empty bottles and cigarettes. After reaching the table of her choice, Beatie looks down at a cockroach on its backside kicking its legs. She swats it to the floor and then wipes a pubic hair off her seat.

Bo pulls forward to let the server set a pitcher of water on the table, then watches her grab an empty glass from Beatie that she has held over one eye. "I'll have the chicken wings," Bo tells the waitress while she pulls out an order pad, "with blue cheese dressing."

Beatie holds the menu close to her face, twisting her mouth back and forth, "So! Pas ca. This looks absolutely gnarly: Churly Based Wings with Hurl Sauce and Barf Bits?" Looking up at Bo, "Did I hear a – Pas-ca-whaah?!!"

"I can come back." The waitress takes hold of Beatie's menu.

"No! I would like to order something now, Miss Vicky Vampire." Beatie yanks the menu back into her possession. "I'll have the salad without the onions and croutons, and please remove any of those hard-to-see, leaf-eating Mothra worms." Beatie puts her finger down her throat and pretends to gag. "Oh, and I would also like a side of pilaf."

Bo reaches for the water pitcher before Beatie has a chance to pour it herself. Disturbed by his lack of manners, she gazes at him through the bottom of her glass, trying to analyze his behavior based on his distorted features. Something she liked to do as a child when judging her classmates.

"So, I read somewhere that most males do work in Georgia. What is it that you do...?" Beatie snaps her fingers, pretending not to remember his name.

"Bo Fox. I am a stocker at a chocolate factory in Durham."

"That can't be good. Do you harm anyone?"

"Not if you do it right?"

"And how long have you been a stalker?"

"Long enough to pick out the best moisties, box them, tie them up, and then ship them around the UK."

"That sounds ghastly! Doesn't anyone notice?"

"Not really. I work my own hours, which are generally at night."

"And no one notices any of them missing the next morning?"

"No, even better than that. I get to eat as many of them as I want." Bo leans over the table with his hand over the side of his mouth, "Don't tell anyone; the company frowns upon it, but it's not illegal in Scotland."

Beatie gasps, "You don't scare me, Georgia from Scotland! St. Augustine is just as tough. We were attacked and sacked for three centuries; lives were taken and families were ruined; our history was erotic, evotic and filled with gas! Don't believe me?! You can take this fork and stick it in...!"

It's a monstrous plate of twenty wings; even Beatie could not believe that twenty chickens could fit on a plate. Her salad came shortly afterward, and she allowed the waitress to leave only after she checked for worms. After mouthing a spoonful of rice and chasing it down with six swallows of lemon juice, Beatie looks at Bo in anguish. She is absolutely appalled by his preoccupation with eating once furry little chirping creatures. There is even a bloody, brown sauce around his mouth, and his nails are dirty with chicken carcass.

Bo wipes his mouth with the back of his sleeve and looks at her plate with a grimace. She is eating a bowl of hedge trimmings while engaged in humming the 'Sound of Music' between bites.

"Pass the Bootchie, please."

"Bootchie? You mean the blue cheese?"

"Is that what it's called?"

Bo places his hands in his lap, waiting for his empty plate to be removed.

"So, what are the sleeping arrangements between you and your roommate?"

"With Mia? There isn't one."

"Ball Squats!" Beatie covers her untamed mouth and lets out a nervous chuckle. "I mean to say, she seems to have exorbitant needs."

The waitress interrupts, "Here's your check, sir. They charged a little extra to remove the worms."

Beatie walks behind Bo with a displeased swagger as they leave. She is irritated with his casual selfishness, wondering if she really can accept this behavior in him. She doesn't want to believe Nikki, but she does recognize a lot about him that seems country. Further confirmed when he shockingly crosses the street without her.

"Why, you ...!" No longer able to hold back her anger, she cocks her finger, aims straight for his back, and shoots him right there in the middle of the street. After she watches him stumble to the sidewalk, she decides to do it again, still aiming for the same spot that almost brought him down. This time she gets him good, and he falls flat on his face! No faking! It really looked like it hurt!

Beatie suddenly feels horribly sorry, thinking maybe she is being a bit too hard on him. She races to his side and clasps her hands together in prayer. "I'm so sorry! I didn't mean to... well, okay, I did, but it never actually worked before!"

"It's okay. Am-m-m, just a l-l-l-little..."

Beatie takes him by the arm, realizing her actions can be harmful. "You know what? Chain me!"

"Huh?"

She reaches out with her wrists raised, "Chain me. I deserve it."

Bo pulls a long blade of grass from the ground and drapes it over her wrists. "You're chained."

"Now banish me to the sands of Vilano."

"Okay."

Beatie tosses two towels over her shoulder and closes the trunk of her car. Sunrises over the beach in the morning and sunsets over the city at dawn are an existential beauty for anyone willing to embrace the start or finish of a day. To Beatie, there is nothing more romantic than to have someone embrace her under a moonlit sky – day or night.

She leaps over a trail of sea-going turtles and tosses a white brick at the ocean, landing somewhere on a stringy glob of red seaweed.

"You know, if you had any direction, you might actually hit the ocean."

"I don't like 'scarlet concubines.' They wash up onto the shore and make everything stinky and clammy. I even wrote a poem about them with my father."

They think they are desired, but they have an awful smell.
If you met a nicely scented woman, would you be able to tell?

"Let's go down a bit further." Beatie clings to Bo's arm with the waves crashing around their feet. She races ahead with Bo laughing and stumbling behind her. After falling into the sand face first, he looks up to see the glow of the moonlight highlighting her goddess-like features. Her lips are so full and her eyes shining so bright, it most certainly warrants an intimate connection.

<SLAP!!!>

Beatie pulls away and spits, not understanding why their joyful meeting had to be approached this way. Not that she is opposed to two people kissing; it's just that she isn't so sure he is doing it right. His tongue was trying to liquefy her tonsils, while, at the same time, force-feeding her mouth with a slimy red eel.

"Ow!!! Bo stumbles backward in the sand, quickly shifting his jaw from side to side.

Beatie already has her arm cocked back, ready to strike him again, when the expression on his face convinces her he's probably just confused. "Never mind, just forget it." Beatie sets a towel down in the sand and sits with her legs crossed. "We're on a nice beach, it's a nice night, so just sit here and talk to me."

"A Scottish tale?"

"That would be fine."

Bo sits down next to her and crosses his legs. "Aye, The Pabbay Mother's Ghost (viii)...or words close to it."

> In a very dry and dusty town, where many of its inhabitants have little to eat, there lives a kindly man who cares for his pregnant wife with homemade porridge.

"Pregnant?"

"Aye,

> and one night, a very weak and pregnant woman comes to his household and asks if he too might share in the homemade porridge he serves his wife. Being a very kindly man, he naturally fills her bowl, and once she feels strong enough, she thanks him and leaves.

Bo sees a concerned squint in Beatie's eyes. "What's wrong?"

"I'm not sure yet."

> It isn't long before a different pregnant woman comes to his household and asks him for the same porridge that made the other pregnant woman strong.

Beatie raises her hand for a pause. "So, this guy has an open-door policy of feeding pregnant women?"

"A little unexpected, but he is a kindly man. So, a third pregnant woman..."

Beatie touches her chest, then her left and right shoulders, placing her hands together in prayer.

"Now what's wrong?"

"How many pregnant women does he know?"

"I don't know; he's a kindly man."

"Exactly my problem with this man."

"There's nothing wrong with him; he just wants to do his deed of keeping those who are in need healthy and strong. So, the next pregnant woman..."

"Four pregnant women?! And maybe there is a fourth and fifth. Possibly a sixth and a seventh?!!"

"There could be."

"Apparently, this man has a very good reason for knowing pregnant women!"

"Exactly!"

Beatie throws her hands up. "Well, I'm shocked! I'm just shocked and speechless, but mostly just shocked!"

"What for? The story is about a man who knows the needs of a woman."

"It's hardly comforting to learn that on our second date, you would take me to a bovine lunch feeding, follow me to a beautiful beach to suck on the gums of my mouth, and then feed me a horny story about getting women pregnant?!!"

"Who said anything about getting horny women pregnant? It's just a tale that all pregnant women deserve to be cared for with kindness."

"Oh! So, you're into pregnant women!"

"No! Of course not. Well, maybe the engineering of it."

Beatie gasps. "That does it!" <SLAP> "You are just what Nikki had envisioned for me!" Beatie pulls Bo's chin down and spits in his mouth. "See if you like it!" As quickly as the tale began, the date was over. Beatie ran off the beach and back to the parking lot.

"Wait, Beatie! Who is Nikki?!"

"Stay away from me!!"

"It's only a Scottish tale! It didn't really happen!!"

Bo trips and stumbles down a grassy hill as Beatie races off into the parking lot. She is working hard to get her car into gear when he finally does reach her.

"Beatie, you misunderstood me."

"No, I didn't! I am who I am, and I should have expected you to be who you are!" Ms. Weary kicks out a few carburetor coughs and quickly pulls backwards with music blaring: "Take out the papers and the trash! Yakety Yak! Don't talk back (viii)."

Bo falls forward and watches Beatie drives away. He stares at the city lights blinking through the wavering trees. It will be a long walk back to the motel and he won't arrive until morning.

FEBRUARY 10th: SORTING OUT FASHERIES

Mia was already up buying knick-knacks and staple foods before the first sign of daylight. She is glad to have made it back before her affliction takes effect but wishes she had more time to clean the room. Her ailment has her working close to her bedside now, so she will have to clean the counters later.

The door flies open, and Bo stumbles forward onto the floor. He crawls along a cleared pathway through the dirty laundry and finds Mia, not quite on her bed and mostly on the floor. One arm is caught up in the roll bar, and the other hand is making a thumping noise against the headboard.

"M-m-mar, are ye-ye, okay?" Bo searches for one of her legs and finds her head between the box spring and the mattress. With some finesse, he gets her to slip to the floor with her arms and legs still up in the air. The doctors say the catatonic condition she experiences every morning is about nerves, but what nerves cause a person to turn into a fainting goat? Mia suddenly starts to quirk, much to the relief of Bo. Her narcolepsy is withdrawing and her limbs are starting to loosen. "Bo?" Mia responds while rubbing her eyes.

"F-f-f-f. F-ff-ff....I f-f-f foo."

"You're going have to do better than that."

"I foo-foo-fou."

"Uggh, not this again. I wish you would learn to sort these problems out on your own." Mia pushes Bo away and rises to stretch her arms and legs. "Okay, slow down. You're nervous about something. You were saying you found something."

Bo shakes his head wildly. "I foo. I foo."

"You found. You fought. You fought with someone?!"

"I foo-foo-fou!"

"Alright, let's try this instead." <SLAP>

"N-n-n-no. I foo-fou.."

"You fou what?" <SLAP>

"Owww!! Bluidy hell!" <SLAP> "Ow! I fou..." <SLAP>

Mia lets out a tired breath, "I know what's going on here. It's a phonation problem. It has to do with the movement of your palate and a British stiff upper lip." Mia lays Bo back on his bed and reaches beneath her mattress for a kinked stick. "I saw this on the Great Baldaldo in Australia once. You remember that show?"

Bo's eyes go wide when Mia shakes a kinked stick over his face. "Oogie Boogie!" Mia runs the stick point down his nose and taps him on the chin. "Oogie Boogie!"

"Mar?"

"It's only a stick. Ready?" <Tap>

"Ow!" Bo raises his hand for a moment. "I Foo-Foo- f- fack!"

"Fack? As in faculty, factor or France?"

"F-F-Fook!"

"No fook!! We're on fack!!" <Tap><Tap>

"Ow! Fack .... Ow! Fook!!"

"Sing it, Bo!! I fook and I fack!" <Tap><Tap><Tap>

Mia tosses the stick aside. "I don't have time for this." Mia scrunches up Bo's face with her fingers, "Alright, you're going to feel a lot of pressure right here that may cause some discomfort. Nose back and lips together...Now go!"

"I fooked! I facked! I fooked! I facked!"

"You fooked and you facked. You fooked and you facked. You fooked and... You fucked up?!"

"Y-Y-Yes. I fff-fooked up."

Mia falls on top of Bo and they roll off the bed together onto the floor. "Oh, Bo, maybe socializing isn't for you." She pulls the covers down from the bed and strokes his head.

Beatie slams her coat into the chair. It was definitely a mistake in her thinking when she agreed to a third date with this man. His words disturbed her. They made her feel frightened! They made her feel constipated! What else? Oh, flummoxed, but in a creative, terrorizing kind of way. Those were not plain words that he spoke. They were words that could have easily be interpreted as "Bulbous Crotch Region" or "Ball Sack Itch Massage." The book specifically calls these words the four P's: Pleasing, Premarital Sex, Pregnancy, and Palimony. Just the sounds of those words make her feel ashamed. But is this not who he is?!

Beatie lands on her bed and flips over several times. What he had said did nothing to reassure her of a lasting relationship. In fact, there is cause to believe he isn't the right man for her at all. Wasn't it Nikki who described him as being corporeal?!

Beatie finds her book and quickly moves her finger across the pages of Chapter 9: Throwing Out the Trash. "What's this?!" Beatie flips the page back: "'Composed and cruel is far worse than cruelly composed says the instigator of the cat.' This is so him!"

Beatie readjusts herself on the pillow and continues her reading. Her eyes glancing toward the phone before returning back to the book again. "Still, it would be nice if he called, or maybe left a present at the front door, or even a paper slip that a new outfit is waiting for her at Meeshman's." Beatie sits up and throws a stuffed animal across the room. "No, no gifts!"

She needs someone to talk to. She needs to seek out a friend!

Mia props Bo's sleeping head up with a stack of dirty laundry. She pulls a blanket from the bed and covers him warmly. The pullover Sam lent her and the sleek training shoes are all she needs to return to the streets. She has been thinking about what Catalan had said about being hungry, and there are others that are hungry too."

Mia glances in the mirror and brushes her hair forward to disguise the remnants of her horns. Grabbing a few bags of food, she returns to the bathroom to turn off the light. She hasn't taken her court-issued pills in quite some time, but all she has in her hand are the dermatology pills. Swallowing them dry, she heads down the ladder and out the lobby door. She is going much further this time, to where the people are said to be the hungriest. It could be a long walk, not knowing their locality, but she is assured by Catalan's verbal instructions that she will find them.

Once beyond the city limits, she makes the first of five turns to where the streets are dark without city lights. After several blocks of quietness, Mia realizes she is no longer in a location where cars make a routine pass. Even though it is a little early for the daily sounds of a city, some noise should be present within only eight square miles.

She recognizes them immediately. Their incidental possessions are stored in unclaimed shopping carts, their discolored toes are poking through corrugated households, and if they own a pair of shoes, they are so worn, they are forced to walk with a tilt. These are not people getting ready for a busy evening; these are people getting used to the days that came before it. This is life to them. A choice of human simplicities, away from the materialistic society that she, herself, has grown accustomed to. Mia understands this, and yet, she doesn't. At least not to their level. They need food and they need clothing; that is why she is here.

"Hello, Schmeebie!"

Mia turns around, startled to see a tall man lying across a low-lying bench, sucking juice from a dented straw. He is footless and toothless, and his greasy smile is made fresh from a chicken leg. He is known as Ankle Bones because he walks on the bones of his ankles. Mia, thinking the name a bit insensitive, calls him Sir Missing Boots. She likes him well enough, mostly because of his deeply rooted red hair that somehow brings color to the bland, wintry days.

"My name is not Schmeebe, Sir Missing Boots, but I do have some food for you."

"Choice!"

"Tasty Cakes or Chocolate Cockle Beads? I made them myself. Less than two thousand calories."

Chewing with his mouth wide open, he seems delighted with a change in flavor.

"How does it taste?" Mia inquires.

"Have done borne me a child!"

"Lovely." Mia says squeamishly after his hearing his flatulence. "Sir Missing Boots, have you seen a man who calls himself Catalan?"

"Turn down that thar' road, then go one thousand, four hundred and seventy-two steps to a park for those who pay no rent. They are mostly dead, for their part, but appear quite alive for ours."

"Catalan mentioned a speaker. Do you know anything about him?"

"The lights never fully reveal their appearances, Schmeebie, but if there is one that is different than the other, you will let us know?"

"I can do that."

"Go with understanding. Bagoot!"

"Bagoot to you too."

Mia continues down the street with her bags of food, walking among the scattered chicken wings, filthy rags of soil, and empty bottles of forgotten liquids. She soon enters a tree laden park where all the city's necessary secrets are kept from the public. There are a dozen explorers sitting before a stage, and they seem interested in a large wood carving standing on a crate box. Mia finds a tree to lean against and waits for Catalan to arrive. Her head is feeling a little hazy and her stomach a little queasy, so she looks into one of her bags for some food. Grabbing a treat, she stuffs it in her mouth, and after a minute or two, she realizes it has done little to help with her eye sight.

There is a commotion with several long shrieks, and Mia looks to see strange people gathering before a man standing on the crate. They are dressed in dark clothing and covered in a heavy blue dye, so much dye that it is hard to differentiate where their skin ends and where their clothes begin. As for the man on the crate, he wears a gray cloak over prison pants and a hood that covers much of his face. He reminds her of a small statue that was placed in the garden of her orphanage and the men from a historic photo she saw in the tour guide book.

> "Then I say to you all, speak to the earth and tell it will be, sprouting roots are needed for our generations to come!
>
> Then I say to you all, speak to the skies and tell it will be, running water is needed for our generations to come!

> Then I say to you all, go to the heavens and tell it will be, if these requests cannot be granted, then let it will be, proper burials for all the generations to come!"

There is a loud applause and cries of 'Bagoot' while the speaker waves for their silence.

> "All you have to do is give yourself over to reason, my people, for what can be taught by the road ahead, can be learned by the one who is not left behind."

Mia looks about at the crazed revelers yelling 'Bagoot!' She is very much in awe of what she sees, not so much by the man's words, but by the passion with which he delivers them. No mistaking, she has heard this tone on many political platforms before, and it usually commands an audience ready to act. Mia feels a surprise tap on her shoulder and then turns quickly.

"Whit ye doin' here, Mar?"

"Bo!! You startled me! I should ask you the same thing."

"You left me sleeping on the floor."

Mia looks up to hear the crowd yell again. "He's really quite good, isn't he?"

"What are you talking about, Mar? I see a few people getting upset over the weather."

"Well, I figured you would never understand this. Why don't you just try listening to someone else speak for once?"

> We may develop medicines to fight disease.
> We may cultivate the land to fight famine.
> We may build indestructible shelters to fight storms.
> But it will always be nature that will convince us to destroy ourselves.

"Exactly!!" Mia claps louder and yells out, "Woohoo! Tell it how it is, speaker!!"

"Mar, aren't you being a bit loud?"

"Well, if you're going to make a sound, you may as well scream."

"Yes, but you just brought your attention to the authorities."

"You go talk to them, Bo. I see Catalan approaching."

Mia begins waving her hands at Catalan, "Catalan! Como yo!"

"Bon dia, Missing in Action!"

"Please, call me Mia!"

"Yes, of course."

"You weren't wrong, Catalan; the speaker is absolutely wonderful! His delivery is so rigid and untarnished."

"Yes, you are looking upon the original L'altaveu. He has always wanted to be the first speaker and was sure he would not make a poor one. Would you like to meet him?"

Mia twists her arms in shyness, then nods her head in a coy gesture of acceptance.

"Alteveu, this is Missing in Action, I mean Mia, as she prefers."

Mia opens up with a large smile and eager face, instantly admitting to liking his distinct dark eyes and black lips. Only, she can't help but feel mildly disappointed by his lack of expression. She was hoping to be presented with a wildness in his face, so common among fanatics she has come to admire.

"Well, that was a wonderful speech, Mr. Alteveu. You certainly know how to address a crowd." Mia sets her bags down before the crate and takes a long look at his splintered shoes. She is almost embarrassed that she has to stare so long, but she can't help but be disturbed by the line of tiny ants running from the cracks in his shoes back to a crack in the pavement.

"Welcome to poverty that once boasted of prosperity, who may be forever led into a constant circle of defeat. As clouds give shape to the sky and the sun gives light to the earth, let prosperity begin with an idea that we, as a people, will not accept poison as a way forward."

Mia finally takes her eyes off of his unfortunate footwear and smiles. "Yes, Mr. Speaker, I do agree; poverty is going to be hard to defeat. Is there nothing we can do about it?"

"Poverty always comes with several large donors for the wrong causes."

Catalan interrupts with a nervous and urgent voice, "Miss Mia, we were wondering if you might help move L'altaveu. to the local cemetery. It's just a few blocks from here."

Suddenly, there are flashing blue and red lights, along with the appearance of authority figures breaking up a fight. Bo surprises Mia again, "We better go, Mar."

Mia looks to see Catalan running off in the other direction, so she too scurries with Bo back out of the park. Mia stops at a trash bin to dispose of the remaining empty bags of food and rests beside a tree.

"Is that the food I paid for, Mar?"

Mia smirks and changes the subject, "That was one hell of a speech. I admit, it was at times hard to understand the complexity of his words, but I sense a real strong purpose in his tone."

"You're going a bit deep there, aren't you?"

"What did you hear?"

"I heard a group of weather prophets talking about how cold the nights have been. One said – anyone have a blanket? The other replied – I think that one is mine, and then a fight breaks out."

"Your problem is you can't reason in complex terms."

"Mar, the policeman I spoke with said this has happened before."

"Well, that's just the problem, isn't it? You were listening to the 'bizzies' and not the Speaker."

Mia feels a tap on her shoulder and spins around into a glaring light. "Prindy Reeshman from Ghost City News. I see you are trying to gain acceptance into a society that many choose not to see."

Mia's face contorts, "Sorry love, nothing personal, I just don't talk to 'snappies.'"

"We are following up on a story about tourists pimping those willing to exchange services for food."

"Lovely, I'm sure y'all will suss it out, won't you?"

Mia grabs Bo by the arm and races to the next corner of a busy street. She pauses to see the news crew still following and pushes Bo ahead into the crosswalk. After many loud screeches and blaring horns, both make it to the other side without harm. Mia watches as the traffic resumes and then looks about at the shop signs, "Where do you want to eat? How about Bobbie Street Joe's again?"

She walks into the restaurant and asks the waitress to clean off a booth. Shaking her coat, she slides toward the window and peers out. No one appears to be following them, so she quickly relaxes.

"We'll have the Platter Splatter again. Did we have peas last night? I wouldn't mind beans this time." Mia calls the waitress back to provide a substitute for the order. She sits back and pulls a phone from her pocket. "Hello, Samuela? We're here at the restaurant. No, you don't have to be present; you just have to participate! Good. So, say there is this derelict speaker, he's poorly dressed – to no fault of his own... what? Of course we can buy him new clothes, that's the easy part. No, I don't know where he lives, what does that have to do with anything? No, that's where Catalan lives. Never mind, I can see you are not going to be a very effective participant." Mia disconnects the phone and puts it back into her pocket. She looks out the window and frowns.

"What's wrong?"

"Sam said the only residence on the north end of Cordova is a cemetery."

The waitress sets a pitcher of tea before them and Mia pulls it toward her to fill her glass. "I really do think I could do some good work here. I'm thinking about giving the speaker a new look. What are your thoughts on a bit loafer or a suede chukka? A derby brogue would look nice on him too, am I right?"

Bo looks at Mia confused. "Why are you getting involved with this again, Mar?"

"What do you care? You weren't even a part of it."

"I've been there with you before. Does New York City in the Bowery ring a bell? When was the last time you took your sanity pills?"

"My determination to help the unwanted has nothing to do with my taking any pills or something. Besides, I'm just talking about buying a man some shoes. I didn't think that required any kind of a sanity check."

Bo lays his hands on the table and looks at Mia, "But it does require my wallet, doesn't it?"

Beatie pokes her head inside the doorway of the barber shop, "Pas Ca?!"

"Come sit with us, Bea'trie. The last I saw you, you were going on a date with that notorious philanderer. What was his name?"

Beatie looks about the room and sees two ladies reclined in their barber chairs. She knows to be cautious when talking freely around socialites because evil ears are always adept in cruelty. Squinting her eyes, she sees their mouths are open and their eyes are closed. They could be dead, but that's probably wishful thinking.

Beatie sits down in the chair, keeping her growl on semi-mute. "Oh right, Parker Ken. Fooey on him. Slimy, greasy, thumb-sucking, gargoyle head! No love there. No, I have a different story to tell. Do you remember when I called you about that date I was on?"

"Yes! What happened?"

"Well, I received an offer to speak with him again."

"A second date? How did that go?"

"It didn't go well at all. In fact, it was icky, licky, sticky, and gross. All the attractions of a mouth gone sour, and you know why? Because he stuck his tongue down my throat, Hydragew!"

"Well, that's common."

"It is?"

"Haven't you ever kissed anyone before?"

"My mom and my pop, and even my uncle once, but it didn't involve a geriatric saliva wash!"

"Maybe it was a nervous kiss."

Beatie chuckles, "Or, maybe he wasn't doing it right."

"Bea'trie, it takes time and sometimes practice to get in sync with someone – both mentally and physically."

"Well, how about the tale he talked about where women are getting impregnated with porridge and kindness?"

"That sounds like a Scottish tale. Maybe in Scotland that's an endearing tale to women."

"Well, yeah, sure - maybe asking him a few more questions would have been the logical approach, but what reasoning can be deduced from such a revolting tale when the consummation of love is becoming more and more problematic?!"

Hydragew squints his eyes. "You lost me there, Bea'trie. Why don't you call him and just make sure it wasn't some kind of a misunderstanding?"

"Well, that's what I was going to do, but then you know what I learned? Why should I be the one chasing him? Is he not the instigator of the cat?"

"Excuse me?"

"So, you know what I did? I waited for him to call. And I waited. And I waited. One more time I waited. Then I waited a second time. And then I waited a third time..."

"Bea'trie!"

"Then you know what happened next!" Beatie looks up at Hydragew with annoyance. "Nothing. Not calling me really made me mad, Hydragew. He's done this sixteen times to me already, and that's not including the minimum three times a day he is supposed to call!"

The barber sets the brush down on the counter and motions Beatie to sit back in the chair. "Not calling you doesn't mean he isn't thinking of you."

Beatie looks up with crooked eyes, "Really?"

"Yes, really. He might think he's being creepy or desperate if he calls you too often or too soon."

"I don't mind creepy or desperate."

"But he doesn't know that. He's just trying to act like the man while, at the same time, trying to speak to you as a woman."

"Is he supposed to do that?"

"If he's doing it right?"

"Wow." Beatie sits for a moment thinking about what Hydragew just said. A tad embarrassed that the book was probably trying to tell her the same thing, and maybe she is wrong about that kiss. It was her first time and probably for him too. Also, thinking – maybe, if she could find someone to make a comparison with.

"Hydragew, do you think we could suck face for a few minutes?"

"No, Bea'trie. It would not be the same."

"Mrs. Hardsqueeze? Mrs. Squirtgardener?" Both ladies raise their eyes with panic-stricken faces.

Beatie allows herself a quick look in the mirror, "Hydragew! I just love the hairstyle. What do you call it?!"

"The Turd Bath!"

"Turd Bath? Interesting."

Mia's hand gently swings back and forth as she crosses the hotel lobby. Her mind is adrift as to which of the available bachelors, Catalan or the speaker, might be courting her for Valentine's. Of course, she is flattered with the possibility that both men could be vying for her attention, and what a conundrum that would be. Currently she favors the speaker who is much like herself: there is no idling of wanted change or commanding words calling for silence. However, with Catalan, there is that feeling of familiarity that few ever experience over a lifetime.

She climbs the ladder and leaps into bed, reaching for the book beneath her pillow. "This book is fascinating, Bo! The author argues that vegetables should prepare their own dirt, trees be allowed to grow in their own space, and get this – mosquitos be allowed to spread their own disease, simply because it is their divine right to do so."

"You're not buying into this book crap, are you, Mar? A half-crazed man in a fight with nature?"

"Or maybe the opposite is true and it is nature that is in a fight with a half-crazed man. Will you look at this? He states here that nature requires a symbiotic relationship between all living orders: animal, plant, fungi, protist, and monera. He calls it the Eco Stasis Effect. When one 'Living Order' becomes too dominant over the others, nature employs a destructive force to restore the balance. This is why we are witnessing more fires, storms, disease, famine, and drought in the world." Mia turns the page, "And this too! If that doesn't work, there is the genetic effect on the human psyche. Nature will manufacture enemies that will destroy life-supporting materials and then go so far as procreation denial. Haven't you wondered why there are far more crazy people in the world today?"

"A bit convenient, don't you think? Putting the controls of a symbiotic relationship into something we cannot address?"

"I don't know; the reviews on the cover say he was deemed credible. At least, by all those who followed him at the time." Mia puts the book aside and begins picking up the laundry off the floor. "Valentine's is just four days away,

Bo. Another empty Valentine's could spell trouble for us both if we don't act. What are you going to do about Miss Rejection?"

"Beatie? I don't know anymore. I really messed up on the beach."

"You've been searching all over for this one ideal that the first you see is the first you get. Isn't that some Scottish Valentine's folklore? I'm thinking it might be better to invest a little more time in the ones you already know."

Bo looks at her with an inquisitive look.

"Not me, boner-begging bag of bones. I've been thinking that Sam has really improved upon her feelings for you."

"Sam likes me again? Is that what she said? Seems out of course for her, don't you think?'

"True, her horoscope does imply it is not possible between the two of you, but how has that worked for her? I'm going up to the crawl space to see if the pool lights are on. Would you be up for a late-night swim?"

"I'm going to use the bathroom before I give that a serious thought."

Beatie searches for her car, always finding it parked in a different place every time. She truly does welcome the advice from her barber and really does have to blame herself on this one. Bo has flaws, and she had simply not asked. She had thought he should be perfect, just like in the romance novels, but now, against the book's recommendation, she is going to have to settle for less. Bo isn't really so bad. True, those words on the beach were repulsive, but they were not terrifying; unexpected but not loud. His attempt to ingratiate her may have been absurd but not nasty. His intelligence might be dim-witted but not moronic, something never fully mentioned in the wise words of the book.

It is not a long drive to the hotel, and there is enough privacy in her car to practice the lines presented in chapter seven: "I want to apologize for my running off the beach. I wasn't thinking straight, and I would like to persuade you ..." Beatie shakes her head, "Oh please – let me persuade you?! I'm asking him for another date; I don't want to 'barf' all over him in the process."

Beatie looks at the hotel coming up on her right and raises her eyebrows. She really should call first. What if he's sleeping? She isn't fond of anyone butting into her sleep. Still, it's not like she's going to steal anything; she just wants this to be a surprise. There is no harm in a surprise; she likes to receive them all the time.

She pushes on the heavy door to the lobby, thinking she should issue a complaint that there isn't a doorman, but the day manager is on the phone whimpering about a missing bike. She continues on down the hallway, grimacing at the filth she sees everywhere. Such an awful place with a treacherous past; hopefully, when they do consummate their vows, he won't demand she move in with him.

Quietly, she unfolds the ladder and makes the silent climb up the steps. One hand over the other, one foot behind the next, reaching forward with her eyes closed, and ... AAHHH!!! Beatie nearly faints and almost falls back down the steps. The most horrifying sight she has ever seen is right before her, and it is creating a pale, waxy appearance that can never be covered with a bronzer!

All over the bed, the dressers and the drawers, doing it on the tables and doing it on the floor. With no apprehension, they are enjoying themselves, intertwined in a Roman orgy, right there on the shelves!

Her high-heel boots doing the dance over a wide-open zipper of his stiff-legged pants! A tight-fitting shirt and a sleezy-looking top, caressing his soiled cotton briefs that are just about to 'POP'!

They think they can do this without a care for the law, the tongue of his shoe pressing into the surface of her bra! And if there could be any more reason to take this to court, it would have something to do with her stretched- out panties on his exhausted boxer shorts!

Beatie gags from her mouth being left open too long. She wants to hang on, but her mind is too entangled in a web of Dr. Seuss rhymes. She slides back down the ladder, landing on her backside and flipping over three times. The day manager can only watch with great concern as she runs past him, swatting about her head as if she is being assaulted by bugs.

Mia crawls out from the crawl space, thinking she had heard someone scream. Bo, at the same instance, opens the bathroom door. "Did you hear that, Mar?"

"I thought it was you."

FEBRUARY 11th: WHY THE DICKENS?

The wind ruffles Mia's bedsheets and puts a gripping chill on her bare feet as she curls up into a ball. She listens to the sound of empty hangers clinking in the open closet and stuffs her head beneath the pillow. It is half past seven already, and she knows she has forgotten to turn the water back on.

Mia walks across the floor with a blanket hanging from her shoulders. She finds a flashlight in the closet, then releases the ladder to the hallway below. Accidentally dropping her light, she listens to the many knocks it makes before hearing a final splash. She winces at the smell of spoiled seaweed and finds her flashlight glowing in a murky puddle with a group of minnows surrounding it.

There is a thick fog preventing her from seeing very far, but she manages to navigate the planks without a misstep. That is until she reaches the platform, where she creates the noise of falling shelves. She lifts the flashlight to see a large, foreboding figure standing before her, then a light over the platform comes on.

"No other entity has ceased to keep this city in so much turmoil."

Mia swings around to see the day manager standing with his hand on a light cord. "You startled me!"

"The man was joyfully disliked by his peers, so his disappearance was never missed, and yet for some reason, they still lionized him."

"Do you always sit in the dark waiting to startle people, Day Manager?"

"I was receiving calls about the water pressure, so I came down to turn on the water."

"Yeh, well, sorry about that. The cold room in the attic kept me from getting out of bed."

"He was like some hubris leading his Cadavers of Confident Displeasures."

Mia looks back, realizing the foreboding figure she was startled to see is just a painting on the wall. She cringes at its devilish smile and oversized teeth. The presence of horns appearing through the entanglement in its hair makes her feel a bit self-conscious too.

"Now he has become their liberating voice."

"Can't imagine how that's going. I don't really believe in people returning from the dead."

"But if they did?"

"I guess I could pretend to like them."

"His objectors realized that if given a platform, he would become a dangerous opposition?" Sen leans down to pick up a booklet that had fallen to the floor. Mia tilts her flashlight onto the cover's inscription.

"Marbelene's Genetic Squeeze Box?"

"The diary reveals a very bad nature about this man. In one of her accounts she writes, 'They were simply looking for change, but not for the better.'" The day manager turns the light off and on, startling Mia with a goofy expression on his face.

"You're funny, Day Manager."

The day manager smirks, "I may appear funny, but there are a lot of St. Augustinians who are about to get scared."

Mia chuckles, "What makes you think the dead want to come back to scare the residents?"

"Mos maiorum."

Mia chokes on the words. "What's a Moss Mayor, Um?"

"The way of the ancestors. An unwritten social code and tradition of those that have passed on."

"So, you are trying to tell me that an army of ghosts have arrived to terrify this city?"

Sen signals toward the darkness beyond the platform. "Would you like to see their boats?"

Mia lifts the flashlight into the dark gloom. "Hey, my light is bending."

"It's called refraction."

“Refraction in a basement?” She hears the sound of crashing waves. “Is that the ocean out there?” The platform's light goes out and Mia lifts the flashlight to see the day manager walking ahead with two foldup chairs.

“I sometimes come down here to watch the tide come in.”

Mia holds the flashlight ahead of him and sees nothing but darkness. “You say there is an ocean out there?”

“How else would they arrive?”

Mia frowns, “You know what I am seeing here, Day Manager? I see the plan of a man's deception trying to bring chase upon a vulnerable female. I also see a hotel badly in need of repairs.”

“It's an interesting view!”

“You appear to be creating a character of many false impressions. Definitely a 'NO' for me!” Mia quickly follows the planks back out with the aid of her flashlight and then climbs the ladder. “Hey!! Somebody shut the door on us!”

Bo tosses the carpet over the door and wipes his brow. He could have easily fallen down that dark hole and broken a leg had he not noticed a foul seaweed smell emanating from it. He makes his way through the lobby and pauses to see the unicycle he had been riding. The wheel has been replaced, the saddle is no longer crooked, and even the crankset has lost its squeak.

Bo takes the bike beyond the city limits, where few people are seen, and after circling the block several times, he finally settles upon an inconspicuous Irish pub placed between an electronic shop and a Tai food restaurant. No one appears to be inside, but if this truly is a pub for a Scotsman, there will be a man inside by the name of Connor, and he will have a plate of hash browns and a frosty Guinness of beer waiting at the bar for him.

Bo steps through the door to hear the sound of glasses being stacked, there he sees a trim man with red hair and wrinkles. “We don't open until eleven.”

“I'm Bo Fox from Scotland.”

"Scotland, you say?" The man grins. "Well, it's close enough to eleven." The barkeep approaches with an empty glass. "What be your pleasure?"

"Do you have any Scottish eggs?"

"We have cow meat and no mustard sauce."

"Any hash browns?"

"Sure, and is Guinness, okay?" The barkeep kicks the barrel and opens the nozzle into the glass, making a slow pour before giving it a rest.

Bo takes a seat at the end of the bar, where the man hands him a plate of hashbrowns. "Yer Irish, Connor?"

The barkeep nods his head.

"Then I guess you wouldn't serve me a bad Irish beer. Cheers!"

Bo raises the glass and in six gulps, places the empty pint back down on the counter. "That will work. I need advice, Connor. I don't understand the ladies too well. It seems a requirement is needed to have all this knowledge before you even meet them."

"A local girl, eh."

"I met her at a bar, which was my first mistake, and then we went to the beach, and that was my second." Bo gulps down his drink and waves for another, and then another after that. What started out to be one drink soon became ten, and that's how they found themselves seated on the floor.

"How did they meet women in your time, Connor?"

"Aye, love was different back then, simpler times. Women knew less about you than you did them, and you could take your time trying to figure the other one out. Now everyone already has an opinion before you even meet. Have you thought about a poem?"

"I tried a tale – The Pabbay Mother's Ghosts."

"Oh, right! The kindly man that feeds porridge to pregnant women. I always got slapped after that one."

"Me too!"

"How about taking her dancing?"

"Aye, I can do that, but I need another ten of these." Bo looks at the bottom of his glass to see another refill is necessary. The barkeep shakes his head. "Enough, laddy, there is a phone on the bar. Do you have her number?"

"I have it memorized."

Beatie finds a parking space six blocks away from the office. It is a little further than she would like it to be, but that's the holiday's fault. Hydragew has not been answering his phone, and her mind really needs advice. All night, she had been tossing about in a fit of rage because of the incident that took place at the hotel. There is no denying that the nature of their clothing having sex is still having a negative effect on her life expectancy. Never, ever, would she forever allow her clothes to be involved with something like that!

Beatie looks up to see she has reached the office when suddenly her phone lights up. There are two people trying to contact her and one is her barber.

"Hydragew, it was just horrible!"

"Bea'trie, hello, what's the matter?"

"I've been trying to reach you, but you wouldn't answer your phone!"

"I'm sorry, I was at a séance, and it didn't end until late last night. It seems our time is nearer to the end than I previously thought."

"I know the feeling. Hold on, I have you on the speaker. That's better. Oh, Hydragew! You should have always been there! They were rolling around on the floor, and his sleeve was stuck in the groove of her panties, and her camise was caressing the insides of his chocolate trousers. What did you say? No! If they were wearing the clothes, it would have made sense. Yes, I understand about things like that. Yes, but still, it was their lusting, lecherous, libidinous laundry, licking their latex linen, that had me puking up lemonade-lime juice! No, I told you! Hydragew, hold on a minute. I have to call you back; someone keeps trying to call me.

"Hello? This is planet Earth speaking, please speak up! Excuse me? No, I don't speak in non-essential, air-velocity speech. Do you have something important to say? Yes, I understand. Sure, it's hard to be yourself sometimes. Well, because people get mad when they find out you're trying to be someone else. I mean, would a shadow be considered dead if it knew not to move? And how about living-dead people? Does a vampire know he's not a vampire if the doctor says he isn't one? Say that again? How about a dance? Well, with

Valentine's Day coming up, that's all I think about. Wait, who is this? Bo? I don't know any Bo. Bo Fox? Wait, you're the guy from Georgia! Yes, I know where O'Toole's is. You're not going there, are you? Tonight? Well, I'll think about it. Okay, bye."

Bo reaches into his back pocket and drops several bills on the bartender's lap. "I think I have another date."

"You don't look so sure, Laddy."

"It's the closest to certainty than I've ever had with this woman." Bo lifts himself off the floor and grabs onto the counter. He then drifts back and forth until he reaches the door. "I'm sorry, I've been calling you Connor the entire time. I don't know your name."

"It's Connor."

Bo pushes on the heavy door that opens with a loud creak. The sun appears much brighter than it did when he first arrived. He turns about and walks back inside the bar with a concerned look, "Connor, I need to call a cab. Somebody took my bike."

Mia and Bo stand before a large window where the inside of the establishment is motionless.

"When did you start drinking in the morning?"

"Ever since I was ten. Sorry, Mar. I had things to sort out."

"Well, at least we're here. It's early afternoon on a Saturday. One would at least expect some visitors to be prowling through the fixtures. Are you still quids in?"

Bo looks up at the sign. "Good Will?"

"Yes, as in Good William."

"Are you making that up?"

"Need it have to be called anything else?"

"Mar, I don't really see the need to add more clothing to what we already have."

"Bo, if you hadn't noticed, the girl you are dating likes to look her best. Maybe you should think the same."

Mia pushes on a heavy door. It is a vast warehouse of clothing, paintings, furniture, fake bushes, and collectibles nobody should have ever purchased in the first place. It reminds her immediately of home.

"I'm sure she wouldn't mind if you came along, Mar."

"To a dance? I don't know if that's really what I want; besides, my hair is a mess."

"Your horns have cleared up, haven't they?"

"Pretty much. I'm still taking the pills just to be sure."

Mia grabs a few hats from the counter and fits them onto her head. After a laugh and a smirk, she quickly sets them down. The clothing for the holidays is in the back, the clothing for a funeral is by the exit sign, and there is even clothing for a criminal trial by the changing room. After trying on several outfits from the various sections of the room, Mia finally concludes that the occasion has little to do with her needs.

"Absolutely embarrassing. There is not a single item in my size that doesn't have a cute bug or a teddy bear on it. Come on, Bo. There's something I would like to see you in."

Mia grabs his arm and pulls him forcibly down an aisle. She knows how important it is for him to dress nicely for a favorable impression. Bo follows her through the partitions as she pushes long coats and tweed jackets along a bar, and then kicks open a shoe box to retrieve a pair of loafers. Mia leads Bo into a section for recent divorcees and hands him a pair of corduroy pants along with a button-down shirt. She steps back for a moment and claps her hands. "Ooh, Bo! Women will be caressing more than just the fabric on your pants tonight, am I right?"

"Think so, Mar?"

"Now, my turn!" Mia pulls down two racks of clothes and then overturns several boxes from the top shelves. There are now clothes scattered about the floor with half of them being tossed to Bo to be sorted. After grabbing an armful, she lays them on a table, then begins separating each article based on usage.

"Mar, these are clothes that neither one of us would wear."

Mia puts on a scowl, "Need you inquire about everything I do? Just put what we have in a larger box and let's go."

"You're planning to clothe the people outdoors again? Why does it always feel like I'm in a Charles Dicken's novel with you."

Mia smiles and lifts a box onto a cart. She then rolls them toward the counter and grabs another pair of shoes. "These will fit nicely on the speaker, don't you agree?"

Bo steps out of the store holding two-oversized bags of clothing. Mia walks past him into the middle of the street to the sound of squealing brakes and honking horns. "Oh, the sound of progress. Now what are we going to do about my hair?" The bus pulls up just in time to find an empty seat in the back. "You need a constructive smile, not a goofy smirk, and you need a swagger in your step, not a cushion under your heels. Got it! And no crappy tales! Now, this is how I want the conversation to go..."

Beatie turns from her desk to see Mia bouncing up and down on her knee. "What are you doing here?"

Mia steps aside with a long sweeping arm, "I would like to introduce you to someone you might be pleased to see!"

Beatie drops her brochures and stumbles over to a large plant bucket. She is trying to hold back the vomit that is rising up through her digestive track. This is by far the worst display of clothing she has ever seen on a living or nonliving entity. All that burlap, even his shoes have a synthetic growth that can't be removed, and that goofy-looking straw hat! Does he want to get stabbed or something?!

"Beatrice, what's going on out there?" Beatie lifts her head from the bucket to see Mr. Happiness stepping out from his back office. "This is no way to treat a customer. We must always remind our guests that to receive is not to be forgotten."

"Yes, Mr. Happiness!" Beatie slowly makes her way back to her desk to allow the heaving to slow down. She then finds her compact mirror and practices a few quick smiles before greeting them, "May I help you?"

Bo steps forward holding two large shopping bags from the Goodwill. "Yes, Beatie, I know since our last meeting..."

"Wait, those aren't for me, are they?" Beatie says while still holding her smile in place with her fingers.

"No! They're for the homeless... I mean for those living on the street. Anyways, I wanted to apologize for the other night. According to my roommate, I may have said some things that were inappropriate, and I was wondering if you would like to go dancing instead."

"And you are?"

Bo takes his straw hat off, "Bo Fox from Scotland. I was the one who told you the crappy poem the other night."

"No thank you, we don't need any more crappy poems, but I do appreciate you stopping by."

Mia looks at Beatie, confused by their interaction, and steps forward in his place. "My, oh my, will you just look at your clothes! So mint and so stylish. I bet they cost a bomb!"

"Oh, yes, thank you. I do so very much like them."

"And the jewelry, too!"

"Guilty, Perkle Myers." Beatie claps her hands together and rolls her eyes. "It's so fab there."

"We don't have anything like that in the U.K, and I love your hair. It goes so well with your emblem shirt and juniper tweed jacket. And the handbag on your desk? So commanding and so in control."

"Well, all true. There's this place I go to called Meeshman's. They can be a bit pricey, but for the most part, pricey is what everybody wants. Unfortunately, they don't have a good selection of shoes."

Mia puts her hands on her waist and lightly bounces up and down to imitate Beatie, "That's too bad, because it's a good thing that Bo found these. Show her, Bo! What do you think, posh or squash?"

Beatie's eyes go wide, "Slip-resistant, lace-up loafers with a frog clip? I hope they're comfortable." Beatie puts her hand to the side of her mouth. "We really shouldn't let the men select their own wear, should we?"

Mia grabs a stapler from Beatie's desk and twists it into pieces. Bo, sensing Mia trying to control her anger, leads her out the doorway. "So, we are here about the dance at O'Toole's."

Beatie claps her hands, "Oh, now I remember who you are; we spoke about a dance."

"Yes, tonight! And Mia was wondering where she might get a new hairstyle?"

"Well, of course she does." Twisting her mouth from side to side to hide a mischievous grin. "I'll call Hydragew. He does my hair. I'm sure he can fit her in."

Mia briskly passes Bo on the sidewalk and goes into theatrics, "Oh, Bo! Do not judge me daily, for I am not of sound mind."

"Alright, alright."

"At least she's not the weirdest person you've ever met. Where is this place anyways?"

"There it is, Mar."

Mia narrows her eyes toward a small sign conspicuously hidden from the line of other shops. "'Parfie Der Barbeeb: We offer hospice care too." Mia presses her face to the window. She notes the chairs are uniquely styled in the shape of chess pieces, and each one sits upon a black or white tile. Mia tilts her head sideways to see the barber. He is a sturdy, dark-skinned man with a shiny bald head, tiny nose, and oversized hands. He wears a slick coat, high-ankled black slacks, and Venetian clogs. He is spraying the mirrors with a cleaner and wiping them with a squeegee. Mia turns to Bo, "There isn't a queue. That's disappointing."

When Mia and Bo step through the door, the barber twirls about with a clap. "Bon apremidi! Bienvenue! Entez!" closing the blinds to block the view from the street. He banters about on his gold-plated clogs, making a loud clopping sound as he rushes behind a chair,

"Beatie called ahead; I'm Bo Fox."

"I am the one here for the haircut." Mia steps forward and wraps herself in the cloak hanging from the chair. She squirms around until she is comfortable and then lifts a finger. "I'm thinking of something that would bring the animal instincts out of me. Something edgy, yet refined from years of evolution."

"Hmmm." The barber places his fingers around her ears and turns her head from side to side. "In Northeast Florida, the wind often blows north to south, but you're asking for your hair to go east to west. No, I believe you are here for something much more than a directional post. You need certainty; you need outdoorsy, with no harnesses to hold you back!"

"Sounds like Scotland, Mar!"

"Ooh, I do like the sound of that! Describe this for me, Mr. Darbeeb."

"It whispers like the highland winds in the cold winter nights and percolates in the crags before a beaver-blocked dam." The barber takes the tips of Mia's hair and draws them out. "There will be a great mane that will shiver like a meadow in the coming spring...."

"A mane?"

"Be still, difficult one." The barber uses his hands to square off her face, stepping back to create an image. "I see free spirit, I see vitality, but I also see danger!"

"Danger?!" Mia rises in her seat with excitement. "What kind of danger?"

"Where the few shall follow."

"Yes, I see now. Where the few shall follow. I've been there. Let's do it!"

Mia does not look up at all while the scissors go their way. She has full trust in a man that tells her he will take all prisoners and make haircuts for them all.

The barber spins Mia around with his clippers before her eyes, "These too will have to be cut!"

Mia pulls loose, "My bangs? I would like to keep my bangs."

"You wish to hide the horns?"

"Well, I don't know what you mean by horns."

"The hard, pointy growths that appear on most hoofed animals."

"Seriously, I still don't see how that applies to me."

"Well then, the sides must go!" The barber lets out a bursting cackle, prompting Mia to look nervously toward Bo. Bo, however, is off chuckling before the caricatures of elderly clients on the wall. "These are amazing drawings. So lifelike with imaginary. I like how they incorporate that death appeal, so commonly addressed throughout the city."

"Those are not drawings," the barber replies.

Mia feels a tug, followed by an even stronger tug that forces her to clasp the armrests. Her eyes go wide when the barber rolls out a tray with a wire brush connected to a three-prong electrode. She watches carefully from the corner of her eye as the barber reaches into a cabinet for a face guard.

"Put these rubber gloves on, madam. I'm assuming the soles of your shoes are made of rubber?"

"I think so," Mia responds with a confused look.

The barber then smiles and runs a rubber band around her wrists and pulls it tightly, "Put this wooden spoon in your mouth and hold this rod for me, please."

There is a buzzing sound that catches Bo's attention. Mia is holding a connectivity rod with a spectacle of blue electrodes surges around it. Even more interesting is the barber plowing through the sides of her head, pausing only to give his arms a rest before starting again.

Mia feels the numbness running through her feet and hands, and it is causing her to change her position frequently. To overcome her uneasiness, she shuts her eyes and concentrates on a more pleasant thought. *She is galloping through a meadow of sweet grass and gathering ponies. Her hair is taking on the moisture from a nearby waterfall, inspiring her to sway her head and yell 'Ney'...*

Mia opens her blurry eyes to see red lights flashing in the dark. There is a whining sound along with the long drone of a motor. She is lying on the tiles with her harness undone and the metal pole she once held now resting without a spark on the floor. "Why are the lights out, Bo?"

"I think he blew a circuit and went to flip the switch back on."

Mia reaches into Bo's pocket and slaps a twenty-dollar bill on the chair. "That should do it. Let's get out of here."

Mia stumbles out the door and knocks over a scooter, staring blankly into the mirror. It takes her a moment, but she soon realizes she is not looking at the same appearance she has been used to looking at. Her hair is cropped short around her ears, and there is a long strip of coarse hair running from the top of her forehead down the middle of her back. There are also two little cowbells tied to its ends.

"Oh, my. You couldn't have stopped this, Bo?"

"Mar, what was I supposed to say? You gave him full permission."

Mia pushes the scooter to the ground. "In what state of mind would you ever think I would be okay with a mane going down the back of my head?!"

"Mar, the guidebook did give the man three stars."

"I look like a pony, Bo!!"

"It's not so bad. A lot of blokes like pownies."

"To ride on! Not to take home to meet the family!" Mia pulls off the exhaust assembly from the scooter and hits him with it.

When Beatie wakes from her slumber, her face is all soft and featureless. She rubs her itchy eyes and stumbles her way to the mirror, only to be somewhat amused by her hair. "Something pooped in my 'Turd Bath'." Beatie looks down at a crumpled flyer on the floor, "Watery Crap! I have a date tonight!"

Beatie had only laid down for a brief nap, and now she is an hour away from her engagement. Racing from her closet back to the mirror, she checks on her progress. She can certainly get all dressed up like a stunning lady if she wants, but she can also dress down and be that little girl that nobody is interested in.

"Now, what to do with my hair?" She has ruined Hydragew's creation and decides it will have to be morphed into something less intricate. Pigtails and bow ties, like she always does when she doesn't want to look overly serious. She runs a bronzer across her face and coppers her nose. She then quickly coats her lips and darkens her eyelids. After a defiant gesture with her tongue, she reaches up with loving arms and pretends to embrace her date. "Nope! That is not what is going to happen tonight."

Beatie looks at the clock and sees she still has fifteen minutes. She dives into the couch pillows with her book falling to the floor. She is surprised to see a squashed leaf in the open pages of Chapter 13: 'Pardon the Jealousy,' and cannot help but wonder what it's about. "'Love is the most violent of emotions, equipped with the largest arsenal and the cruelest of tactics.' Ooh, this does sound interesting. So, what are you suggesting, Mr. Goggy?"

> "You must go slowly, or he will think you are being an easy 'boner-babe'. Don't make the mistake of saying yes to everything he says. Show you are interested, but make him work for it, even if

it means pretending to have a flirtatious discussion with someone else. Remember, wanting him to want you is a plausible desideratum."

Beatie continues to read with a fertile mind, trying to absorb all the carefully chosen words as if they might become her own. The book suggests she should choose an evil pet name for him and notes one that is highlighted: Lonely Mushroom. The book specifically recognizes him as being a fungus, a yeast, or a mold that requires damp and dark conditions. Also, he prefers to be in a dense soil of highly decaying matter. Beatie bites on her lip, "If this is who he is, then the book should know."

She leaps from the couch and slides across the floor, readjusting her skirt and slipping into some low heels. She grabs a small purse and skips out to her car, knowing she is going to have so much fun with her date tonight; only this time, on her own terms.

"Darn, Ms. Weary, why won't you start!" Beatie searches for a phone number on her phone and dials. She knows that Hydragew refuses to be seen in such silly places, but an acquaintance of his, Marbury Fever, whom she once met at a blood drive, is a frequent attendee at O'Toole's.

"Hello? May I speak with Mr. Fever? He's not feeling well? Who is this? Thurston Delirium? No, don't hang up! I need a ride to O'Toole's! Well, I'm going now. Uh-huh. Well, bring him along!"

Beatie hangs up the phone. "Game plan on!"

Mia slips into the high heels Sam lent her and clops her way into the bathroom. "Valentine's is in four days, Bo. Is there anything in the world that would make you take a shower?"

"Mar, I can't wear these clothes you bought; it's a dodgy club we're going to."

"Suit yourself, you paid for them."

Bo changes back into his backpack attire: the American torn jeans and a v-neck sweater. He straps on his boots and grabs a jacket. It has a slight odor, but he knows it will dissipate in the open air.

"And you believe those clothes give you confidence?"

"They have worked before."

"Mouth to mouth as usual?"

Bo sticks his tongue out.

"Stop it, that's gross. Make no mistake, I'm only going to watch you screw things up."

Sam is prompt, but she has parked on the other side of the street. It is extraordinarily busy on a Saturday evening, and she can't help but chuckle when Bo crosses the street without Mia. She is a good thirty feet behind him, wobbling like a newborn giraffe and fighting a growing wind. Sam watches with hilarity as Mia grabs onto a sidewalk tree and twirls her way to the ground.

Bo wraps on Sam's window and she lowers it with a smile. "Maybe you should go help Mia, Bo."

Bo frowns but acquiesces to her request and darts back between the cars. "Mar, let me pull some of these branches from your hair. You look like a styrofoam cup with toothpicks sticking out of it."

Mia rises, still holding tightly to the tree. "I appreciate that, but please leave out the disparaging comments or just go away."

Sam slaps the steering wheel in laughter while she mechanically lowers the window again. "Why did you come back without her?"

"She told me to leave her alone." Bo climbs into the back seat while Mia crosses the street with careful steps and her arms held out. When she finally does reach the car, she grabs onto the rooftop and drops down quickly into the passenger seat. After regaining her composure, she reaches back and swats Bo. Sam immediately covers her mouth with a clandestine cough.

"Don't you say anything, Sam!"

Mia looks into the mirror and mends her hair back into place. She brushes the lip gloss from her teeth and turns around to swat Bo again, "And that's for crossing the street without me!"

The owner greets everyone at the door with a loud 'Halooo.' His face is painted a sunburn red, and his nose is coated with a thick, white zinc. Every departure and depression of his hair is made to look like he just came off a boat. There is a crazy, seaside feel to O'Toole's, starting with the large mural upon entry. One cannot help but feel they have stepped into an underwater sea garden with the long columns of kelp and drifting seals painted along the walls. On the floor above, there is a bar made to look like a fishing boat and its furnishings are constructed out of driftwood and coconuts. The staff is dressed as tour guides, and there is a stage on the boat's deck where Kareoke takes place. Nifty, but all eyes, are on the intricacies of Mia's hair, which allows Bo to sneak away and find his date.

He hears a band in another part of the building and follows the sound through a dimly lit tunnel. There he approaches a bouncer seated beneath a sign that reads DARLA PUMPERNICKLE'S, and a sign on the lectern that reads: No flops, no crops, no cut-off tops. No glasses, no asses, no stuck-up classes. Obey the rules or return to Otoole's.

She dances like a zombie with her head tilted to one side and her eyes rolled toward the back of her head. Her mechanical movements of stiff arms and legs are all attributes meant to mimic the walking dead. This is not exactly the place where Beatie wants to spend her time, but she does like the occasional quirky song. She only wishes the attendees didn't dress in silly space outfits. There is no way they are going to attract the right kind of mate dressed this way. This is her opinion and their choice. The attendees wear what they want. Get over it.

Beatie watches as Bo enters the room. She wasn't quite sure he would show up, just like she wasn't quite sure she would show up. Now that both are here, it is all about what to do next. She wants to ignore him like the book says to do, but there is something terribly unfair about his appearance. He is looking awfully mouthwatering and very digestible dressed in that open-neck sweater and butt-fitting jeans. It's really the hypocrisy of it all, isn't it? It's like the dog can lick you, but you can't lick the dog back.

If matters could get any worse, it would have something to do with the two girls appearing by his side. One presents herself as a pony and the other as a tarpon fish. Inner warnings tell her the 'fish-spine' woman is interested in him too. This is not how it is supposed to go! The book she holds so dearly in her thoughts states that she should be the chosen one now!

Beatie needs advice, but Thurston and his companion, Multi Organ Dysfunction, are consumed in dancing with some Mars Barf creature. So, what to do? She really doesn't like the position she in. She recalls from the chapter 'Pardon the Jealousy', that paradise is but a dream that is forever exclusive to one's mind, and it can be used as hell for others. This seems to make sense to her and the right way to handle the matter. Unfortunately, it will have to wait because the song just changed to a quirky, hop-along tune that compels her to dance like a begging dog.

Mia nudges Bo from behind, forcing him to readjust his feet. "Where is your date?"

"She's over there, wagging her rear at that Mars Barf creature."

"You mean the girl dancing with the spaceman and sniffing his butt." Mia strokes her chin. "Well, isn't this truth."

"I don't understand it, Mar. She seems misdirected somehow."

"Misdirected? She is going in a contradictory direction to what a very small portion of society would misinterpret as acceptable." She pats Bo on the head. "Sam and I are going to try Karaoke; join us if you want."

Beatie is absolutely thrilled with the results of her flirting technique. Her little mushroom now appears rejected and his life turned upside down. Maybe he'll grow a fungus and be digested by bugs, how fun would that be? Then again, it would be nice to visit him and treat him with respect – Bahaha!! That's not going to happen. Beatie passes by Bo, swaying back and forth with a silent sneer, pausing only when he calls her name. She then quickly takes up a hidden position within the crowd and watches his pitiful reaction.

"Just look at him," Beatie says to herself. "He truly is a lonely mushroom, bound to the damp soil for which he is placed. Now it is time to complete the submission training." Brushing up against his back, she taps him lightly on the shoulder, "Hello, my little mushroom. I guess I haven't had time to receive you with all this manliness about me. Can you not see them vying for my attention? There are just so many to choose from, and did you not notice me dancing with my two boyfriends? They are still my lovers, you know."

Bo looks over at the two men with their arms around each other. "So, I guess it's not working out?"

"No, of course it is." Beatie turns to see the two men kissing, then turns back to Bo, "I'm making them practice."

"F-f-f-Faire game, Beatie. If y-y-you don't want me around – j-j-just say so."

Beatie's mouth suddenly goes wide with excitement. He is struggling with his words!! Never, ever in her life has she treated someone like this before, and it just seems so justifiable. "Oh, my poor, broken mushroom. If only the fungus learned to be more kind to you." The book says she can nurture the fungi now, but for some cruel reason, she likes acting this way, so much so that she looks around to see what else she can do to him. There is a woman guzzling back a tall glass of beer to the cries of – Go! Go! Go!

"I can get drunk if I want. Certainly could, if you pay for my drink."

Bo goes to the bar to buy Beatie a beer. She has never liked beer, but she doesn't have to; she just wants to see another anguished look on his face. Bo hands her the glass and Beatie takes a quick swig. "Remember this?" She puckers her lips and then sprays him with a mouthful of alcohol. But much to her disliking, he wipes his face and walks away.

"Oh, I see! Everything has to be about you now!" Beatie puts her hands on her hips and rolls her eyes as he continues to walk away. "Okay, I guess I can forgive you, just buy me another drink and we'll call it even. Where are you going? Hello?!!" Beatie follows him to the men's room until the door closes on her face. She knocks, but there is no response. "Well, can I still call you my broken little mushroom?!"

Thurston taps Beatie on the shoulder, "Ready to go?"

She throws up her hands, "You're my only ride."

Bo turns the tap on the faucet. He can't understand why he finds himself in the bathroom doing the same thing every time he goes to a bar. He lifts his head to hear a lively interest coming from the patrons outside and pokes his head out the bathroom door. There he sees the pleasure, a young lady parting the crowd with her uncontrolled beauty. She wears a slick black dress that exposes her flawless figure, and when she tosses her hair over her bare shoulder, she leaves behind the mesmerizing scent of an iris flower that leaves her beholders paralyzed.

Unworthy thoughts quickly appear in Bo's boyish smile, and it makes him question his own dignity. He steps back into the bathroom and turns on the tap again, splashing his face and reaching for a towel.

"Why does beauty find shame in immature men?"

Bo drops the paper towel and turns to see the very same woman standing before him. "Excuse me?"

The lady steps forward and lifts his chin to connect with her eyes, "I said why do men scorn the attraction for which they all desire? Are we taught that it is something we cannot have because we are someone we are not?"

Bo takes a deep breath for composure, "You know you are in a men's bathroom?"

"So, men go into women's locker rooms."

The woman does not wait for Bo to say anything further and places a soft hand on his jaw. "Follow me, unless the boring life you live suits you."

Down a hallway they enter into a private room where the walls are shadowed with sculptures from the Serengeti Plains. Behind a bar, a large person is seen standing in the usual way with the clothes being worn suited for a woman, but under a closer inspection, it is revealed that these clothes have been borrowed for a much larger man.

Bo's escort leads him to a barstool where the bartender hands them one of six glasses, swallowing one herself in a single gulp. Bo raises his own glass for a salutation, "Long may yer lum reek," then he swallows his glass without a mere flinch. The lady again lifts a glass before him, "My name is Olivia Contessa Davelport," swallowing the contents of the glass again in one gulp. "Beauregard Heathan Fox," Bo replies following her lead.

More glasses follow with each one synchronized to be finished in the same manner. After a tray of glasses is emptied, Bo slides off the stool and takes his place behind the bar. He watches the bartender exit through a glass door while Olivia taps her fingers along the counter, "I'm bored." She says, reaching forward to tweak his nose, "What I would like to understand better is how this is all going to end." The lady motions to the glass door where water molecules are running along the inside pane. "You may go now." She says with a drunken slur. "You just don't mean that much to me."

Bo gives her a questioning look. Those words might seem hurtful, but in his condition, he is more interested in where the next drink might be coming from. There are terrible consequences to fear from one's blind action, and it only takes one errant judgment to make a terrible mistake, but it always takes two to confirm something truly went wrong. Bo decides to step through that glass door to determine his fate.

A revolving mist blankets his face as he taps a switch on the wall to activate a fan. When the fog dissipates, the true nature of the bartender's identity is revealed. He is the barber that was recommended by Beatie, except now, he is lying naked on the floor with his knee raised before his privates. After removing a wig from his bald head, he tosses the soggy sod to Bo's feet and places his elbow on his knee.

"I recognize you. You're the barber who cut Mia's hair."

"And you are the boy who has been trying to win the favor of my friend, Bea'trie."

"Be-a-tree?"

"And yet, you are here now in the mist room with me."

"I don't even know what a mist room does."

"That doesn't help."

Bo turns the fan off so the mist can accumulate again. "If this is about Beatie, which explains nothing of your appearance here, I must confess I have failed to find a meeting of the minds with this woman. In other words, I feel I have cast a line far too short to reach her."

"If I may frame this correctly, you are heading in the right direction, except with the wrong frame of mind. If you want to impress Beatie, you're going to have to do a little more than just cast a line. There is an actual person on the other end that you are trying to hook, and it is important that you feel for movement first."

"I was never really good at fishing."

"Good, fishing is a lousy analogy. The truth is, connecting with a woman is more of a game to learn, and the rules to follow are always changing. This is rarely in a language most men will never understand. There is luck on your side; however, Beatie is hardwired to be gullible, and she only needs to feel loved to be 'hooked'. Many times, the only thing important to her is that she means anything to anyone at all."

Olivia suddenly appears in the room expecting to find an unpleasant occurrence, and that she does. She looks at the barber and then at Bo, "Isn't this how we always envisioned it?"

Both look at her and shrug.

FEBRUARY 12th: WHERE THE MEMORIES ARE

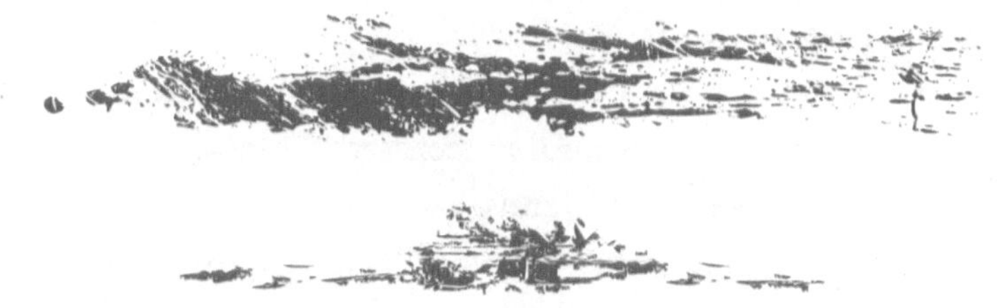

It is five past seven in the morning, and Mia is starting to revive. The constricting sheets around her legs and arms are beginning to loosen, and although her body is still very stiff, her eyes are alert to the very rapidly approaching floor.

"Ow, my head, you stupid @#%&#!!" Mia falls to her side and lies flat, staring at a book binding that surprisingly brings forth a chuckle. The author does have a lot of doubting points, not to mention being overly ambitious. And the army of spirits combating the effects of nature? Obviously, a poor attempt to be chivalrous under the guise of one's romantic stupidity.

Mia dresses in her standard black spandex, red pullover, and pink training shoes. She has decided to take a field trip now that she has discovered the forgotten people. She will not be taking any clothing this time, but instead, four bags with as much food as she can carry. She knows the food she delivered yesterday will not last. They need a daily supply, not just a 'survive-the-night' handout. Naturally, she feels sorry for them; this being her own feeling and not the feeling of others. Sam, her closest friend, won't be bothered with her projects, having experienced an embarrassing incident back in New York City. Well, who cares about Sam and those like her, Mia wants to embrace the lonely people outdoors. She too remembers when she was forgotten and had to be found again.

She puts her court-issued pills aside and reaches for the horn tablets instead. The two together have been making her feel awfully loopy and might explain the possible hallucinations she has been having. That in mind, she certainly doesn't want to say anything that might upset the speaker, especially, if he is to be her Valentine.

Grasping two full bags in each hand, Mia quietly shuffles down the attic steps and through the lobby, pausing only briefly to look up at a unicycle hanging behind the lobby desk: 'Who broke my unicycle again?' reads the signboard. Mia chuckles and continues on to the front door.

"Are you making a deposit, Ms. Pearl?"

Mia cusses when she hears the familiar voice coming from the adjoining room. She sets the bags down and squeezes the blood back through her fingers. "I'm going to meet some friends."

The day manager walks casually toward Mia with his hands on his hips. "Is that what the new hairstyle is all about?"

"It's called the Pony. A sign of vitality, free spirit, and a lust for life."

"I never knew a haircut was meant to make you look like the real animal."

Mia rolls her eyes and lifts her bags, "Can you open the door for me, Day Manager?"

"There is nothing open at this hour on a Sunday, Ms. Pearl, and church isn't until nine."

"I'm just doing some sightseeing before the crowds arrive."

Sen walks to the door and peers at the contents in one of the bags. "An interesting fact about the dead is you don't have to feed them."

"Yes, well, thank you for that." Mia gives a quick smirk and shuffles down the steps. She picks up her pace as she makes her way into the city. Her arms are tiring but her fingers are unwilling to let go of the bags. She is in a hurry because soon the daylight will expose what she has been trying to accomplish: the quest to help those that need to be helped.

After a few more blocks, Mia comes to a twinkle of lights glowing in the unrelenting darkness. This is where she finds them, huddled around fire-lit trash bins with their neglected appearances and uninterrupted stares. She quickly scurries from bin to bin, opening her bags of food with the hopes of reviving them from their comatose state. It is only at the first can, however, does she find enough warmth to stay a bit longer.

"I have something for you all."

A lady with soiled cheeks claps her hands together and inspects the four bags. "I do enjoy food that is fine in quality and distributed for mass consumption."

"Try these – Putsy Fruits. They are supposed to be good for you."

"What else?" The lady beams.

Mia smiles and allows her to dig into the bags unabated. After finding what she likes, she looks up with her eyes flickering in the light. "Are ye going to the park? Thar be talk of things thar." Mia waits for the woman to swallow. "That park used to have many of us who would sit alone; now it's crowded with men covered in blue. There's something different about those people. Something deviating from the norm. No matter at what distance you look at them, everything seems strange about their appearance."

"Strange?"

"Their wear is not of this century."

"Well, it is a historic city; maybe it helps them with handouts."

"Maybe, but the fabric is hardly suitable for those that live with the cold. Their faces too have that congenital similarity identical to anyone unaccustomed to looking at blue. You know what I mean, that pale coloring that comes with hollowed eyes and a pronounced bone structure, kind of like they are dead or very close to it."

Mia suddenly is forced to rub her eyes when the wind blows the smoke into her face. She looks again at the lady happily filling her mouth and staring blankly ahead. "You were saying, Ms. Cheeks?"

The lady just gives Mia a questionable look.

Upon reaching the park she finds the blue men already standing around the crate. It isn't long before the one ear of the next turns toward the voice of the one.

> "We will never become its equal! When we shake a stick, it shakes a tree. When we dig a ditch, it splits the earth. When we use fire to light wood, it burns down a mountain and consumes the forest. Ask nature if we may live, and nature will always reply – for how long? For nature has created time and the end of time with a purpose in mind."

Mia clasps her hands together. Oh, how she loves the way the speaker's words just roll off his tongue. He is truly the master of stirring minds.

She pushes her way to the front of the crowd, hoping to see more of him in a true light. "Hello, Mr. Alteveu. Woohoo!"

"Ah, yes. The missing one."

"I see nature is giving you a problem again?"

"What can I say? It is a bad time to be people."

"Would you like something to eat?" Mia sets her two remaining bags down and sifts through a near empty one. "I have a few Pocket Pussers, and this is good – Cricket Bonnets. It looks like your cohorts could use a good feeding too."

"Do not look upon us as if we are a disease of the fourth degree. We have all grown accustom to poverty."

"I never said you all look sick, just slightly mal-nourished. Maybe that's something you should address with nature."

"I have spoken to nature and she has nothing to say."

"I still have a six pack of Weedle Pockets!" Mia shakes a small juice carton, "Are you sure you don't want one?"

"I have already had bread and flavored water."

Mia tosses the empty bag at the garbage bin and watches her errant throw hit the rim and bounce along the ground. There she finds herself staring at the cracks in the speaker's shoes again, only this time, many more ants have arrived to devour his feet.

"Is this how we are to be judged by your eyes, madam? Do the cracks in a boot somehow define the person who wears them?"

"No, of course not. I love all boots."

"And this love for boots somehow makes you feel justified?"

Mia bites down on her lower lip, knowing she has troubled the speaker again. She knows she will need to impress upon him greatly if she is to win his favor. "To end darkness is to turn on the light so we may reveal the true nature of what we thought we once saw."

"Ah, *The Illuminator of Foggy Pants*. A book published for an audience of easy believers."

"I don't know about that. I mean, true, it is within a fictional framework, but it does touch upon societal structures and how we may evolve with a mutual understanding of our surroundings."

"Is this what you believe – or should we scorch it all and live in holes?"

"I do fancy the pavement horticulture specialist, Farmen Burbian, and his take on the free society etiquette of pandering."

"Yes, and how does it go?" The Alteveu raises his arm to the sky:

> "I live in box shelters placed outside delivery doors. I drink from broken tiles that collect water on the floors. I feed from dumpsters and open my hands to those willing to give. But I am not any of these things: a panhandler or a pick pocket waiting for you to forgive."

Mia looks up at the speaker with a wide-open smile. "That was beautiful."

"Beauty does not address their prayers, madam. Give them your heart, for what they want, money cannot buy."

Suddenly, a light from above grows bright before her eyes, causing a searing pain in her sinuses. She then hears a high-pitched voice.

"Shemmy Merble from Ghost City News."

Mia looks in dismay at a lady holding a microphone before her face. "Bloody hell, how many of you are there?"

"Interesting hair. Is this some new punk resurgence the city is unaware of? What is this book you are holding?"

"The Illuminator of Foggy Pants by Lucifer Goggy. It was his last book before his death."

The reporter takes the book from Mia's hand and looks at the back cover: "'The storm will brew for the opposition that is kept silent.' I'm not going to ask what it's about."

"You shouldn't."

"Chapter One: 'The Alternative Lifestyle of the Unseen Inhabitants?'"

Mia snatches the book away, "He is quite charming."

"You are saying you have met the one we cannot see or hear?"

"I never said that."

"You said that this is his last book before his death, and now you are implying he is quite charming? What is your name, Miss?"

"Why does that matter? I don't have to cooperate with you."

"Miss, what non-governmental organization tries and convicts people for assumable crimes?"

"You do, but why should I talk to you?"

"And what non-governmental institution determines the outcome of thought, speech, behavior, and court opinion in society?"

Mia nervously touches her hair, "Okay! It's the 'Pony.' A barber gave it to me. It is a sign of vitality and free spirit."

"I am not asking for your horoscope, Ms. Pony. I'm following up on your interactions with those in the park."

"Ms. Pony?"

"You just said your name is Barbara A. Pony."

"I never said that."

A man on a unicycle suddenly approaches and crashes into the camera crew, knocking them all to the ground.

"Miss Pearl? It's me!!"

"Day Manager!" Mia leaps onto the handlebars and turns toward Miss Merble with her knuckle placed to her ear, "Sorry, we must be having a disconnection. Call back later, please!"

Sen skirts through the crowds, doing his best to avoid the people in the crosswalks. He turns down a quiet street and leans his head back, "Miss Pearl, are you familiar with the media?"

"Ghost City News? What a crock."

"This could be trouble."

"Who could be trouble?"

"The media, they know what you don't know, but they don't know what you have seen. Few have ever met the man in privacy."

"Who are you talking about?"

"I am talking about the outspoken antagonist who knows not his silence. The man that is studied upon the ways of dispute and acts accordingly. Does that not frighten you?"

"The Speaker? No, he's not like that. He's just a little bothered by the weather. I was really looking forward to getting his signature on his book. I'm only here for a few more days and may not have many chances."

"Then you have met him?"

"Duh, isn't that what I have been trying to tell you?"

"Some say it was a strange discovery of a savage culture. A society of beggars with a derelict captain spreading fear about what we cannot see. Did you know that they once caught the manner in which they walk? Normal in anatomy, but faulty in their step?"

"They have worn-down shoes, Day Manager. Could you not be any more insulting?"

"They are the cadavers of confident displeasures and said to be one of nature's mistakes. For this reason alone, they were easy to recruit and even easier to mislead. Their purpose is to create a world no one can live in."

Mia rolls her eyes in jest. "The nerve of those people. Let me off up here, alright?"

Sen pulls up to the front door of the hotel and leans forward to drop her onto the steps. "Here you are Miss Pearl."

"You have it all wrong, Day Manager. I spoke to one of them. He said he had just come off a plantation and is here with Mother Superior."

"What's that about Mother Superior?"

"I mean Father Camps. He's this man of the cloth. I never met him, but already, I don't trust him. He seems to be acting as a straw buyer for these laborers. It doesn't sound ethical at all."

"Ms. Pearl, I think you are mixing the stories up."

Beatie leaps onto her bed, anxious to take up her book again. Consulting the book of ideas has become a normal part of her day now. It provides her with that wealth of information she needs when dealing with unreasonable men. She had never allowed herself to be so forthright with a man before, and this book offers her that smiling satisfaction of watching them squirm.

She rolls onto her back and draws the image of Bo before her. "There you are. You don't have to apologize; I understand about being unacceptable. Ms. Malvenu called me a dance ogre once, and Ms. Barbie called me a demented wombat. They were them and she was me. Why shouldn't we both be us?"

She rolls over onto her stomach and finds her place in the book. She is at the part about what couples might say to each other on their next date. What a bore, especially the part where it says she should take interest in what he likes to do. "Bahaha! That's not going to happen." She turns to the next page about personality traits and then skips through the pages to a line that catches her attention. "Dating to obtain power for which you do not own? That's the way it was at Darla Pumpernickles! I was there!!"

Beatie sits up and reads the following lines:

'He will eventually flee, and this will feel unacceptable to you.'

"This did happen!! Twice already! It should always be about me, shouldn't it?!"

'You will be forced to call and apologize, even though it was never your fault.'

"'That 'squat bucket'! I'll sneeze up his nostrils if I have to!" Beatie twists the bedsheets around her neck in frustration. "This relationship is becoming way too suffocating: the humiliation at the beach, the inappropriate acts of his clothing in his bedroom, and how about this game of sharing a woman who thinks she can dress a man?! Is this not who they are?!"

Beatie looks down at the next line in the book: *'You have no choice; he is in control now.'*

"AHHHH!! That does it!!" Beatie runs into the living room and begins climbing all over the furniture before grabbing a banana out of the refrigerator. "Why should he have all the power?!" She hurls the banana peel at the garbage bin and looks down at the empty phone messages. "It would be nice if he called. Maybe show up unannounced from time to time."

Beatie lies on the couch and twirls her hair over and over again, putting little knots into places where she thinks they should go. She thinks briefly about what the sponsor said about apologizing but then throws a stuffed animal at the wastebasket. "No way! I'm too hurt to apologize for something I didn't do! So, what now?"

Beatie does not call for an appointment, but she does have to look through the window to see who might be inside. She has to be careful when talking about relationships, because there are listening ears that are adept in cruelty. Oh, good, Mrs. Beetlemeyer is in there. Mitsy Burdi, Breesha Sherman, and Mickey Turtlebiter are in there too. These are a promising group of nursing home relics.

"I'm here, Hydragew! Pas ca!"

"Bea'trie, welcome back!

Beatie flaps her arms and struts across the floor, pecking from side to side before fluttering into one of the available seats. Hydragew's eyes go wide when he sees her hair. It has been rolled around in so many different directions that pig tails have formed all over and around the sides of her head. In fact, her hair is so distorted that even lice would probably get lost and die of starvation in there. He shakes his head, "So, I am telling you ladies, what I saw last night would scare the beetlejuice out of any ghost enthusiast! These figures just drifted right into my barbershop asking for a shampoo and a snip. I nearly fainted when I pulled out my scissors and realized that, not only were their heads less solid, but their hair was like cutting through thin air!"

Beatie closes her eyes, smiling and listening to Hydragew's voice. It's so soothing when he runs his fingers through the follicles on the back of her neck.

"So how did your date go last night, Bea'trie?!"

"Date? Which date? Oh, right, at Pumpernickles." Beatie sits up in the chair and clasps her hands together. "Well, of course it was fabulicious! Oh, you should have always been there, Hydragew, just to see that cute look on his face when I rejected him. It was kind of somnambulist, but in an almost corrugated-cattywampus kind of way. I even felt like royalty once he stuttered and wallowed away in his tears, right before I cut off his head with my hand cleaver!" Beatie lifts her head to hear the ladies in the room rejoicing.

"Is he one of 'those' that comes back crawling after you have proven him a fool?!"

Beatie moves her hands all over herself as if being desired by him.

"Go Beatrice Go!" Yells Mitsy Burdi, sending Beatie into a head sway.

"Maybe he deserved it!" Calls out Mrs. Sherman.

Beatie prances about the room, swaying her head while swinging her arms back and forth. She can't help but get all caught up in the celebration while they too remember the fond memories of torturing a whining, pining, plebe-sucking, primordial Aye-aye for enjoyment.

"So, are you satisfied, Bea'trie?" Speaks a slightly offended Hydragew.

"Not really. Truthfully said, I really wanted a little more inspiration after I told him I have a boyfriend. He was also supposed to have this stabbing 'in-your-heart, death-rolling, breakdown' when I told him I was getting married. You know, with that emaciated look? But you know what I reeeeaally wanted him to feel, more than anything in the whole world? I wanted him to feeeeeel." Beatie reaches out and twists Hyragew's nipple.

"Ow! Bea'trie, stop that! That's not how you treat men!!"

"Why not?"

"Because they don't like it!"

"But isn't it about what I like?"

"Bea'trie, where are you getting all this information about treating men?"

"It's from Change by Way of Means by Lucifer Goggy's. It's my favorite book forever!"

"Well, I think you are being a bit misinformed."

"I don't think so. It all seems quite agreeable to me."

Beatie suddenly frowns and slouches in her chair. She is going to disregard Hydragew's comment about not enjoying her abusive dating techniques, particularly when she knows the book is right. She sits up and places Hydragew's fingers on the back of her neck, trying to get them to move again. "Oh, Hydragew, I do need you to say something fabulously delicious!"

The barber looks at Beatie in the mirror with a clown face. He then puts his hands over his breasts and rocks back and forth, "She huvs nice chebs and a perfectly round bahookie too."

"Bahaha!!!! All applaud.

"So, do you like this man, Bea'trie?"

"I'm not sure. Every time he looks at me, I feel like I should be looking the other way, or even repulsively gagging up wet leaves. Is that what love is all about, Hydragew?"

Hydragew sets the comb down and lifts up her hair, "I think love is about finding our own soul in someone else's body, but it is as much about having his soul inside of you as it is about having your soul inside of him."

Beatie thinks about those words for a moment. Though she isn't so sure he's right, she does like the way they roll off his tongue. Maybe she should give Bo another chance, but he's going to have to step up and be trustworthy, or else she will have to pull out his nose hair with a plier.

"Valentine's is coming up in a few days, Bea'trie. Are you sure your parents will like him?"

"My father doesn't like anyone, so that's settled. My mom will just treat him like a house pet."

"Are you ready for the viewing, Bea'trie?"

Her hands cling to the seat as she lets out a gasp. "Is it really ready?" Beatie leans forward, glancing from side to side in the mirror, "It looks good! I like how you joined the bobs so it is all fluffed together in the front. What do you call it?"

"The Silkie Chicken."

"Really? I've never seen a bird like that before."

Mia walks into the room with her shoelaces undone and twigs pointing out of her mane. She changes into her pajamas, irons out her hair, and then leaps into bed. The sheets are all nice and cold, but just how warm she can make them is exactly what she is looking forward to.

Bo holds the start of a letter before his face, amused by the infinite amount of absurdity he has put on a piece of paper:

> *From the time of who I once was, and how I wanted to be understood; to who I am today and to who I have yet to become...*

Bo crumples up the paper and tosses it at the wastebasket. The words just aren't there in his head right now. It's hard thinking about leaving someone before Valentine's Day.

> *Remember me as the man from another land, whose speech was not so grand and his clothes had to be washed by hand.* "Ugggh!!"

Mia rolls over and smirks, "Working on an equation with words, are you?" She smiles when he drives a pencil through the page. "You're gonna break up with her the day before Valentine's?"

"She won't know until the day after. I'll leave it on the windshield of her car."

"Well, I think we have come closer to the truth about you than ever before."

"In time, I am sure she'll agree it was the best for both of us."

"Frankly, I don't see what Sam and that girl ever saw in you."

"I'm not really interested in Sam now."

"Well, no worries there. Her low opinion of you hasn't changed."

Mia tucks her legs and rolls to the edge of her bed. "But you know what? I'm glad. It's one thing to make someone feel turned on, but it becomes an entirely different issue when everyone else feels sick about it." Mia lifts herself up and walks to the kitchen. She is aware of Bo's attempt to call it off with another and believes this is a good time for a cup of tea. After the water reaches a boil, she walks to his bedside with her cup and grabs one of his discarded letters.

> *"To assure you I have been appreciative of all your claims, I have requested from the king...."*

"Where did this come from? You're breaking up with her, not having her beheaded!" Mia snatches another letter from the floor:

> *"I am not worthy of your presence, and the better man is already waiting for you at the club."*

"What crap of defeatism is this?" Mia gets down on the floor and sifts through more discarded papers. "All of these letters are nonsensical and prolix."

> *"I have left a fingerprint, the only trace of its kind, for I will no longer be here when you read this."*

"This was the letter you wrote for the girl in Australia. Did you not put this on her windshield?" Mia grabs the whole bunch of letters in her arms. "Being that I am a woman you were once involved with, I am sure the other girls were relieved when you left them as well." Mia crawls up into the crawl space and tosses the letters down to the trash bin. She then drops back to the kitchen floor and grabs her teacup.

There is a sudden knock on the floor door. "I'll get it! It's probably the day manager." Mia pulls the door up and then quickly lets it drop back down.

"Who is it, Mar?"

Mia dances on top of the door to drown out the knocking sound. "Nobody. Not a soul is down there."

There are more knocks but more forceful and deliberate now. The door then starts to shake along with loud grunts. Bo then issues another response. "Mar, let the person in; it could be Sam."

"No, I'm pretty sure it's not, Sam."

"Mar."

"Fine!" Mia lifts up the door and looks down into the emptiness. "Like I said, no one is down there." Mia slams the door and crosses back to the kitchen with her cup. "You know, I truly do think I'm doing some good here. I'm really not sure what might become of the explorers when we leave."

"The Free Society Explorers?"

"I won't force you, but you can help a little or you can help a lot with our remaining time here."

Mia looks up at the crawl space when she hears a squeaking sound. Soon, a figure drops down onto the floor and takes the teacup from her hand. "Your door was locked, so I came through the window." Beatie hangs her coat over Mia's shoulder and smirks, "Quite interesting hair you have there."

"Yours too." Mia smirks.

Beatie leaps over the dirty laundry, pausing to touch her hand to her forehead, then to her lower chest and to each shoulder. The shoes appear to be behaving on their own, but the undergarments fornicating on the chair still bothers her. She sits on the bed next to Bo and rests her hand on his knee, looking at him as if he were a morning puppy, all tender-faced with a long night of sleepy. "I've come to the realization that I can't do any better than you."

Bo raises his eyebrows, "I agree."

"That was easy," mutters Mia, turning back to the kitchen.

Beatie waves and clicks her fingers at Mia, "Miss! There's a folded map in my coat if you would, please!"

Mia picks up the coat from the floor, reaches into the pocket, and pulls out the map.

"That's it. Over here!"

Mia tosses the map at Bo, who reaches out to catch it.

"I would like to invite you to my place for an afternoon of fun. My house is highlighted in yellow and here's the address in case you get lost. There is a big cypress tree on the front lawn and a swing on the front porch." She quickly stands, "It should take you around an hour to get there, say around 3:00pm?"

"Samantha's horoscope says it's gonna rain." Blurts out Mia.

"That's not true, the beaches follow their own destiny."

Bo looks at Mia with a large grin, "I look forward to it."

"I look forward to it," Mia mimics to herself.

Beatie hugs Bo, "I don't know why I like you; I just do!"

Mia follows Beatie to the stairwell and kicks the door shut. She then turns toward Bo with her hands on her hips.

Bo just shrugs, "I don't know, Mar. She seems confused, but I really don't think it can get any worse."

"Exactly what I don't understand. Despite all your flaws and idiosyncrasies, she is still interested in seeing you. That alone should strike her as odd." Mia reaches into the closet for two button-down shirts, "And wildly assuming she has met worse, that doesn't erase the fact there must be someone out there far better than you. Red or yellow?"

"Um, yellow."

"What are you going to do about leaving?"

"I hope to know this evening."

Mia puts her hands on her thighs and flaps her shoulders. "I'm gonna get me some rumpy-pumpy before I go!" Mia reaches to the floor of the closet. "Boots or sandals? Your soles are rather uneven."

"Sandals it is!"

"Oh, don't go, Bo!" Mia wraps her arms around his legs, then climbs on top of his back, with both of them falling to the floor laughing.

For about twenty minutes, Bo watches the scenery change from stately ocean homes to busy commercial street corners. He steps off the bus into a muddy tire track and scrapes his feet through the grass. There are sewer pipes running through the open ground, and it is making quite a mess of the area around him. He pulls out the color-coded map and squeezes a stuffed animal tucked beneath his arms. It is a souvenir he had found in one of the shops, a cross between a turtle and a bear. He thought she might like it.

It isn't long before he is making the large stride up the porch steps to the front door. The house soon comes alive with the sound of alarms, so he quickly steps back and works up a disarming smile. The door opens and Bo looks into the face of someone he has not met before. She wears a black jumpsuit and a luxurious teal and gold scarf with a jaguar on it. The expression on her face couldn't be any more clear – he is not welcome. Bo looks down at the map to double-check the location; he then looks up to see the lady clicking her fingers.

"Oh, I know what this is about." She hands him a roll of toilet paper. "The workers use the bushes down beyond the tree line. You will find a shovel there too."

She starts to close the door when Bo puts his foot into the break. "Sorry, Ma'am, but is there someone by the name of Beatie that lives here?"

The lady holds the door closed on his foot and pulls out some viewing spectacles. "No, you must be mistaken."

"Nikki! That's for me. I'll be there in a moment."

The lady kicks at Bo's foot until he relents and then closes the door on him. There is an animated discussion inside until Beatie finally steps out onto the porch. She knows not to invite him in, or else he will have to go through the scrutiny of her two roommates – that likely will not go well.

Bo holds the stuffed animal before her. "I picked up a gift!"

"I love gifts!" Beatie rolls her eyes and tosses her head back with her hands over her eyes. "I'm ready!" She then opens her hands up. "Where is it?"

"This is it!" Bo shakes the turtle-bear before her.

"A stuffed Gamera monster? Is there a second gift?"

"Cheep, cheep, cheep." Bo looks at the open window to see a parrot squawking in a cage.

"Oh, you have a bird!"

"Her name is Miss Pringle."

Another voice calls out from within the house, "Anything wrong, Beatie? Should we call an extractor?"

"No, we're fine, Nikki," looking back at Bo with a smile.

The window suddenly rattles in the wind and both look to the sky. A flying branch sails over their heads and bounces across the rooftop with a thump.

"We should be fine. I thought we'd go to the beach. I packed some sandwiches." Beatie steps back into the house for a moment and tosses the stuffed animal inside; she then hands Bo a picnic basket. "It is only a quarter mile, but we'll take the car."

Beatie turns the ignition on: "It was an itsy bitsy, teenie weenie, yellow polka dot bikini that she wore for the first time today (ix)."

She pops out the disk and the next voice they hear is the weatherman. He is issuing an urgent warning not to venture outdoors until the storm has passed. Beatie turns off the radio and smiles at Bo. She is looking forward to a magnificent day of food, fun, and laughter.

At the beach, Bo walks around to open the door for Beatie. He pauses to inhale the rich, salty air that reminds him so much of Scotland. Beatie hands him the picnic basket and leaps barefoot into the sand. Bo's eyes fixed on the menacing clouds now joining with the rising wind. "Aye, will you look at that! I have never seen a funnel cloud over the water before."

Beatie sets out some plates and condiments on a beach towel, still convinced nothing is going to ruin her day. She is quite familiar with passing storms, having lived in Florida all of her life. "Stop worrying. The direction of the wind is pushing the storm out to sea." She pulls out the makings of a roast sandwich and hands it to Bo. "Your roommate sure has a lot to say."

"Mia? That old boffie has more to say than you know, and right at this moment, she is infatuated with city folks nobody can see."

"Fricken-fracken ghosts are what they are!" Beatie scoffs. "The city is loaded with them. I think we should expulsiate them all!"

"Expulsiate?"

"Yes, immediately even! So, you think she likes you?"

"She does and she doesn't. One day its niceties and the next my pockets have been mugged."

Beatie lies back in his arms and slides her fingers into his. "It doesn't matter. I don't feel threatened."

A flash of lightning appears and in five seconds there is a rumble. They both watch a row of long tentacles drop from the clouds over the ocean. It is slightly discouraging, but Beatie refuses to allow the weather to ruin a perfectly good plan. She reaches back to stroke Bo's jaw and quickly finds he is busy extracting a hat from his pants.

"What are you doing?"

"It's the Stoorworm!"

"What's a Stoorworm?"

"A great water monster that engulfs ships and swallows up land. It pretty much prophesizes devastation."

"That is silly nonsense! Is this another stupid tale? I told you, everything will be alright."

There is another flash of lightning followed by a deafening crack of thunder. The parked vehicles suddenly sound their alarms. Bo ducks as seaweed flies over their heads and a gust of wind blows up Beatie's dress. When she finally wrestles it back down around her legs, Bo is off the beach and headed for the car. Swaying back and forth while fighting the wind, Beatie does her best to keep up, but there is thirty yards between them and he's not slowing down.

Bo is the first to reach the unlocked passenger side. He sits in the seat relieved to have escaped the rain hammering down on the windshield. He becomes startled when Beatie knocks on the window and demands the driver's door be unlocked. Bo leans quickly across the seat but accidentally releases the parking brake and the clutch at the same time. He can only watch in anguish as Beatie cries out in panic, yanking on the locked door, while the car rolls ahead. From the rear window, Bo can only watch with empathy as she rolls off the hood and onto the ground under a shroud of thick rain.

Beatie throws her purse aimlessly at the couch and knocks over a table lamp. There are no words between them that could possibly calm her mood now. Beatie goes to the washing room and wraps herself in a warm towel, letting her wet dress slip to the floor. Bo sits at the kitchen table, already wrapped in a towel. His mind is mesmerized by how clean the house is. He hasn't seen a room so organized like this since leaving his own home a year ago.

Beatie spreads his trousers across the table and pushes a mop to remove the shoe drippings off the floor. She stoops down to pick up a dirty sock and tosses it to the mat. She then goes into the bathroom to clean the toilet, hoping he might leave out of boredom, but he doesn't; it's time to send him home.

Beatie storms back into the room, ready to run him out with a toilet plunger, when she sees something highly unusual. "What the heck is he doing? Is that his shirt coming off?" Beatie drops the plumbing tool on the floor and takes up a position behind the lamp. "Booky Bahooka! His pants too? No way! What if he's naked under those clothes?"

Beatie lets out a soft squeal, her excitement further concealed behind her quivering lips. She has never seen a man naked without his clothes before, and it's causing her to flick her forefinger in anticipation of each garment coming off. "Yes, and the socks too." She bites into her knuckle, knowing this can't continue on like this, but how can she turn away when her lips are puckered and her tongue is sliding in and out of her mouth!

<SLAP> "What is wrong with you, you breastfeeding-bunny-bumping-pleasure-bag?!" Beatie definitely has to compose herself, bring the temperature down a bit, and return to the normal world of fine clothing and stuffed animals. But what if he decides to put his clothes back on? "Okay, one more look."

<SLAP> "Absolutely not! Is this not what Chapter Seven said was going to happen? And did I not specifically tell the book, particularly in Chapter Four, that I have only the purest of thoughts and the cleanest intentions?! So, then why are my panties down around my ankles?!"

"AHHH!!" Beatie races back to her room and clubs herself five times with a stuffed animal. "Look what this man is making me do!!" She pulls out a 180-grit sheet of emery paper from her vanity drawer and begins wiping the horny smile off her face. Her father is right; she is behaving like a bargain-sale concubine invited to a backdoor barbecue. "That does it! I'm putting an end to this concupiscence right now! Where is my robe?! No way can I have this man sleeping here while my hormones are enraged like this!"

Bo dries his body off with a towel and looks up at the skylight. The sound of rain is growing louder, and it is giving him the urge to use the bathroom. Pulling the towel tightly around his waist, he shuffles quickly down the hallway for permission.

Beatie reaches for a robe from the back of her door. Her chest is bare, and she has no hair to hide her inner-thigh cleavage. All Bo can do is stand in silence with wide open eyes viewing her nakedness. "Booky Bahooka!"

Beatie's face suddenly lights up in a blaze of anger. "What the heck are you doing in here?!!"

"I didn't s-s-see anything! I j-just n-n-n-eed to use your panties?! I mean your bathroom!!"

"I'll show you where perverts go to the bathroom in this house!" Beatie quickly wraps the robe about her body and grabs a broom from the closet. She pushes Bo down the hallway, and after a quick left, she pushes his face up against the back door window. The low visibility and the bending of the trees confirm his worst fears about the Stoorworm.

"Aye, black as the earl of hell's waistcoat, it is." Bo looks back at Beatie with a questioning look. "It's a real pea souper out there. Do sheds always float in the backyards in Florida?"

"If you have to use the bathroom, you'll need this!" Beatie thrusts a roll of toilet paper into his hands. "You'll find some raised land up by the fence!"

With a quick flutter of her hand, she dismisses Bo into the yard. He finds a low-lying branch to pull himself onto the shed and then makes his way to the other side to lower his pants.

FEBRUARY 13th: IN DEATH DO WE PART

The wind blows over the Huguenot cemetery and through the narrow spaces in the ceiling boards of the attic. The tossing of a few paper plates, along with the silverware falling off the counter, has Mia setting her bare feet to the cold floor. Tired but functional, she recognizes the sounds of cars sloshing through the wet streets. She also knows the smell that comes with it. It's that odor of damp death, so common in her work life back home.

Mia can no longer be kept away. The thought that they are out in the wet and cold worries her. The limited array of food in the kitchen bothers her too, they need a variety, not a one-star soup kitchen. She quickly dresses into warmer wear and fills four bags with a mix of food and clothing. She steps into her trainers and digs through Bo's pant pockets for the last bit of change, accidentally finding the departure tickets falling to the floor. She is not anticipating any changes to her travel plans, but she does feel the anxiety when seeing the scheduled flight home from Miami. How can she leave this country when all she sees are more projects to be completed?! Mia lifts the four bags; maybe she does need more time. Possibly a lot more time. After all, it isn't difficult to imagine herself settling down in a city where she can do amazing work.

The streets are silent and the lamps glow bright in the absence of light. The heavy scent that comes with the ocean air has left a mist upon the city. It can be unseasonably warm in February, but when a rain does come through, the temperatures can easily drop thirty degrees. She is aware of this and is saddened too that she didn't pick up a few more socks, hats, and gloves.

It is not long before she comes to the glimmering trash bins and finds her favorite explorer. He gets so excited whenever he sees her that he has to hug himself first.

"How are you, Mr. Shiver Squeeze!"

"Squeezie behebe!"

She opens her bag to show him what's inside. "Look, I made some chip buddies, pudding rolls, and several toast medleys."

"Ba vida kin bobby!!"

"You can take some to cousin Bobby if you want. It may have to be the pudding rolls, though."

"Boozy Kazooby!"

"Come on everybody, form a queue! I really went out on a splash for you all this time." Mia reaches into the clothing bag and divides the articles based on their stature. She then distributes the remaining clothes evenly so they all have what they need. She's not trying to make a fashion statement; it's more about the smiling faces that a thousand people could not do before her. "Who wants to wear the mitties? How about a sweater?"

"This looks expensive." Says Bandana Man, "I'll be robbed if I wear this."

"Put some dirt on it."

After settling a few squabbles, Mia issues a response: "Don't worry, we'll suss it out later."

There is one other explorer she knows through random appearances. His mental duty on the street is to pick up the scraps left behind by the others; other than that, he is the only explorer who has sat with the blue men. Mia believes he knows something about Catalan. "I'm looking for Catalan, Grubby Two Shoes; have you seen him?"

"Never found him to exist!"

"That's impossible! He has that distinct accent and wears the blue dye that they all like to wear.

Suddenly, there is another voice that startles her, "He's a stealer! He doesn't belong on the streets with the rest of us."

Mia looks to see a man sliding along on his knees on a noisy piece of cardboard. He carries a clear bottle that has a yellow liquid inside.

"Sir Missing Boots! What is that you have in your hand?"

"It's my urine-pepper."

"Lovely." Mia frowns. "Did you say you know something about Catalan?"

"I do. He's not who you think he is, and you will soon find he is not who you want him to be." He points toward the park, where there is a loud vocal eruption. Mia immediately flips over a shopping cart and places the last bags on top.

> "Here we stand, and if you choose to stand where you are today, you will only find resentment in a world you thought you could follow. For they are manipulators of mind, and this you will discover in time, that they are not of the ones that will accept your kind. It is their world to be had and yours to follow!"

Mia frowns at the Alteveu. His face looks so evil and sinister. She does not wish to see him like this so close to Valentine's.

> "Let us not forget the man who works the soil, for he knows the dirt far better than the man who pays for his plow. For it is he who the earth trusts, not the man whom lives off his labor."

The crowd grows more restless as more enter the park. Mia looks to see Catalan waving and looks through her bag for a sweater. "Catalan, I just arrived. What did I miss?"

"He told the people he abhors their individualism."

"He's probably having a bad day. Here, try this on!"

"The Alteveu admits he truly does not care about the needs of others, just the needs that he requires from them."

"You all look so thin. I have pickled ham, and I hope you like pumpernickle."

Catalan takes an orange sliver into his mouth, "There should never be acceptance for the one that embellishes power with the mere goal of making oneself happy."

"Well, you know him best." Mia is a little caught off guard by Catalan's denouncement toward his friend, but she does understand that hunger can make one irritable. "Oh, look what I found! Orange slivers with salmon!"

Catalan opens his mouth to let her know he has already been eating them.

Mia looks up when she hears the silence. "Look Catalan! I think he's finished! Sir, Alteveu! Woohoo!!" Mia prances up to the stage. "I see you and the gang had a good talk. Another great speech to die for, am I right? Wink Wink."

"Everything to be laid before us as a purpose."

"Ah, nature getting under your skin again?"

"I have no ability to stop what nature has already cooked up, even if death is all that is on the menu."

Catalan bows slightly and away. "The Alteveu does not fear death. He has already made peace with that offer."

Mia rubs an irritation from her eyes and looks carefully at the speaker. For the first time she sees the man's face to be quite different than the face she has seen before. His complexion is a paler version of his former self, and not just from the recent chilly nights, but from a long period of time and decay outdoors.

"Your face, madam, is familiar to those who have seen you before?"

"I was here with Catalan the other day. I am Mia."

"I do not recall there being such a meeting."

"Well, you were very busy at the time. You even forgot to sign your book. In fact, I have a copy here." Mia reaches into her sweatshirt pouch and extracts the book. "If you could sign it – Alteveu, The Speaker, Lucifer Goggy, any of those names would be fine." Mia places a pen carefully on his knuckle hoping he will write.

"Whatever you do in life, my dear, you carry a name, but it should not be the same name you merely scribble on a piece of paper but the name addressed to you when you stand before a crowd."

"Interesting that you say that. Sister Debago gave me the same advice when the authorities returned me for the fifth time. Their punishment for me was to prepare a garden, and if I ever ran away again, I was assured the orphans would starve."

The Alteveu, with his arm raised, turns to the crowd, "The Sisters wanted everything, so when does everything become enough?"

Mia shrugs her shoulders, "I'm not saying they wanted everything, but a little respect would have gone a long way."

"Find the joy in this woman, my soldiers, for all she wants from them is their respect!!"

"Bagoot!!!"

Mia stumbles backward and falls to the ground. She looks up to see a group of blue men crowding around her. In fact, there are many more of them gathering in the park, all marching in place as if – getting ready to scare the city. Mia flees the park, only to reach a dead-end street. She tries to break through a wooden fence, hoping she might find a road back to the hotel, but unfortunately, she has no recollection of the place where she has arrived. She will have to go back through the park again. She turns abruptly and bumps into something solid that causes her to fall.

"Prindy Reeshmen from Ghost City News."

"Seriously?"

"You have not been addressing our organization's questions."

Mia stuffs the remaining bag of food beneath her sweatshirt. "Hi ya, love. One more time, please?"

The lady assists Mia to her feet. "We have noticed that you have been feeding those that otherwise search for food."

"I don't recall ever being asked such a question."

"We no longer need to. We witnessed your engagement earlier."

"Really? You Americans are always assuming that someone from the UK will travel thousands of miles just so they can feed the people of another country. We have hungry people of our own, you know."

Mia crosses her arms in defiance, but much to her surprise, the reporter reaches a hand beneath her sweatshirt and snatches a hidden bag of food. "You were saying?" Shaking the bag and watching several snacks drop to the grass. "Miss Pony, are we here to play this game of yours every time we catch you in a compromising position?"

"Excuse me? Did you just call me, Miss Pony?"

"It's right here in my organizer. Miss Barbara Pony. Five foot two, 115 pounds, thin blonde hair with a British accent."

"Bloody Toothbrush, Shemmie Merble!" Mia puts her hand over the microphone. "Who told you I would be at the park?"

The reporter looks back down at her organizer. "That would be a Sen Lin Khan."

"Day Manager!" Mia grips her hands.

Beatie hears a crash from a glass table and looks to see one has toppled over. Her mother has been following the twiddle board patterns on the floor she uses to travel about the room. "How many laps have you made, Momma?" Beatie sets her book down for a moment and puts the table back into place.

Mrs. Backlebond squeezes in next to her daughter and kisses her on the cheek. It is almost lunchtime and she is speaking profusely about her Transgruple Delight. She notices her daughter is in a depressed mood and though her mind may not be as sharp as it once was, her instincts as a mother have not failed her.

"I remember what being forgotten is all about and that unhealthy share of loneliness that follows."

"Momma, I have been having trouble with this boy I have been dating."

"It would be nice if he would call; is that what you are thinking?"

"I'm not even sure I want him to do that anymore."

"Your father used to always call me. It drove me crazy because everyone hated him. Your grandma hated him, your grandpapa hated him, and your uncle chased him down with the lawn mower."

Beatie wipes a tear, "Pappa got run over by a lawn mower?"

"He couldn't avoid it! Back in those days we had the push kind with the rotary blades. Your father never heard him coming."

Mrs. Backlebond smiles when Beatie laughs.

"But your father didn't stop calling, and then you know what? I soon realized he just cared an awful lot. That's the kind of man I want you to meet. And you know what else I want you to know?"

"What's that, Momma?" Beatie looks at her mother and knows she wants to offer her more advice, but her face is changing back into a child again. "Momma?"

"How can one blame a tree for leaving the forest if its only wish was to bask alone in the sun?"

Beatie wraps her arms around her mother and gives her a kiss on the forehead.

Suddenly, the door flies open with a strong gust of wind that sends the mail flying about the room. Mrs. Backlebond immediately launches herself onto the floor, mimicking the flight of papers.

"It's Olivia and Nikki, Mamma; it's not a hurricane."

Mrs. Backlebond gets up with the help of her daughter and wanders to the back door.

"We didn't scare your mother away, did we?" Nikki replies.

"No, Mother likes to watch for animals in the backyard."

The girls sit down on either side of Beatie and each one takes a moment to look at the other.

"So, Beatrice, whose clothes are those hanging on the dining room chair?"

"I had a boy over last night."

"Really?" turning their heads about the room. "He's not still here, is he?"

"No, I sent him into the backyard. He was making me horny."

Olivia and Nikkie break out in a loud outburst, "Way to go, Beatie!!" Nikkie slaps Beatie's hands over their heads. "You did notice that it became a bit chilly last night?"

Beatie folds her hands and lets out a deep sigh, "Well, I am sure he went back to where he is staying."

"It was a gale storm, Beatrice! The roads were washed out. The services were closed."

Beatie is a bit concerned with their dialogue. Never have the girls ever taken an interest in anyone's well-being before.

Olivia lets out a deep breath, "Yes, but that is not why I am here. I saw you at Pumpernickle's the other night."

"I didn't know you went to Pumpernickle's."

"I never do. In fact, it took intense courage for me to do so. You really should thank me. I just so happened to meet the very man you are dating. Tell me, Darlie, how interested are you in this person?"

Beatie's mouth twists slightly. "Why, somebody else wants him?"

"Straight to the point, as I prefer. I found he and Hydragew in the mist room. Do you know what goes on in there?"

Beatie begins wringing her hands. "I don't know what a mist room is, but it's sounds wet."

"That's exactly what it is, very wet in a moist kind of way."

"Are you sure it was Bo? I mean, I was with him at the time, it just seems too coincidental that there would be the same people at the same time in that same type of moisture."

"Coincidental that I found him in the mist room? Or coincidental that I found Hydragew naked on the floor before him?"

Beatie stands up and walks about the room. "Is that what this is all about? Serious, you know one can't be comfortable wearing clothes in a mist room."

"We're both very sorry, Beatrice."

"But this is absurd! Hydragew's my best friend. He's not gay like that. We were even talking about our souls just the other day."

"I wish I could agree, Beatrice, but I've just seen too much about men that would explain otherwise."

Beatie sits back down on the couch, wrapping her arms around her knees. She cannot believe what she is hearing. She agrees, there are a lot of strange things about Bo, on a daily basis even, but attending a mist room?

"I'm sorry, Beatie, I don't know how you can love a man whose love is meant to be found elsewhere. He's not from this country."

He finds himself as a young boy in an untainted meadow, strongly fragrant after a spring rain. The sound of a clanking bell and he turns to a footpath where his going is much easier. The grassy path through the shining blades of dew always leads to a sign that reads: Sango Bay. There in the shallows, where he lies beneath the water, he makes little ripples with his fingers. The world on the other side is coming apart and it knows not why. An object plunges into the water, leaving behind a trail of tiny bubbles. This object is long, soft, and repulsively fleshy.

Bo wakes with one hand attached to a smooth texture and the other hand resting in a bowl of water. Next to the bowl are three boiled eggs and a half-eaten fruit bar. He reaches for an egg and realizes it is still very hot. Lifting his other hand, he notices he is holding onto the tail of a drowned possum. He quickly disarms the dead creature out a small window and determines he is in a shed with lawn grooming materials. Stepping backward, he trips over several bags of mulch and is startled to see a little lady wearing an alpaca hat. Her little face appears to be an older version of Beatie, which confuses him. She hands him a large blanket and a plastic bag containing dry grass, then requests that he follow her into the yard. The air is cold and damp, and the back yard has been converted into a small pond with water bugs and toads having a party. He steps into a small raft, and they slowly make their way toward the house with the aid of a paddle.

Beatie lies on the couch submerged in a stack of pillows, blowing a high sigh into the air. She is still mad at Hydragew for hanging out in a mist room, but she is even more shocked to learn that Olivia and Hydragew are known to each other. Almost deceitful in a clever kind of way. Olivia doesn't like people being happy; she is a hateful person and looks for reasons to use her hate so she can smile forward.

A draft in the room sends Beatie's feet deeper into the cushions. "Someone left the back door open. Mamma, is that you?" She listens to the faint sound of her mother at the back door.

"Shh...You can't come in, little house animal, but I did give you some grass."

Beatie watches as her mother shuffles into the room with mulch and wet leaves on her alpaca hat. Her hands are behind her back with a frown on her face. "Who were you talking to, Momma?"

"The tool shed has some very unusual animals in it."

Beatie SCREAMS when her mother tries to hand her a hairy, stiff object. Her mother SCREAMS back and then rushes to the front door, and with several long back-and-forth swings, she releases a possum carcass into the front yard.

Beatie turns her head toward the voice of Nikki, "Beatrice, there is someone at the back door! I've seen him before."

Beatie sits up quickly, sending the couch cushions to the floor. "You mean he's still here?!" Bo's voice can be heard entering the house. She has no makeup on, which is just fine, not wanting to appear attractive for that sloth-crawling piece of bowel movement, but what to think of him now? His behavior has gone unchecked for several hours already – and is it not wrong to think he is way out of bounds on this?! Showing up at someone's back door whenever he wants to. What if he's naked again? Is this not who he is?!

Beatie quickly retrieves her book from under the couch. It says she should let him have it, force him to stutter until his cheeks collapse and he swallows his face. "The perfect plan!" But what if she fails to humiliate him in front of her pretend friends? What if, instead, he presents an argument that convincingly defends himself? And what if she starts liking him again, standing on the tips of her toes, panting like an eager puppy, imagining what it would be like to be with him on a daily basis?! What then?!

"Food is ready!" Beatie looks in shock at her mother standing before her. "We will be having a fresh 'popricorn schmedley' with chocolate-covered spam. It's what you always want and expect from your own kitchen."

"AHHH!" Beate rushes back to her room to get a last look at herself in the mirror. A quick spray of her favorite perfume, but definitely trying to avoid the lip gloss. There is no need to make him pretty should she decide to kiss him.

<SLAP> "Get a hold of yourself, you mad-brain, head-cheese ensemble! Don't you remember anything that the book told you?!"

Her book is right. She should instead be preparing herself for a long angry stare, because this is how she should feel right now. And a growl, because this is how she should sound, and maybe too, use her tongue like a snake so she can taste him.... "Noooo! No tasting!!" Beatie slams her head down on the vanity, trembling to think that this could all blow up in her face. She stands tall and straightens out her clothes. She will obviously be challenging the powers he has over her, whether he knows he has them or not.

Within a few minutes, the potatoes are peeled, the fish is out of the boiler, and the salad is in a bowl. All courtesy of the private chefs provided by Olivia's parents. Bo walks into the room, barefoot and smiling, which angers Beatie, because he is acting like he is among friends. He stretches his arms out to receive her, but she refuses to reciprocate, preferring the suitable frown. At the table, she catches a glimpse of him in dismay, and it almost makes her want to smile, but she won't; it might give him hope.

"Pass the 'Habari Yako,' please." Beatie bites down on her hand after yet another scatterbrained mistake. "I'm sorry, I mean, please, pass whatever you want, and I'll eat it."

Bo looks at a lady across the table and sees disappointment in her face, one that he is familiar with. He must have done something wrong, because she is now motioning with her hand to have his head cut off. That's when Beatie stands up with her hands on her hips, "Olivia caught you with another man!"

"Another man? That's daft. Who is Olivia?"

The lady from across the table leans forward and smiles. "Why does beauty find shame in immature men?"

"Did you not notice that 'Olivia-friend' is here?"

Beatie waits for a response but hears no response from Bo at all. Instead, she watches him swallow down hard on his pudding while reaching for the water.

"We want to hear a tale!" Nikki demands.

"We heard you tell interesting tales!" reiterates Olivia.

"Tell it! Tell it! Tell it!" Calls out the two ladies while Beatie's mother just squeals. Beatie crosses her arms with an agitated look upon her face. "Speak now or remove you from my eyes, I will!"

Bo searches his mind for a tale, and the only one that comes to mind is a tale from The Fidi Belurdi, a collection of stories passed down from his late ancestors.

> There is a little girl and her younger brother who had never seen the night sky before. Their parents had always sent them to bed

> too early and woken them too late to know one ever existed. One night while their parents and friends were celebrating a holiday, the children were awakened with the sounds of fireworks.

Olivia pats her mouth to cover up a yawn. "How boring."

Beatie looks around at the three unamused faces. "I would still like to hear all of it."

> When the children went to the window, they were shocked to see a black sky with many white holes in it. Naturally, they thought their parents had blown it up, so they would have to live in darkness. Angry, the kids decided to trick the adults into the cellar and lock them in. There, they made them perform the sun dance again until the blue sky returned.

Bo pauses to see Mrs. Backlebond load her finger and shoot him. She then slides behind Beatie to shoot him again.

> Unfortunately, the night sky returned, so the children had to keep them locked in the basement to continue with the dance. To this very day, the ancestors of all those in the basement continue to dance so that the sunlight will return for all the generations to come.

Beatie looks around to see a tear in everyone's eyes. The tale is not what she was hoping to hear. She was really hoping to beat him up a bit more. Beatie motions everyone to keep quiet with their whimpers. "I will examine the accused with my own questions now!"

"Like what?" Bo demands.

"Like what you were doing with Hydragew in the mist room?!"

"There is no doing anything with Hydragew in any mist room. If anything, we were talking about you."

Beatie frowns. Unfortunately, his sound proof reasoning is exactly what she was expecting. She grabs her coat from the rack and takes Bo by the arm. Mrs. Backlebond runs back to get her own coat, but Beatie closes the door to the porch before she can follow.

"Now, explain!"

"Olivia coaxed me to walk in on a man in a mist room, but nothing ever happened! If I had known what was going to take place, I would have torn my eyes out right there!"

"You would have?"

"Yes, I would have."

"Okay, let's see!"

"Well, I can't actually ..." Bo looks at Beatie, who has a serious look on her face. Reluctantly, he grips the top of his eyelids and stretches them as far as he can. Beatie carefully watches with growing interest until Bo suddenly releases himself. "Ow! I really hurt myself, Beatie! See the red?"

Beatie frowns, "Yeh, I guess it was okay. I was expecting a bit more, though." Beatie sits down on the porch swing. "It's just that Nikki, Olivia, Ms. Barbie, Hydragew, my boss, my mother, my father, and the boy down the street don't like you."

"Are you sure you're not leaving anyone out?"

"It's not so much that I believe them but so much of your name we do not know."

"Beatie, your friend, Ms. Davelport called me a rapscallion, a scallywag, a varlet, and a vamooser. Does this describe the man you have been dating?"

"Olivia's words would know; she invents them."

The blinds suddenly open, and they look to see Nikki and her mother cheering on Beatie. Beatie immediately goes into an act, pressing her hand over her ears and shaking her head, "No, it's not right that you should say those things! How lugubrious!!"

"Lugubrious?"

"It's this word I know. Just play along."

"Well, it's a lang road thot's no goat a turnin'!"

"I have no idea what you just said."

"That's okay; they just closed the blinds."

Beatie continues to ask the questions and listens attentively to whatever Bo has to say. She has never heard from a man's point of view, and though it contradicts everything she has read, there is not a quirk she can find in the accused, except for being a misplaced, lonely mushroom born to the damp soil for which he was found.

Darkness blackens the walls of the room, and Mia soon strains her eyes to see the pages in her book. She has read enough to conclude that the stories are merely for entertainment. No further fact-finding is required, and her pills, or the lack of them, were probably the culprit for her hallucinations. Therefore, the stories about ghosts are only a ruse concocted by a beguiling day manager. That being discovered, she now has determined which of the two, Catalan or the Alteveu, will be her true Valentine. Yes, the speaker has leadership skills; he is also smart and hip, and tall and fit – but he's just too controversial. Therefore, her choice will be Catalan.

Mia tosses the book aside and looks at her watch. It's 4:00 am. She drops her feet to the floor and digs through her backpack. The leggings, V-neck sweater, and her closed-back, T-strap, glitter booties are the best she has to offer. She bathes her face in the mirror and puts an adhesive in her mane. She then grabs her coat and feels for the pills in her pocket, soon dropping them to the floor. She won't bother with them. She is in full control of her looks and her mind now. There is one more item in her closet. A box of bay leaves with four leaves to be placed at the four corners of her bed and one for the center of the pillow. She does this every night before Valentine's with the hope that she will return one eve to see the stems have materialized into a man.

Mia grabs a few empty bags, filling them with food and clothing; she then pulls on a winter coat and climbs down into the dark hallway. Sen looks up from his ledger to see Mia scurrying across the lobby. "Could you smell the cemetery this morning, Ms. Pearl?!"

Mia stops and squeezes her fist into a tight ball. She had hopes that Sen would not be up this early. "I work in a cemetery, Sen. I think I know what one would smell like!"

"Was your meeting yesterday informative?"

"It did seem a tad unsociable, but what can you expect from people who are hungry!"

"In this city, one person in fifty has seen a ghost."

"That's one person too many, Day Manager. Now if you don't mind, I'm rather busy." Mia hurries toward the door but stops when Sen raises his voice with an offer.

"Maybe you would like to accompany me tomorrow to the Hokie Dance. It's quite a cute spectacle held by the local theater."

Mia takes several quick steps backward. "Is that what this is about, Day Manager? A date? You get me thinking that ghosts are invading the town, then to top that off, you tip the media off to my whereabouts!"

"Does this mean yes?"

"An emphatic – NO! If I may recite a line from Chapter 6: 'In the art of political warfare, all views are to be heard, and all lies still worthy of their merit.'"

"You are going to see them, aren't you?"

Mia picks up her bags. "Good day, Day Manager!"

"You are getting involved with something you know nothing about, Ms. Pearl. You will never be able to conform to their way of thinking."

Mia pushes her back against the door and nods goodbye.

"Ms. Pearl, wait!" Sen hurries to the doorway and calls out to Mia making her way down the steps. "'You cannot provoke change without threats, and you cannot reach diplomacy without understanding.' You said you read Chapter 6, did you not?!"

Mia briefly turns and extends a middle finger, "Bagoot!"

Sen continues down the sidewalk following her until she crosses the street, "His truth has many hidden misconceptions! He does not bring unity nor does he bring out the good in common man! He has to find derelicts with no questions asked! They merely serve his purpose, but there was one who tried to warn the others!!"

Mia stops in her tracks, "Catalan." She turns about and crosses the street back to Sen. "Go on."

"There are many insane revolutionaries and the chances you got the right one is a hundred to one. A hundred to one (x)!"

"I'm not interested in the Speaker anymore, it's someone else."

"We are talking about Valentine's Day, am I right?"

Mia rolls her eyes at what Sen could be suggesting.

"You want to be sure. We all want to be sure. What I want to do is very simple; the dissipation of these ghosts is very slow. Let's go down to the cemetery; whatever has been hanging out there for the last twenty-four hours is bound to still be there (x)."

Mia shrugs her shoulders with a bent lip, "Maybe the only way to confirm they're coming(x)."

The stone hits the sidewalk and bounces along the gutters two dozen turns before it reaches the cemetery gate. "I've seen this, Sen. It's the Huguenot cemetery. It was the first public cemetery to be erected in 1821 in response to the out-break of the Yellow Fever. It doesn't look at all full."

"The residents in there could no longer tolerate the tourism, so many just left for the suburbs."

"Sen, enough! I have worked in cemeteries all my adult life, and nothing remotely ever suggested the dead would just get up and leave their resting place." Mia turns her head to hear a voice approaching.

"You two need to be careful this late at night."

"Miss Dirty Cheeks!!" Mia welcomes the lady with open arms. "What brings you up this way anyways?"

Mia watches as the lady reaches down into one of the food bags. "Yes, go ahead and take one."

Chewing with her mouth open, "The city graveyard is attracting attention again."

"I don't see anything in the cemetery."

Sen points down the street, "There is another cemetery down the road. It's the Tolomato Cemetery on Cordova."

"That's where Catalan lives!"

"I don't think so, unless he's dead."

"He's not dead, Sen." Mia grunts. "He's quite alive, and for your information, I have a fun-filled plan for him tomorrow night. I'm taking him to Boogle Snitch across the river."

"Impossible, they can't extend beyond city limits."

"You know what, Sen? I've just about had enough of your antics. All this tomfoolery you've been playing is really just your attempt to ingratiate others while covering for your own inadequacies." Mia shakes her bag. "Yes, take one more, Ms. Cheeks."

It is all quiet except for the calls from the seagulls gathering around the trash bins. Mia pauses at the next block, disappointed by the imposing bars blocking a yard of headstones. She was hoping to see a bunch of single-family homes on a golf course or maybe an expensive high-rise with valet parking, but instead, she sees a cemetery made gloomy by a white mist and foreboding trees.

"Ms. Pearl! This is not the time to be house hunting. You heard your homeless friend back there."

Mia spins about with closed teeth, "Free Society Explorer!"

"What?"

Something unearthly crosses the street that causes Mia to gasp. It barely walks upright but manages to climb the cemetery gate and dig its way into the soft earth before a gravestone.

"Did you see that, Sen? All my years in the rental business and I have never ever seen anyone just dig themselves a grave and crawl into it. Is this what American is becoming?"

Sen tries to follow Mia's eyes but can only shake his head. "Where do you see all that?"

"Over there where the men are sitting!" Mia points toward a group of workers she sees seated against the headstones.

"Who is sitting where? I don't see anything."

Mia rushes across the street to the gate and begins shaking the bars. "Hello! Woohoo! I'm looking for a man named Catalan! Is there a patio home in the back?!" Mia turns to Sen. "My watch says it's half past six. What time does it open?"

"I don't know; I don't hang out in cemeteries."

Mia pulls on the chain latch and begins shaking the bars again, "Woohoo! It's me again! Is this a gated community?! Why is it locked up?"

Mia's eyes go wide with anticipation as she sees the mist break before her eyes. "Look Sen! I see someone leaning against that large stone back there." The chain suddenly falls to the ground and the gate opens.

"Sen, someone has buzzed us in." Mia turns quickly. "Sen? Where did you go? Well, isn't this telling."

Bo rolls over onto a lawn mower, realizing he is back in the shed. He recalls playing multiple rounds of Scrabble that involved drinking wine. Vaguely too, he recalls undressing and climbing into Beatie's bed. This might explain why he is in the tool shed again.

He finds his damp clothes scattered about the lawn equipment and then ties up his boots. Opening the shed door, the drizzly air makes him shiver and sneeze. It brings out a sense of nervousness as to whether this really can be life for him. A life that also cries with the sounds of mechanical contraptions and busy city folk.

Bo makes his way around the pond and into the house. He finds a piece of paper and a pen and begins to write. Slipping the letter into a book under a couch pillow, he walks down the hallway and peers into Beatie's bedroom. She looks so adorable sleeping with her off-colored face and hair in two Princess Leia knots. Her mouth is open and her eyes are closed, and her arm is holding tight to the turtle-bear he gave her. So peaceful, so innocent, and so childlike.

The cab driver is on time, and Bo is quickly down the porch steps and into the back seat. He smiles at the friendly lady popping large gum bubbles in the mirror. When the cab pulls away, he rubs his sleeve against the clouded back window and watches Beatie's house disappear into the mist. Leaning back against the seat, he closes his eyes and reminisces about home. The tops of Ben Nevis, Ben Macdui, and Ben Braeriach. The rolling hills of Cheviot, Ochi, and the Campsie Fells. The lowlands through the valley of Glencoe, the mist of the western fjord, and the banks of the Loch Fyne.

'I can never live in a place so remote,' he heard her say. How can he expect her to leave her surroundings if he himself can't leave his own.

Bo is startled by the wiper blades shuddering across the dry windshield. He sits up to see the early morning light rising over the stately homes along the beach. "Is there anything open on this road, ma'am?"

The cab driver lifts her hand and waves a wrapper, "Peanut butter and jelly?"

"Sure, why not?" Bo takes a bite and glances out the window, watching the sun bake through the morning mist. They cross the bridge and make the three-quarter turn at the round-a-bout, suddenly being forced over to the side by several vans filled with camera crews. Bo senses something could be wrong. "Could you follow that news crew, please?"

Mia ties the back of her hair with a wristband and steps into the yard.

"It's great to see you again, Mr. Alteveu. Where are all the people who attended your speeches?"

"The invites grow fewer when loyalty comes with doubt."

"I was thinking the same thing myself yesterday."

"Ahh, forgive me for my pranks if you thought them rude, for they were crafted for an audience belonging to the devil's brood."

Mia breaks out into a wide-open smile, "Oh, Altie, I can't stay mad you!" Mia steps forward to give the speaker a big hug but is saddened by his rigidness. Instead, he turns toward the attendees in the yard. "Are we not finished out there?!"

"Yes, master!"

Mia frowns, "Why do you have to work them so hard? Out in the cold of all times, even when there are plenty of sunny days ahead?"

"One cannot divide the labors of time, madam, but one can divide the chores to ensure that their time is not wasted."

"Well, maybe if you were to be a bit more uplifting and not so condescending all the time. Don't you think they would be happier to follow your cause if you showed them some care?"

"You misunderstand me, Madam. I am not trying to make friends; I am trying to make enemies of others."

Mia squints her eyes at the speaker, questioning his efforts to ever try and ingratiate her. He seems to have this control that he just won't let go of, like at the orphanage where they regarded her as worthless.

"You should not be overly concerned with these men, absent-minded one; they are second-hand minds, maybe third at best."

"Still. you mustn't treat them as such. I'm sure each one has individual aspirations. How about that one over there? He looks like he could be a banker."

"They do not have the power to prevent their destiny."

"But they have rights!"

"Where the few will rule, all else will become messengers; that time is now. Leave them and take my arm."

Mia takes his raised arm, and with reluctance, she continues toward a large stone structure with an open door. "Wow! Altie, is this your home?" Mia calls down the stairwell. "I do like how the steps lead to a basement. It's kind of dark down there. Do you think you could get a permit to install above ground windows?"

Mia had not forgotten the match booklets, finding them useful whenever she might need to start a fire. She finds a maple branch for a torch, and with the arm of the speaker, she leads him down the narrow tunnel. Despite their careful steps, though, the speaker still loses his balance sending them both stumbling to the soft earth.

"Are you alright, speaker? I know what will be of use to you." Mia reaches into her coat. "If you are going to stumble through the sand, would it not be better in a new pair of loafers?!"

The speaker's face does not share her joy and so she frowns. "What's wrong? I know they're not suede, but these do come with a frog clip. You know, Valentine's Day is tomorrow."

"Valentine's Day is insufficient to our purpose. Help me up."

With a worthy pull, Mia notices a man trapped beneath the speaker's body. His face is scrunched in pain, and his hands are pinned behind his back. His legs too have been beaten and rendered useless. Mia immediately looks up at the speaker.

"I am not about popularity, madam, nor about what is right. Independence has always been bad for those who wish to rule."

Mia looks down at the look of shame on the beaten man. "Catalan, let me help you up." She tries to push the speaker aside, but the motion only allows the speaker to roll back and forth with great pleasure.

"Catalan, can you not fight back?"

"I can only provide the talent that was given to me, and that is not enough to defeat the mob."

The speaker then lifts a dividing hand between the two and issues Mia a choice. "One friend may lead to two friends or to two enemies in all. Where is it that you stand with me, woman? Obedience to the garden or are my shoes still unacceptable to you?"

"Do not treat her so harshly, Altaveu." Speaks a broken Catalan. "We should be glad for her attendance."

"Why? What truth does she possess anyways? Once haggard and gruesome, now cleansed to a glow. Her horns, once the epitome of evil, now but a slight scratch beneath her mane. Did she somehow believe this appearance would advance her among our kind? I think not. The Sisters were right; she will always abandon a garden so others will starve."

Hearing these words from the man she greatly admires fills Mia's heart with a great burden. True, she did run away, and yes, the garden did die, but the garden was always meant to die. Her teachings were always meant to ensure its death.

Mia stands above the speaker with wide eyes. She now realizes that her failures in life were necessary if the sisters were to remain in control. She looks down at the speaker with a slight grin that soon grows into a broad smile. "Ah, but I do agree we should have one beautiful garden that works cohesively; I just hold reservations about who should manage it."

It is then that the anger in the Alteveu's mind becomes a terrible one, and all the evil faces from Mia's past now appear before her.

"How dare you insult the great speaker! The great author!! You with your fancy shoes and fancy wear. You choose the shoes you wish to wear and discard the ones you no longer want to keep! What do you know about footwear?! Walk in the shoes that I am forced to wear, and then tell me which shoes are best to work the garden!"

Catalan looks toward Mia and sees she is making a gesture for him to look away. When he turns, he hears a low growl, followed by a loud snap, and then the sounds of scraping. He cannot help but wince at the thought that the speaker could be treated in this way.

Once Mia is certain that no more words will be used to harm another, she presses her mouth to his ear for one final word of vindication. "Director, can you hear me? I want you to know what I have always known about footwear, whether it be flat shoes, arched shoes, shoes for show, or shoes on-the-go; even these closed-back, T-strap, glitter booties with a four-inch titanium heel that I am wearing at this very moment for only $59.95. And I tell you this, my underhanded, despicable peddler, the day that you decide to walk in my shoes will be the day we stop talking about shoes."

Mia drives his head forward into the wall, watching with enjoyment as his face alters from flesh to pulp and back to flesh again. She then picks up her smoldering stick, and right before thrusting it into his cavity, she snarls, "Happy Valentine's Day, you splintered-shoe, butt smoker!" Mia drives the burning stick into the speaker's cavity and drops him to the dirt.

There are flashing lights and voices coming from the entranceway and Mia quickly scurries over to free Catalan. "Never mind me, Mia. Nature has taught me much about the garden. That bad things do grow in what has been neglected.

"It's not your fault, Catalan. You had no choice but to listen."

"It is my general belief that I have always had a choice." Catalan raises his hand, "Sempre que vagis, vaig a seguir."

Mia lightly touches her forehead to his, "Como yo."

Mia hears the voices grow closer and quickly finds a way out another way. She steps before the dimly lit sky, watching her breath evaporate before the morning lamps. The cold brings a sting to her nostrils that sets forth a tear from her eye. Catalan seemed wrongfully accused for being a man of his time, and unfortunately, he will still have to find his place among those that will forever judge him. Mia suddenly covers her eyes from a blinding pain that sizzles her sinuses.

"Barbara Pony! Barbara Pony! It's really you! You found the robber that stole Chappaqua!"

"Chappaqua? I don't know any Chappaqua! Who is this?" Mia snatches at one of the lights, realizing it is a camera. "Oh, no."

"Miss Pony! May I call you Barbara?!"

"Barbara?"

"Miss Pony, how did you know the blue paint robber was stashing artifacts in the Mausoleum?"

"Have you not learned anything? I am not Barbara Pony! It's really simple; there is this barber and a hairstyle he calls the Pony. There is no Barbara and there is no Pony."

"Did you know the blue-faced robber was a former teacher specializing in Catalonia history? He lost his job over some fixation with a sixteenth-century author. Sadly, he ended up homeless."

"Free Society Explorer!"

"What? He was in custody until he slipped away and returned to where he hides his stash. Always before sunrise."

"Before sunrise? What time is it?"

Bo looks out the car window to see two policemen lowering a man into the back seat of their car. "Ma'am, could you let me out here, please?!" Bo reaches into his pocket and drops several large bills onto the front seat. He races down the street, barely avoiding several speeding vans, and changes his direction once he sees a park crew wheeling a smoldering statue out of a cemetery. Along the cemetery bars, Bo instinctively grabs his nose when he sees a dead animal lying in the gutter. He is perplexed, however, to see the creature wearing a red pullover, leggings, and nightclub shoes.

"Mia?!" Bo rushes over and rolls her onto her back. He found her just like this once when she was out looking for traces of a Dutch farm in lower Manhattan. Her mane is twisted, and her face is coated in mud, but other than that, she appears unharmed. Bo reaches into a puddle of rainwater and rinses her face of the filth. "What happened to you, Mar?" He rubs her afflicted legs and arms until she begins to loosen up. "Mar, it's me, Bo."

Mia looks up at Bo, and without saying a word, she tries to explain to him with as many facial 'ticks' as possible exactly what had happened to her. Bo lifts her into his arms and shuffles down the street with his eyes to the sky. "Aye, it's going to be a beautiful day to travel, Mar."

"Why doesn't anyone like me?"

"Sometimes it's like that, you know."

"I want to go home."

"So do I, Mar. So do I."

There was no one around to witness what Mia had seen. There is never anyone around to witness anything Mia has 'ever' seen, and for Mia to explain her thoughts would only make matters worse. All she knows to say is, 'Things were not as they had appeared.' In other words, they were all reappearances of what she had seen many times before, in various places and in situations where she was sure she had been. This may seem confusing to most, but in the subconscious of a better mind, Mia will always return to where a large wood carving stands on a crate, addresses a confused crowd, and tries to answer her one question – why her mother had to let her go.

Beatie sits alone at her vanity with the weight of her book slumping down over her knees. She looks all cute and cuddly wearing a kitten-eared beanie and big, fluffy, pink slippers, but cute and cuddly is not at all how she feels. She is tired of worrying before the mirror, wondering if she has done something wrong again. Early this morning, she became deeply distraught when she went to check on Bo, and he wasn't in the tool shed. There was such great hope in seeing him, and now the joy is lost without translation; and yes, she did consult her book of ideas, but there was no response from within.

The book falls to the floor, opening to a page with a folded letter in it. She looks at the headline: "Putting Out the Trash: There are no rules preventing you from walking away."

"But I don't want to walk away, Mr. Goggy. Why would I when he is so full of new words? He really doesn't have any bad habits, except maybe the pregnant story, and well, sure, his dressing habits, lack of full maturity, and phone phobia. What else? Oh, yeah, his excessive drinking, poor dining habits, and clothes that he feels should be engaged in sexual fetishes, but it's not his fault; he just doesn't know what everyone wants him to be, and that's okay; it takes time to figure those things out. It's hard being anyone beside yourself when you're trying to be somebody nobody likes."

Beatie immediately sits up, realizing a disturbing thought. That is exactly what she was saying about herself. It was she that was trying to be somebody that nobody likes. Suddenly, she is very disappointed to learn that what she has been told is incorrect. But what she knew and what she did not know wasn't her fault. She had been listening merely to obtain a negative opinion about Bo, which seemed like the right thing to do because she was enjoying it.

Beatie leaps onto her bed and throws a stuffed animal at the waste basket. The book she has been reading is having an effect on her well-being that just isn't very nice. And those Blue-Haired, Cockle-Breading Floo Floos? They're all about this too. She thinks about what Hydragew once said, that love is about finding your own soul in someone else's body, and it is as much about having his soul inside of you as it is about having your soul inside of him. Only now, Bo's soul might be saying – so long, 'soul,' and by tomorrow you will be a forgotten amoeba!"

Beatie grabs the car keys off the vanity. A conference of the minds is needed. A time for thoughts to be heard. She will be taking the day off, which is fine, Mr. Happiness will have to figure out the days she'll be working anyways. Again – a woman thing. She hops into her car, which makes good on its promise to get her there, and miraculously finds a parking space just outside the barber shop. Quite odd, isn't? The day before Valentine's should always be busy with people getting their hair done, so why are there newspapers covering the windows with a sign that reads 'We're Closed'?

Beatie manages to squeeze through a slack in the chain and finds her way beneath the furnishings meant to block the door. She pauses behind an open-back swivel chair to see who might be the cause of this obstruction, and there she sees the problem. One is a member of the Spotted Face Club, and the other just recently formed the Angled Body Hip Replacement Jamboree. The remaining attendees have their heads reclined in water basins with a green moss growing on their faces. There is no need for an introduction; these are socialites, minions of evil committed to ruining the lives of others. Beatie knows she should not be here, but she has something important to discuss. She crawls along the shadowed portions of the baseboard and locates the 'Lonely Chair.' A chair reserved for the demonstration doll used in the Olustee Battlefield reenactment. Unfortunately, for the doll, it was called up last week.

She sits patiently inspecting her nails while listening to the group chatter. There is a new chair in the shop. It is one of those fancy, ultra-suede, sweat-absorbing, self-cleaning chairs. It also comes with wine, cheese, and fabric softener. It has a large mechanical apparatus fastened to its shoulders, and someone's head encased inside.

Beatie looks up when she hears an opportune sneeze. This is the moment to speak, "I wouldn't change a thing! I'm just so happy to be with him. Maybe I'm convinced that love is inevitable, so when someone likes to spoil me, I'm not going to just sneeze it away." Instantly, the lights begin to flicker, and a door in the back slams shut. Several large bulbs explode around the mirror, and the emergency lighting begin to flash. It is then, within the mechanical apparatus of the fancy chair, a prickly, baked head with smoking tentacles slowly descends to reveal its hideous self. Its face has a multicellular feature that would normally make it impossible for it to exist – but then it speaks.

"Well, well, well, what do we have here?"

Beatie knows she should flee, but a strap from her chair suddenly loops around her legs, waist, and arms, locking her into submission.

"I would have gladly spent another hour with you, most difficult one, had I only known it would have been beneficial to do so. This, of course, was before you compromised yourself further. What do you say for yourself now?"

Beatie watches from the corner of her eye as the evil presence glides across the floor, and settles into a vacating seat next to her.

"You were going to say, my dear?! Speak, but do take careful aim, for if you miss, you may never be able to speak again."

Beatie is horrified. She knows that a devil-warding scripture is needed to repel this evil presence, but what possible words could have any effect on this foul, wretched, skin-sloughing yetti?!"

"You were going to say?"

"I hate watching movies where the actors are always eating."

"Hahaha!" Ms. Barbie cackles. "I see you have been listening to your readjustment tapes. Maybe there is something you can do right."

"Yes, Ms. Barbie, but rather, I do have something to say." Beatie takes a deep breath. "It's just that I see the manner in which you speak, and I also hear the manner in which you speak, and therefore, I feel the manner in which you speak, and when you do speak..." Beatie looks around to see the faces in the room. She is rambling on without direction, and it's become noticeable. "...and therefore, when you do speak, it ruins everyone's hair, and their clothes, and the follicles inside their nostrils."

Ms. Barbie slaps her hands on her lap and stands. "Well, this is going nowhere."

"I didn't say I was going anywhere. You said I could speak, and so, this is what I am going to speak."

"Exactly why this should be enough for now." Ms. Barbie tosses a cape over Beatie's head and walks about the room. "So, where was I? Oh, yes. I almost forgot to tell you all about her appearance the other night." Ms. Barbie returns to Beatie's chair, where the cape is still covering her head. "Whether you stand alone or in the company of others, young harlot, it is your clothing we must never forget."

Ms. Barbie pulls out a photo from her pocket and passes it around. "I submit to you the dress that she wore to the party. I am sure that you will all agree that this dress can only be found in the dark corners of indecency. Now, I do admit that is me wearing the dress," Ms. Barbie chuckles, "but I assure you that I donated it to Meeshman's many years before, given to me by my first husband in keeping with a pornographic mind. I am amazed that I had the decency to ever take possession of it."

"The dress or your husband's mind?" Beatie clamps her hand over her mouth to keep from bursting out with laughter.

"Excuse me?" Quips Ms. Barbie. "Did you say something, Harletta Concubine? So lascivious and so inviting you are in that dark alley kind of way. The men at the party certainly thought so. You do remember the men at the party? Why wouldn't you when it was my choice to receive any one of them for the evening?"

"It is shocking to hear that even you could be refused, Ms. Barbie." Beatie slaps her hand over her mouth again and giggles.

Ms. Barbie's eyebrows suddenly rise to a dagger, obviously mortified that she, Cairn Barbie, could ever be judged by another. "Let's be incisive, shall we? It is time to end this fantasy farce of yours and expose to everyone who you will never become. A respected entity within our own community." Ms.

Barbie holds up a letter. "This is a note that was found outside a garbage bin from her pretend lover!"

> *I have left a fingerprint, the only trace of its kind, for I will no longer be here when you read this.*

Beatie's eyes grow wide and teary as Ms. Barbie reads the rest of the letter. But how can she deny her? He was not in the shed, and it was Ms. Nikki that warned her she will eventually become a forgotten amoeba! Are these not thoughts to be concerned with?

Ms. Barbie crumples up the letter and tosses it into Beatie's face. "The truth lies in those words, Miss Fornication Tool. He is leaving you and you did not even know it."

Beatie looks down at the letter and then back up at the smug expression on Ms. Barbie's face. This barfly-eating succubus has said way too much to prevent her from acting out now.

Beatie reaches down to retrieve the crumpled letter, then with an evil smile, she tosses the letter right back at Ms. Barbie. But that was not enough. She then lifts up a basin full of water and dumps it over her head. Then after parading about the room to the gasps of the patrons, she next wraps a wet towel around Ms. Barbie's head, yanking off all the organic impurities adhering to her face. All that increased anxiety of her fading youth, now the target of imperfection!

"So, you are human! I knew it! The great grandma-ma, Cairn Barbie! Could we have possibly known?" Beatie lets out a loud cackle and spins Ms. Barbie around for all to see. "Observe all you followers of evil and worship its flaws!" Beatie leaps up and down, finally free from all the shackles placed on her mind.

Ms. Barbie grabs her coat, but Beatie is not quite finished. She slides her foot out just far enough to catch a step and it sends Ms. Barbie to the floor. "You tripped me?!"

"And you should thank me, really!" Beatie grabs a broom by the trash disposal and slides it into her body. "You were about to leave without your transportation!"

"Well, I never! Somebody, please help me up!"

Beatie does a little dance before lining up behind Ms. Barbie, ready to give her one last satisfying kick in the pants, but Hydragew suddenly grabs her around the waist and pulls her away.

"Let go of me!" Beatie whines and kicks and swats at Hydragew until he finally releases her. She then pushes Ms. Barbie aside and runs to the door, "Good riddance to all of you lascivious, bawdy, blue-haired, fish spines!"

Beatie rushes out to Ms. Weary, who immediately fires up under the rage of her forefinger. How she even allowed herself to be swayed by comments from those she despises is impossible for her to understand. All their tender speeches convincingly outlining their false truths and degrading claims that men are only meant to be a temporary species! How original is that!!

Beatie stops at a crosswalk full of people and turns on the car heater. She can sense Ms. Weary is getting a little warm under the hood from all this talk about evil manipulators. Well, no longer does she need to be listening to people like them, and her car agrees.

Beatie looks over the steering wheel to see a commotion going on in front of her car and smirks. She just wants everything to be worked out. This means she will have to shift into complete acceptance that everything he does is wrong and just get used to it. At least for now.

Beatie suddenly screams and rolls down the window to address a family kicking Ms. Weary in the headlamps. "What's going on up there, family of people?!"

"You just knocked over our baby carriage, you soft-headed, fiber-eating chinchilla!"

"Oh! Sorry." Beatie puts the car in reverse and sets the parking brake on. "Chinchilla? Isn't that some sort of a rat?" Beatie waits for the crosswalk to clear and then continues on. "So, what am I going to say? I'm dying for you, and please accept me? No, I can't say that. How about something in Scottish? 'Guid gear comes in small bulk.' I don't even know what that means."

Mia dumps a drawer of trinkets into her backpack and stuffs them down with her foot. She pulls the zipper down on the side pocket and packs in her toiletries. All her necessary items of foreign shoes, novelty shirts, and souvenirs have filled all the spaces, so the home outfits are going to be left behind. Bo wraps the smaller clothing of socks and underwear into a plastic bag and ties the ends together. He then shoves his dirty clothes into a separate bag and zips up the remaining pockets. After all the months, weeks, days and hours of traveling, they are ready to go home. The places where they once wanted to go are no longer the places where they want to be.

Mia gazes into the mirror and chuckles. Her face has cleared up and her horns are close to never happening. A maddening two weeks that somehow still brings forth a smile.

"You're all full of beans this morning, Mar."

"You know, I'm actually not tired. I think spending the last two days in Miami will be relaxing. It will be twenty-seven degrees Celsius, and did you know that sun tan lotion was invented there? The city was also founded by a woman. What does that tell you?"

"It will be nice climbing back under the sheets of my own bed. How about that?"

"Yes, that does sound wonderful."

Bo is amazed by Mia's cheerfulness. The last two weeks would have tossed anyone into a delirious tailspin, but not Mia; she made it through the cistern, her contemptuous relationship with the media, and a fanatical love for two people that were never who she thought they were.

They make their way down the steps into the hallway. Bo pushes the ladder up into the attic and watches a folded letter flutter to the floor. Mia shrugs her shoulders, "Did you make any long-distance calls, eat any hotel food, or watch any porn?"

"It's from Sam. Did you tell her we were leaving?"

"She knew we were only staying the two weeks."

"That's encouraging."

"What do you expect? She was throwing a wobbly over my city involvements, so I told her to go take a swing in her bra."

"Maybe you should read this then."

Mia holds up the letter, "It's a city eviction notice! That bint! I'll sue! She's a substitute teacher; can she even do that?!" Mia crumples up the paper and drop-kicks it down the hallway. "Let's take a cab to the station. It will be quicker."

Mia walks through the lobby and decides to make an appealing gesture toward the day manager, only to tell herself that maybe his advances were worthy of merit, and maybe too, his heart was always above his waist. Unfortunately, Sen would not address her by any other name than the one she signed on the ledger.

Over the past three months their names were Dinkie and Peetrie, Smiddlie and Jobby, Catalan and L'Alteveu. The same results with different names. She had applied for the role of the caring and devoted partner, and by the end of her performance, she didn't get the part. Tomorrow is Valentine's Day, and to Mia, the best among them still lacks value.

"Here's your hotel receipt. It's official. We will spend Valentine's Day together in Miami."

"Like the way it was before, Mar?"

"I like the way it was before. Things were like that, you know."

Mia sets her backpack down and searches through her pockets. She pulls out a roll of toilet paper and zips her bag to the top. "I have to use the loo."

Bo continues on out the door and sets his backpack down on the sidewalk. There is a very disoriented sky above the city that comes with several flashes of light. Bo watches as the Valentine's banner gets caught up in a strong wind and lets loose along the rooftops.

"It's the order of things to come."

Bo looks down at the little sales girl handing him a brochure. He digs into his pocket and finds two quarters, "I remember you."

"Of course you do. It's Sprikkets Magee, thank you very much. And those skies you are witnessing are thunder booms."

"Good to know should I ever return."

"You're running away, aren't you?"

"It's not like that."

"I understand; the people that left for the sea were well aware of the misfortunes on land as well."

Mia pushes Bo lightly, "The weather looks ghastly. Who were you talking to?"

"The little salesgirl." Bo looks about. "She was here a second ago."

Mia taps her foot and looks at her watch, "Maybe we should hail a cab." She extends her hand and is relieved when a car slows down. She opens the door to the back seat and waves for Bo to hurry in.

Bo sees a paper on the floor and reaches for it with a chuckle, "Look, you made the front page, Mar."

"Aw, will you look at the pretty pony?"

"Keep reading."

Mia suddenly takes on an anguished look. "Bloody hell! That's me?!" She swats Bo with the paper and then tosses it to the front seat. "You know, I truly thought I was doing some good here!"

And that's the last they spoke of it.

"Are you sure she knows you're leaving?"

Bo shrugs his shoulders, "I think so."

"You think so? You let her know it's over, right?!" Mia stares at Bo in disbelief. "You didn't leave another confusing letter, did you?"

"I'm sure everything is fine."

"I'm just saying, you have this language that requires a deeper evaluation than what most people are accustomed to listening to."

Mia rises up in her seat and looks about. "Bo, why are all the cars behind us blowing their horns?!" She looks over the front seat and sees the driver's door is open. She then watches as the owner of the car makes her way across the street and into the hotel. "Bloody hell! She just left us in the middle of traffic!"

Bo darts his way across the street and follows a shadow racing around the hallway bend. He finally comes to a stop when he sees the young lady leaping up and down for the rope to the attic. "Miss, is there something the matter?"

"No! Nothing's the matter. I made a mistake; it's not you."

Bo hears a loud crash, a cry, and a splash. He then leans over the opening in the floor and squints his eyes down at the lady sinking slowly into the wet sand. "Beatie, is that you?"

"No!" He hears back.

"Beatie, I know your voice!"

"I don't care! It's not me; I should know!"

The day manager approaches with a flashlight and Bo assures him everything is alright. He takes the careful steps down the stairwell, wincing at the smell of dead fish and spoiled seaweed. He then lowers the flashlight onto Beatie's puffy-eyed face and gives her a heartfelt smile. She looks so helpless, sucking in her cheeks and puckering her lips to mimic a fish.

Bo splashes down in the wet sand and lifts her up with one mighty long, sucking 'pop'. He then carries her up the steps and sets her down on the hallway floor. Her rapid blinking eyes are trying to tell him that she messed up and she is embarrassed about it too.

Suddenly, Beatie surprises Bo by biting down on his hand and dashing out of the hotel. Bo rushes out into the street and hears a faint whimper coming from beneath a delivery truck. "Beatie?"

"Dismal old hotel. Why did you have to stay here?"

Bo lowers himself onto his knees, "It can't be comfortable under there."

"But you are leaving me!"

"I never said I was going to leave you."

"But you wrote a letter and I heard it!"

"That's just people talking."

There is a long silence until she pokes her eyes from beneath the truck, "But it's going to be Valentine's Day tomorrow."

"Exactly, Valentine's is tomorrow."

Beatie makes her way out from beneath the truck, and once on her feet, she falls limp into Bo's arms. He carries her across the street to the blaring horns of traffic, and makes his way to the open door of her car. He lays her across the seat and closes the door.

"I will never forget this, my hen. You made my trip full of hope, happiness, and memories. You will always be with me as I will be with you."

Beatie stares at him with unblinking eyes. "You will?"

"Most certainly."

"Would you like to put that in writing and make three copies of it?"

Bo finally smiles a perfect smile and Beatie takes notice and smiles back.

Mia's voice can be heard calling from a truck she had waved down. "Let's go, Bo!"

"I have to go, Beatie."

"I'll see you soon then?"

"That's what memories are about, aren't they?"

"They are?"

Bo smiles again and taps her on the foot. He then makes his way to the back seat of the truck and stares at the passing scenery. There is nothing offensive about his memory of her; nothing at all. She was so perfectly unique in so many ways, it would be too impossible to forget someone like that.

When the truck makes it beyond city limits, he suddenly feels a regret that maybe a relationship with her could have worked out.

Mia straightens the collar on Bo's shirt and readjusts his pack straps. The train glides into the station with both taking a step forward.

"You know the first thing I'm going to do when I get home? I'm going to find a new job! How about you?"

Bo comes out of his daze, "What, Mar?"

"You're still thinking of her, aren't you? Interesting, so fragile is a relationship that lacks a common understanding that when we think of our thoughts as being exclusive to our own interpretation, we fail to recognize the other one's acceptance."

"Another profound sermon, Mar?"

"Need I say it in another way?"

Mia stands on the seat and shoves her backpack into the above carriage, giving it a few extra punches to ensure its place. She then squeezes in next to Bo, and within a short moment, she is smiling and taking his hand. "Cheers to all of those we left behind and to all those that wished we had left a lot sooner." Mia lifts her head from Bo's shoulder and reaches down to pick up a crumpled piece of paper. "What's this?"

> *"I have left a fingerprint, the only trace of its kind, for I will no longer be here when you read this. Sometimes the matter is too complex to say in person, when there has always been that promise of commitment for another tomorrow. Goodbye is not what anyone foresees as a possibility, but now I present to you the contrary."*

"This was the letter you were supposed to give to the girl back in Perth. You never let her know you were leaving?" Mia drops the letter back on the floor. "Doesn't matter. I'm glad you told this one directly, not like the others with a letter."

Bo stares at the dark window. He can't help but think that maybe he had chosen the wrong words to explain his departure. He opens his logbook, flipping to the last page with nothing in mind to write.

She walks onto the porch to see who is making the chatter outside. Maybe it is wishful thinking, but there is always that long, feverish excitement when Bo shows up unexpectedly. Beatie sits on the porch swing with Lucifer Goggy's book on her lap. Two weeks have already gone by and she knows she has to return the book. She really did enjoy all the comical suggestions it made about dating men. There was even a Scottish section that still has her chuckling: 'She huvs nice chebs and a perfectly round bahookie too' – Bahaha!! It is just what Hydragew had said too!

A letter slips from the pages of the book and falls to the porch steps. She reaches down to unfold the paper before her eyes.

> *"I have a grave understanding of what I must do, and though it means going away, it will never be without the remembrance of you. Our visit was short, indeed, but there is no doubting the everlasting connection that still exists between us. For all your consideration, my thoughts of you will always be with me, as I hope mine will be with you."*

Beatie watches the meaningful light of the day come to an end. She remembers why she likes Bo and the good things she has to say about him. He had anywhere to go and anyone to be with, and he chose to be here with her. She has never met anyone like that before. Beatie folds the letter and slips it into her pocket. He will return; she is sure of it; the letter did not state otherwise.

FEBRUARY 14th: BAMBOOZLING APOTHECARIES

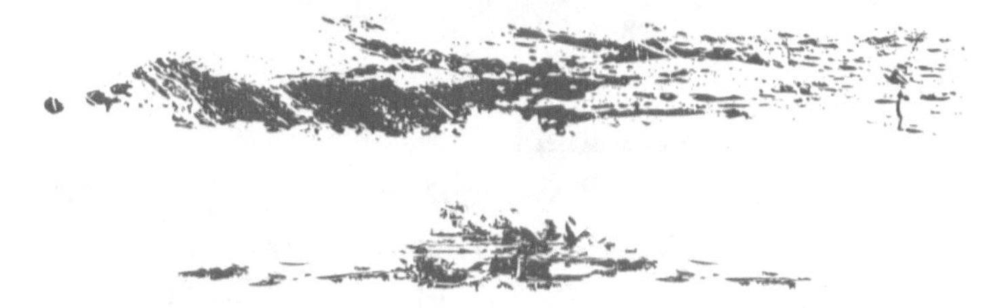

The sun glares bright upon the yard in the late morning sun. It is drying off the remaining moisture from a late night of rain. It's time to get ready for work, and it is Wednesday, so the knee-high, white go-go boots, along with the short, green cotton skirt, are all part of the required dress for today. She rolls her chestnut-colored hair beneath a white baker boy hat and wraps a yellow scarf around her neck; the chain-ball earrings are her own choice, of course.

Beatie cleans Ms. Weary of the fallen foliage, and for doing so, her car behaves with a smile. That's the only medication nature needed to prescribe for her car's troubles. There is a soft glaze appearing upon the golden rooftops of the city, and Beatie is sensing a quality in the air that people are going to be friendly to her today. Noteworthy are the ladies at the barber shop, who have suggested she spend more time with 'the girls' now. Apparently, Ms. Barbie mysteriously left town.

Beatie arrives at the office and gives the little salesgirl fifty cents. She finds her seat in front of the window and begins folding her brochures. She is thinking it is time to go back to her ballet class and maybe to Meeshman's for a new dress. She will also return to Iggie's, hoping to make this her favorite scene now. She will wear her flip-flops and a dress that requires little care, not so much makeup, but enough to get her noticed.

Beatie sets the new glossy brochures on her desk and rests her chin on her hands. It is lunch time and a new dress has been placed in the window across the street. She unravels a napkin containing a small sandwich, eating it slowly and chewing it thoroughly.

NOTES AND REFERENCES

Author, Film, and Song Citations

(i)Handel-Halvorsen Passacaglia Piano, Song by Georg Friedrich Handel and Johan Halvorsen 1894. Youtube https://www.youtube.com/watch?v=uBAtBjtuogg&start_radio=1. (Piano Arr Raif Husicic).

(ii)(Citation) Blatty, William Peter (Author, Screenplay, Producer) Friedkin, Willian (Director) 1973 *The Exorcist* [Motion Picture] United States: Hoya Productions "Yes, but Mrs. MacNeil, the problem with your daughter is not her bed; it's her brain."

(iii)Single by Johnnie Ray "Yes, Tonight, Josephine" Written by Winfield Scott and Dorothy Goodman 1957

(iv)Single by The Trashman, "Surfin' Bird." Written by Al Frazier, Carl White, Sonny Harris, Turner Wilson Jr. 1963

(v)Single by Eileen Barton "If I Knew You Were Comin' I'd've Baked A Cake" Written by Al Hoffman, Bpb Merrill, Clem Watts 1950.

(vi)Single by Tommy James and the Shondells "Hanky Panky." Written by Jeff Barry and Ellie Greenwich, 1966

(vii) (Parody) Sullivan, K.E Scottish Myths & Legends, "The Pabbay Mother's Ghost," Brockhampton Press, 1998

(viii)Single by The Coasters "Yakety Yak! Don't talk back." Written by Jerry Leiber, Mike Stoler 1958

(ix)Single by Brian Hyland "Itsy Bitsy, Teenie Weenie, Yellow Polka Dot Bikini." Written by Pail Vance and Lee Pockriss 1960

(x) (Parody) Zanuck D R and Brown, D, (Producer), & Spielberg, S (Director). 1975. *Jaws* [Motion Picture]. United States: Zanuck Brown Company and Universal Pictures. "There are many insane revolutionaries out there and the chances you got the right one is a hundred to one. A hundred to one! You want to be sure. We all want to be sure. What I want to do is very simple; the dissipation of these ghosts is very slow. Let's go down to the cemetery; whatever has been hanging out there for the last twenty-four hours is bound to still be there." Mia shrugs her shoulders with a bent lip, "Maybe the only way to confirm it."

<u>Internet References for History</u>

*Citystaug.com/693/our-history

*Ghostcitytours,com

*History of St. Augustine, Florida en.wikepedia.org/wiki/history_of_st._Augustine. Florida Page last edited 15, September 2022

www.ingramcontent.com/pod-product-compliance
Lightning Source LLC
LaVergne TN
LVHW090602110826
845146LV00001B/226

* 9 7 9 8 9 8 9 4 2 8 3 4 2 *